The Last Duke She'd Marry

Scoundrels of Mayfair Book 3

ANNA CAMPBELL

ALSO BY ANNA CAMPBELL

Claiming the Courtesan

Untouched

Tempt the Devil

Captive of Sin

My Reckless Surrender

Midnight's Wild Passion

The Sons of Sin Series:

Seven Nights in a Rogue's Bed

Days of Rakes and Roses

A Rake's Midnight Kiss

What a Duke Dares

A Scoundrel by Moonlight

Three Proposals and a Scandal

The Dashing Widows Series:

The Seduction of Lord Stone

Tempting Mr. Townsend

Winning Lord West

Pursuing Lord Pascal

Charming Sir Charles

Catching Captain Nash

Lord Garson's Bride

The Lairds Most Likely Series:

The Laird's Willful Lass

The Laird's Christmas Kiss

The Highlander's Lost Lady

The Highlander's Defiant Captive

The Highlander's Christmas Quest

The Highlander's English Bride

The Highlander's Forbidden Mistress

The Highlander's Christmas Countess

The Highlander's Rescued Maiden

The Highlander's Christmas Lassie

A Scandal in Mayfair Series:

One Wicked Wish

Two Secret Sins

Three Times Tempted

Four Christmas Kisses

Scoundrels of Mayfair Series:

The Worst Lord in London

The Trouble with Earls

The Last Duke She'd Marry

The Duke Says I Do

Christmas Stories:

The Winter Wife

Her Christmas Earl

A Pirate for Christmas

Mistletoe and the Major

A Match Made in Mistletoe

The Christmas Stranger

His Christmas Cinderella (in the anthology *A Grosvenor Square Christmas*)

Other Books:

These Haunted Hearts

Stranded with the Scottish Earl

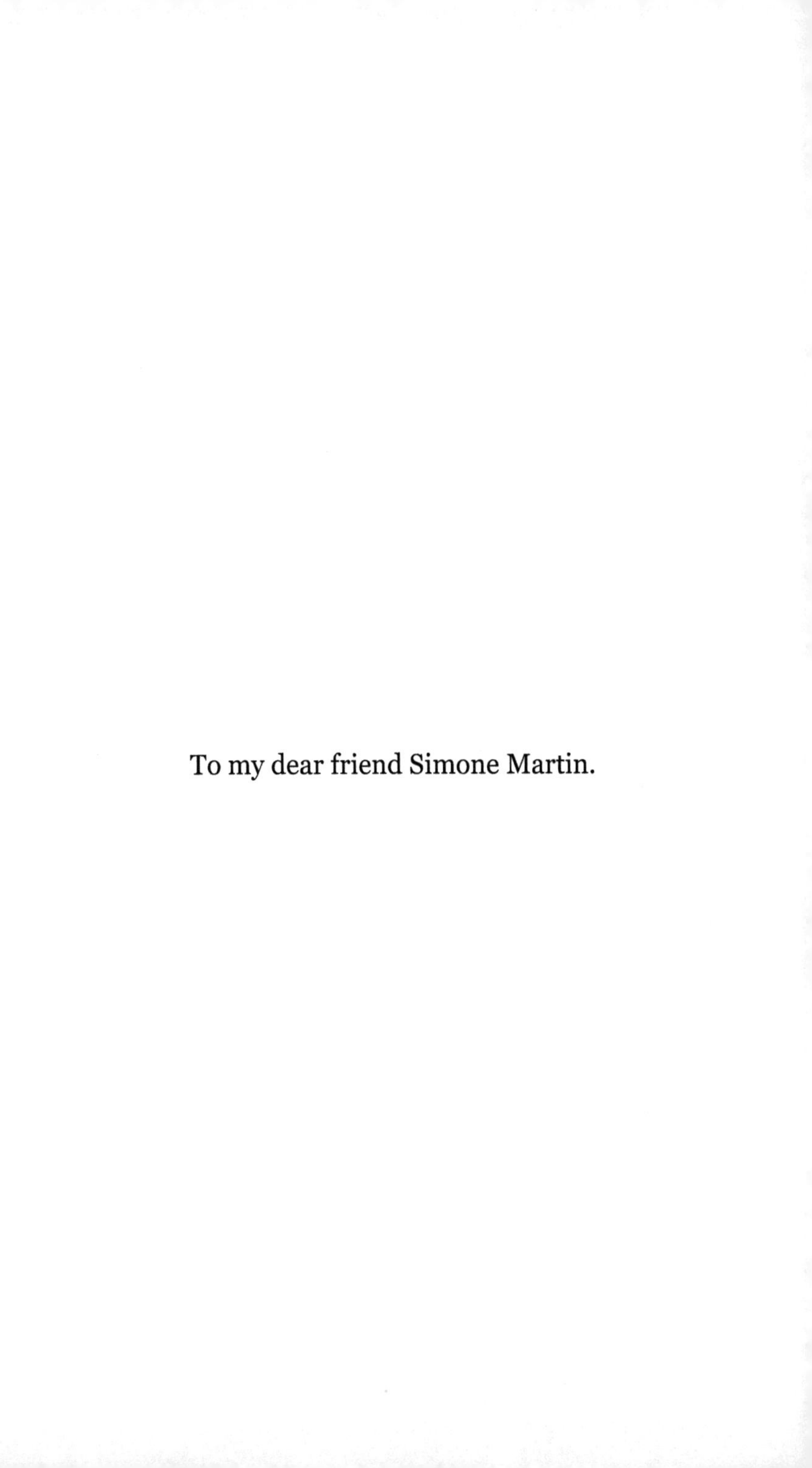

To my dear friend Simone Martin.

CHAPTER ONE

White's Gentlemen's Club, St James's, London, May 1817

"**R**omeo!"

The joyful exclamation shattered the sanctified silence of the library at White's.

Heads turned, glowers proliferated, grunts of disapproval rumbled. Creating a ruction in these hallowed halls of masculine privilege simply wasn't done.

Lucas Hebden, Duke of Evesham, stirred in his winged leather chair near the fire and cracked open heavy eyes. An army of blacksmiths slammed hammers on the anvil inside his head, although as usual, he only had himself to blame for his misery. The brandy at the gaming hell that he'd visited last night had been poor stuff indeed. Which hadn't stopped him from downing a lake's worth of the rotgut swill.

Through his headache, he struggled to make sense of what was happening. A stout, balding fellow wearing an unfortunate daffodil yellow coat loomed in front of him. The fanatic light in his eyes brought back memories of Eton. Just so had Evesham's sports master looked at him after his schoolboy self had scored a century in a cricket match against Harrow.

"Romeo!" the man shouted once more.

Because Evesham didn't know the cove – and because his name, thank heaven, wasn't Romeo – he closed his eyes and struggled to resume his snooze.

"Romeo!"

"Shh!"

"Pipe down!"

"Dashed intolerable behavior!"

Evesham muffled a sigh. The chorus of protest from the club members swelled until a man couldn't recover from an almighty drinking spree in peace. More was the pity.

Once more, he forced his eyelids upward. This time, he winced. That yellow really was too much when a chap suffered from a sour stomach.

"Are you addressing me, sir?" he asked, impressed that he could string so many words together through the clanging in his brainbox.

"I am indeed."

Given Evesham's parlous state, the sprightly tone struck him as obnoxious in the extreme. Still, he made an attempt at politeness. He was more accustomed than he should be to encountering people he'd met on the carouse then completely forgotten, once the night's high jinks were done. "Are we acquainted?"

This man wasn't like his usual companions in crime. He looked excessively healthy and cherubic. Not to mention that he must be closer to sixty than to Evesham's thirty. And even at the bottomest of the bottom of the deepest tankard, Evesham couldn't imagine ever introducing himself to anyone as

Romeo.

"I'm Portdown, don't you know?"

No, he didn't know. And why did the blockhead have to keep shouting? "I believe you have mistaken me, my lord."

"Never. I must speak to you right now."

Evesham was a very democratic duke, happy to mix with all levels of society. But this upstart proved so presumptuous, that even his rusty sense of consequence was offended. "In that case, leave your card at Hebden House."

"Whatever the devil you do, shut your traps or get out of this library," Lord Castellaine snapped, rattling his newspaper in an aggressive manner from an armchair a few feet away. "If you don't, I'll call a footman and have you both thrown out."

Evesham glanced around to discover a circle of hostile glares centered on him and Portdown.

Disapproval was nothing new. In his one and only London season nine years ago, witty and wicked Verena Gerard had dubbed him His Dis-Grace rather than His Grace. But however disgraceful he might be, he had no wish to be banned from White's.

"Come with me now." Portdown muffled his bellow to a loud whisper. "It's urgent."

"I doubt it." Evesham folded his arms across his powerful chest and stretched out his long legs. He leaned his head back and closed his eyes again. "Go away."

He rarely summoned up his ducal tone, but when he did, it always evinced instant obedience. So he was too astonished to put up much of a fight when Portdown grabbed his arm and hauled him out of his chair. Even through his annoyance, he couldn't help but commend the man's strength. Evesham was three inches over six feet and built like a prizefighter.

Clearly enthusiasm won out over fifteen stone of

solid muscle, because he found himself on his feet and towering above Lord Portdown. With some trouble, he found his balance. "What the hell—"

"Come along."

Even through the thickheadedness that came of too much liquor and not enough sleep, Evesham recognized that if he intended to give this encroaching mushroom the setdown he deserved, he couldn't do it in the club library.

So he didn't resist as the pestilential man dragged him along a corridor and into an anteroom that at this hour of the morning was empty.

Portdown released his arm and shut the door, turning to survey him with more of that confoundedly off-putting elation. "You're perfect."

Despite his irritation, that made him laugh. Nobody in their right mind would describe the Duke of Evesham as perfect. In fact, the world believed that he was just about as imperfect as imperfect could get.

Because he was a man with a close acquaintance with the effects of drink, he spared a moment to study his tormentor. If the fellow was three sheets to the wind, he could almost sympathize. He'd done plenty of madcap things himself, while on the booze. "Are you foxed?"

"No, of course I'm not. It's eleven o'clock in the morning."

"And we're not acquainted?"

"No."

"Is this a matter of life and death?"

"Not precisely."

Evesham's audible inhalation expressed impatience. Even if he'd gone to bed at ten last night, this conversation would baffle him. With a Goliath of a headache afflicting him, he couldn't be arsed trying to unravel this strange encounter. "Then I'm going back to the library. You, sir, may go to Hades."

The rotund man shifted to block the door, raising his hands to stop Evesham leaving. "This is more important than life or death. This is...*art.*"

Shocked, Evesham paused in reaching out to shove the man out of the way. "Art?" he repeated, as if the word was a profanity. "What in blazes do I have to do with art?"

Startled, the man stared at him, as if he at last heard him. "Sorry, old man. I'm guessing you're all at sea. But the moment I saw you, I knew."

Despite recognizing that his best move would be to leave this madman to rave on his own, he couldn't contain a spurt of curiosity. "Knew what?"

"I told you. Romeo."

"My name isn't Romeo. I'm Evesham."

"Evesham?" The man frowned, as if he struggled to bring the name to mind.

That was a surprise. Evesham had been away from England for a long time, but he'd left such a trail of scandal behind him, he assumed that his title would spark some recognition.

"Yes."

"There was a Duke of Evesham. A friend of my father's."

"There *is* a Duke of Evesham, and I am he. You must be thinking of my grandfather, the previous duke."

"Oh, you're a duke. That's capital." Portdown looked even cheerier. He might be a lunatic, but at least he was a jolly lunatic. "Juliet likes dukes."

Juliet? The fellow lived in a complete fantasy world. Evesham's head was whirling.

Portdown went on, as if he was as sane as the next man. "And you of course are Romeo."

"For God's sake—"

Portdown's smile remained sunny. "I've been

looking for someone to play Romeo in my scenes from Shakespeare gala, and you're just perfect."

Perfect again? Before Evesham could object, his tired brain clicked into operation and this conversation, however unconventional, finally made sense.

"Theatricals. You're talking about theatricals!" He collapsed into a chair and ran his hand through his ruffled hair. "Look, my good man, whoever you are, I don't do theatricals. Find someone else to play Romeo."

Portdown sank into the opposite chair and for once, he didn't look as happy as a pig in mud. "The only other person even halfway suitable is His Grace of Granville."

Evesham bit back a growl. Of course the sainted Alaric Dempster was suitable. The numbskull was bloody suitable for every blessed thing on God's green earth.

All his life, people had told Evesham that he should be more like the Duke of Granville. All his life, he'd kicked against the odious comparison.

"Then let Granville do it."

"He's blond."

The darling of society was as golden as an angel. "I know."

"And you're dark."

As dark as an Italian. He'd been called a suite of nasty names at school because he was as swarthy as a chimney sweep. "So?"

"Juliet is blond. Two blonds together aren't right."

"Cast another girl as Juliet then."

Portdown smiled. "No, Juliet is my daughter, and she's set on playing—"

"Her namesake." To his consternation, Evesham started to follow this nonsense.

"Precisely."

"The answer is still no."

A few of the boys at Eton had been artistic. They'd painted or written poetry or put on performances. Not Evesham. He'd been a sportsman through and through. A cricketer. A rower. Handy on the football field. A fencer. A boxer.

A boy who had forced the world around him to shift from bullying to admiration. Scratching away at a violin or rhyming "bonnet" with "sonnet" would never hew him out a respected place in the violent society of his schoolmates. Beef-witted bastards that most of them had been.

He was rather surprised to learn that the stiff-rumped prig Granville involved himself in something as inherently frivolous as amateur dramatics. On this long-overdue visit home, he was yet to run into his bugbear. Unless the prancing poodle had changed beyond recognition, he was more likely to be speechifying in the House of Lords than dressing up and treading the stage.

Perhaps the fellow had his eye on the mysterious Juliet. If so, she must be pretty.

About the only thing that Granville and Evesham shared, apart from their exalted rank, was a taste for good-looking females. Hadn't this mutual weakness already sparked the scandal that sent Evesham on a career of debauchery across the Continent and left Granville behind in London, with his halo intact and the object of general esteem?

The thought of putting a spoke in Granville's elegant wheel was almost enough to tempt him into Portdown's clutches. Almost, but not quite.

"I won't give up." Portdown regarded him the way that a foxhound stared at a sirloin steak. "I'm a man of great determination."

"And I'm a man of renowned stubbornness." As

his constantly disapproving grandfather had so often pointed out.

Portdown sighed and steepled his fingers in front of his chest. "I can't persuade you?"

"No."

"You'll soon become sick of my pursuit."

Undoubtedly. He was already tired of it. "You're wasting your time."

"Hmm," Portdown said with a thoughtfulness that worried Evesham.

A silence fell. Almost soothing. Evesham should go, but it was quiet and warm in here. And just at the moment, Portdown wasn't harassing him.

He'd drifted close to another nap when the cove finally spoke. "You don't want me to ask you again to join what promises to be a supreme artistic experience?"

"No," Evesham said drowsily without opening his eyes.

He should go home to Hebden House and find his bed. At the very least have a wash and a shave and change his shirt. But his servants were so in alt to have the master back after all these years that they fussed. He couldn't bear fuss.

"Then how about I suggest a deal?"

He opened one eye to see Lord Portdown looking positively beatific. "How about you just leave me alone?"

"Can't do it, old boy. Not when art is involved. Although I'm willing to make you an offer."

"Oh?" With an effort, Evesham sat up and regarded the bizarre individual before him. If Granville ended up with this eccentric for a father-in-law, it would be fitting punishment for a life that always fell out exactly as the sod wanted.

"Let's wager on a hand of piquet. If I win, you'll come down to Afton Park next week and learn your lines and take part in rehearsals without a whisper of complaint."

"And if I win?"

"If you win, the subject of Romeo is forever closed. What do you say?"

"Why the hell should I agree?"

"Because you don't want me pestering you."

"I don't. But I don't want to make an ass of myself spouting bloody Shakespeare in front of an audience either. Nor do I wish to leave London right now."

"Then you just need to win, Your Grace. Surely a young buck like you doesn't lack confidence with the cards. I imagine you've won more often than you've lost."

It was true, he had. He might choose to souse his wits in various intoxicating substances, but that didn't mean that he lacked intelligence. His grandfather had despaired that he wasted a fine scholarly mind in pursuit of sporting records.

That fine mind warned him now that this odd, plump little man was playing him. But he was good at cards, and the prospect of Lord Portdown barking at his heels day after day was too appalling to contemplate.

"If I win, you'll never mention theatricals to me again?"

Portdown lifted one hand in solemn pledge. "My oath as a gentleman. I'll endure a blond Romeo, while you continue to enjoy the pleasures of the capital."

Even better, if Granville had to play Romeo, he'd make a fool of himself in public. How could Evesham resist? "And all I have to do is play a hand of piquet with you and win?"

"Perhaps to be fair to you, we should make it best of three."

"I warn you, I'm accounted an excellent player."

Portdown looked perturbed. As well he should. "Then the outcome is already assured. Shall I call for a pack of cards, Your Grace?"

Sighing, Evesham rose and crossed to the card table in the corner of the room. "Go right ahead."

CHAPTER TWO

Afton Park, Wiltshire, a week later

Lady Juliet Frain glanced up from her heavily marked script, as her father appeared at the top of the stone steps leading down to the hollow. Next week, this was where his Shakespearean gala would take place.

Papa looked mightily pleased with himself, but that was nothing new. At least this current project meant that he wasn't digging up the flower beds at the rented Lorimer Square house to test his theories about staging ancient Greek drama. Anything he dug up here on his Wiltshire estate belonged to him.

"I've got a treat for you, my dear," he said, bustling toward her, face alight with glee.

A tall, dark-haired man bounded down the grassy slope after her father. Despite his commanding size, he moved with a lithe, energetic grace that took her breath away.

Her father hurried up onto the open-air stage and stopped in front of the bench where she perched among a chaos of props. The night of the gala, Hamlet's mother would sit here to observe Ophelia's madness. "I've brought you your Romeo."

She looked past her father to the stranger, who had stopped a couple of feet away to settle a glittering gaze upon her. All the other parts in the performance had been assigned to family and neighbors. She'd hoped that her father might cast her suitor, the Duke of Granville, as her lover. When Papa had ordered the best guest bedroom prepared for a mystery visitor, he'd told her that a nice surprise was on its way.

Juliet hadn't seen Granville since she'd left London three weeks ago to prepare for her sister Viola's scandalously rushed wedding to the Earl of Renfrew. She could already tell that this unknown man was a million miles distant from her own always-correct swain. Who perhaps was no longer her swain. Viola's antics had tarred the Frains with scandal, and His Grace of Granville sought a wife of impeccable reputation.

Juliet put aside her constant niggle of worry and rose to her feet, wondering who their visitor was.

"My Romeo?" She winced at the uncharacteristic uncertainty in her voice. Lady Juliet Frain was never uncertain, plague take the newcomer. But something about his unabashed masculine appreciation made her falter.

The man was dressed in the height of fashion, however untidy, so he was clearly from society's upper echelons. He was also making no attempt to hide the way his bright dark eyes conducted a survey of her person. A heated, concentrated inspection that made her want to slap him.

She was surprised at his temerity. Her natural dignity and well-earned reputation for always doing the right thing meant that most men treated her with respect, if not downright apprehension.

Her father couldn't stop grinning. "Your Grace,

allow me to present my daughter Juliet."

Your Grace? Was this brazen devil a duke? Juliet was something of an expert on England's premier noblemen. How could this one be a completely unknown quantity?

He didn't act like a duke. Every duke she knew was conscious of his great consequence. This one looked like he'd just got out of bed and as if he'd happily go back there, given the chance. Taking her with him, the rogue.

His clothing, a dark blue coat and biscuit trousers, while expensive, had been flung on as a matter of convenience rather than fashion. The thick black curls looked as if he'd given them a quick comb then forgotten about them, unusual when elaborate male coiffures were the style.

If only she could say that he was unappealing. But in all her life, she'd never seen such a striking man.

Granville's looks were much praised. But compared to this tanned, vivid man, her suitor's blond classical appeal faded to insipidity.

As she chided herself for the disloyal thought, her father went on. "Juliet, this is the Duke of Evesham, who is kind enough to lend his talents to our small company."

Evesham? Oh, no!

Juliet had been uneasy since her father had produced this picturesque scoundrel. Now dismay made her heart sink.

Silently cursing her father, she curtsied. Did Papa have the slightest idea what a disaster this promised to be, especially for her hopes for the future?

"Your Grace," she said in a cool voice that in no way reflected her inner disquiet.

"Lady Juliet," Evesham said with a bow. The deep rumble of his voice stroked her skin like velvet. When every muscle tightened in immediate response, she told herself that it was disgust.

She wished him to Hades, although he was yet to do anything improper. Apart from level that fixed attention upon her. The glint in his eyes told her that, unlike her, he was overjoyed to make her acquaintance.

Papa was in general immune to social undercurrents. Which always puzzled her, because he was perceptive and subtle when he directed actors or performed himself. Perhaps everyday events didn't engage his attention the way that a play did.

He didn't pick up on the buzz of swift awareness, hostile on her part, edging the air between Juliet and the duke. "The moment I saw Evesham, I knew he was perfect for the part. You two will set the stage alight."

Juliet's dismay turned to complete horror, as she recalled why the duke was here. She and this disreputable brute were set to perform the balcony scene, exchanging some of the most romantic lines ever written. Granville would have a fit when he found out.

"Papa, can I have a quick word in private?" For once, her famous composure cracked. Outrage too strong to conceal made her voice tremble.

"Of course, my dear." Papa glanced at Evesham, who continued to ogle her with that disturbing interest. "If you'll excuse us, Your Grace?"

"Of course," he said.

Once Juliet got her father off the stage and out of earshot, she glared at him. "Papa, do you know who that is?"

Her father looked surprised at the question. "Of course I do. I just introduced you. He's the Duke of Evesham. Met him at White's. Capital fellow."

"He's not a capital fellow," she hissed. "He's Granville's worst enemy."

"Granville isn't in that scene with you. He's not the ardent Latin type at all. He might make a fair Paris, but we're not doing that part of the play."

Juliet only just prevented herself from stamping her foot. She often found herself at cross-purposes with her eccentric parent, but never had she felt so much like strangling him. "Pray shift your thoughts from Shakespeare for one second. I'm talking about real life. How will Granville react when he discovers that you're offering Evesham hospitality? Even worse, what will he think when he hears that I'm playing Juliet to the man's Romeo?"

"Granville?" Her father looked bewildered. "What has he to do with anything?"

"Honestly, sometimes I think you live under a rock." She clenched her fists in her skirts with frustration. "Granville has indicated that he considers me a suitable duchess."

Her father still looked nonplussed, although surely he couldn't be quite as ingenuous as he pretended. He'd attended almost as many balls this season as she had. He must have heard the gossip about a possible match. "Of course you are. You were born to be a duchess. Everyone has always said so. In fact, you would have become a duchess two years ago, if dear Bolton hadn't suffered his unfortunate accident with those cart horses."

Juliet hid a wince at the mention of her late suitor. "I have ambitions to become the Duchess of Granville. I believe His Grace and I will suit admirably."

"He'll be lucky to get you."

"You're not following me, Papa," she said with some heat. "Thanks to Viola, I'm tainted by scandal."

"We hushed that up with a quick wedding."

"Which caused so much talk that Portia and I had to leave Town before the season ended. It's possible that Granville has already shelved any plans to propose. If I'm embroiled with his worst enemy, I can kiss an offer goodbye."

"How do you know that Granville and Evesham are at daggers drawn? I thought you and Evesham were strangers."

"How do you not? The scandal was bad enough to keep tongues wagging for years. Heavens above, they were still talking about it seven years ago, the first time I went to London. Nine years ago, Granville was engaged to Vanessa Gould, before she ran off with Evesham."

Her father frowned. "Now you mention it, I might have heard something along those lines. Did Evesham marry the chit?"

"No. That was the worst of it. There was a duel, and Granville winged Evesham. Evesham fired into the air, as well he should, given he was at fault. Then he and Lady Vanessa took off for the Continent and a life of sin. I heard they parted company soon afterward, and she disappeared from view. Whereas he's devoted the time since then to offending every rule of morality. He's not a fit person to introduce to your daughters."

"He's a duke. Dukes are always fit persons." Papa gave her a critical glance. "Don't get yourself in such a state, poppet. You'll have plenty of chaperones while he's here. Anyway, you're more than capable of deterring improper overtures. I've seen you crush masculine impertinence a hundred times. I'm sure you'll be safe."

"I don't care about my safety." Telling herself a howling fit of rage would do nobody any good, she spoke through her teeth. "I care about people calling me one of Evesham's strumpets."

"You have such a pristine reputation. Nobody would say that."

"What about Granville?"

"If he's a man of sense, he won't fly up into the boughs over a bit of playacting."

Except knowing that the woman he courted was whispering romantic nonsense to Evesham must bring back painful memories. And while Granville liked Juliet and had made no secret of his intentions before Viola's misstep, she'd been out of his sight now for several weeks. A lot could happen in London in several weeks.

Not only that, at twenty-six, Juliet was dangerously close to being an old maid. The world might say that she was born to be a duchess. She might picture herself sporting the famous Granville emeralds. But thanks to Viola's misbehavior, Juliet Frain wasn't quite the desirable match that she'd been at the start of the season.

Linking her name with Granville's bête noire wouldn't improve her chances of becoming his duchess. Granville was the last unmarried duke in England. Or at least unmarried and eligible.

Evesham wasn't married, but she'd rather remain a spinster for the rest of her life than tie her future to that reprobate's wagon.

Not that the reprobate would ever consider marrying her. She was altogether too stiff-rumped for the ramshackle Duke of Evesham. Even if he was in the habit of wedding the women he ruined.

No, Granville was her only remaining chance at a duchess's coronet. And with every second, she felt him slipping out of reach. It was enough to make her want to throw a tantrum. Even if elegant, composed Juliet Frain never allowed her temper to get the better of her.

Another reason why she'd make a superb duchess.

It seemed so unfair that having lost Bolton in

tragic circumstances, fate should deprive her of the perfect replacement. She admired Granville more than anyone she'd ever met, and they had so much in common. A firm grip on duty, an understanding of propriety, a reforming temperament. They could establish a useful partnership that would benefit the nation.

Damn Viola and Renfrew. Damn her father. Damn the beau monde and its addiction to tattle. And damn Evesham for agreeing to play Romeo. Right now, she'd happily pitch every one of them into the lake that lay a mere stone's throw from where she stood.

"If you lose me my chance to marry Granville, I'll never forgive you, Papa," she said with a bite that she hoped would pierce her father's habitual self-satisfaction.

It didn't. Instead, her father gave her a blithe smile that didn't put her any more in charity with him. "You're fretting unnecessarily. It's all water under the bridge, my love. What's important is the play. You and Evesham will make magic together. You mark my words. Then you can toddle off to wed Granville, and the two of you can set up home as happy as two pigeons in a nest."

"Papa—" she began, but he raised his hand.

"We can't leave His Grace waiting any longer. As it is, he must wonder why you needed to whisk me away for a coze the minute he appeared."

She'd wager good money that His Grace knew exactly why she wanted to talk to her father. Evesham looked wicked. He looked worldly. He looked like he didn't give a fig for public opinion. What he didn't look was stupid.

Which only made him more dangerous.

Juliet swallowed another protest, convinced that this was all going to end in catastrophe.

"I want to rehearse Portia's scene with her this morning. She's far too collected when she appears on stage. She's meant to be out of her mind." Her father had already put her objections to Evesham completely out of his mind. "While I do that, I thought you and His Grace could go somewhere quiet and run through your lines to get a feel for each other."

A feel for each other? It was as if Papa wanted to destroy her reputation. Especially as the spark she'd noticed in Evesham's eyes hinted that he'd be more than happy to get a feel of her.

Juliet had trouble keeping her voice down. "You just said I'd have plenty of chaperones."

But if she'd ever had a chance of getting her father to banish the disreputable duke back to the stews where he belonged, that moment had passed. Papa belittled her perfectly legitimate concerns with an airy wave of one artistic hand.

"Don't nag, Juliet. Whoever you marry, he won't appreciate a woman who carps at him all the time. This is your home. Nobody will lay a hand on you. The only reason His Grace is here is to perform in the gala. Anyway, you've got a good pair of lungs. If the fellow steps an inch out of line, shriek for help."

"You're taking all this very lightly, Papa," she said through stiff lips.

Outside matters theatrical, her father took most things lightly, to her regret. It was one of the reasons that she'd had to sacrifice the luxury of a childhood to ensure that Portia and Viola received a decent upbringing.

"And you're taking everything far too seriously. As usual."

Juliet firmed her lips to muffle another protest, even as chagrin stung her. She knew that she was old before her time, but whose fault was that?

"Very well," she said in a cold voice.

What else could she do but cooperate? Her father wasn't even listening to her anymore.

It seemed that when it came to managing the troublesome duke, she was on her own. That was nothing new.

But if Evesham imagined that he could bend the rules of propriety without suffering nasty consequences, he was about to discover how wrong he was. Lady Juliet Frain was no brainless ingenue. She was a mature woman of the world, well up to thwarting a rake's tricks.

The duke's manner might promise sin in abundance. But he was Napoleon and she was Wellington, and he was about to meet his Waterloo.

CHAPTER THREE

*E*vesham leaned against a mossy column on the side of the stage and wondered just what Lady Juliet was saying about him to her father. Nothing complimentary, he'd wager his considerable fortune. He hadn't mistaken the horror on that exquisite face when he appeared. Clearly, she'd heard the gossip.

A week ago, when he'd fallen into the clutches of that baby-faced card shark, Lord Portdown, he'd been right about one thing. In all these years, the Duke of Granville hadn't lost his eye for a pretty woman.

Lady Juliet Frain was a perfect rose. Golden hair. Tall. Built like a Valkyrie, just how he liked them. And plenty of flash and fire, which surprised him, because everything he'd heard about her, since agreeing to this farcical arrangement, indicated that she was the staidest woman in England.

As he listened to tale after tale of Lady Juliet's unshakable virtue and impeccable understanding of etiquette, he'd almost reached the point where he felt sorry for old Granville. The fellow was a dry stick, always had been. But even a dry stick deserved better than an iceberg in his bed.

So when Evesham arrived today, he'd expected a pattern card of a society beauty. All the gossip had mentioned Lady Juliet's looks, as well as her lack of approachability.

Instead, he found himself in the presence of a gorgeous thoroughbred of a woman. All pride and contained passion, not to mention an immediate and powerful disdain for that notorious lothario, his Dis-Grace, the Duke of Evesham.

Ever since Portdown had beaten him in two quick hands at White's, Evesham had dreaded this visit to Afton Park. They hadn't even had to play the decider.

He'd spent the last nine years staying ahead of the tides of war on the Continent and having a deuced good time in the process. Lord Portdown had maneuvered him into a corner in a way the French army never had.

Once Evesham lost at cards, his fate was sealed. While he might be a libertine, he'd never welched on a bet. Within an hour of meeting Portdown, he'd agreed to come to Wiltshire, lines memorized and ready to take direction.

Which would be a first.

One glimpse of Lady Juliet Frain, and he perked up. What had been an unsought imposition suddenly offered an array of possibilities. Playing Romeo was going to be fun, something he never thought that he'd say.

Having fallen foul of Portdown's powers of persuasion himself, he wasn't surprised when the earl soon returned, trailed by his daughter. "Juliet will be delighted to work with you."

Evesham swallowed a snort of amusement. Lady Juliet looked delightful, but she didn't look delighted. In fact, she looked ready to commit murder.

He straightened from the convenient column and

bowed again. "I'm at your disposal, my lady."

Her magnificent bosom swelled against the modest green bodice of her gown, and her shoulders squared. Deep blue eyes, the color of the Mediterranean at sunset, narrowed on him, and in his head, he heard her silent "damn you."

By Jericho, who on earth would call this woman staid? She burned with defiance. Irresistible, really, to a man who had spent his whole life daring fate to do its worst.

She was too much woman to waste on that prating bore Granville.

At that moment, he swore that he'd keep this ravishing creature out of his enemy's desiccated claws. Or his name wasn't Lucas Hebden.

Inevitably, he couldn't help feeling that history repeated itself. But he had no regrets about his actions nearly a decade ago, and something told him that he wouldn't regret what he did this time either.

Another spectacular blond, obviously Juliet's sister, appeared at the top of the slope in front of the stage. She paused, as she realized that there was a stranger in their midst. Three dogs gathered at her feet. A red-and-white one that looked mostly beagle. A collie mix. A disreputable black rascal that looked like a poacher's dog.

Evesham had heard that Lady Portia rescued mistreated animals. Very laudable, but a little too do-gooder for him. Odd that despite her resemblance to her sister, she left him admiring but uninterested in taking matters further.

"Portia, about time." Portdown greeted her with audible irritation. "I expected you to be here when I arrived."

"Sorry, Papa. Mrs. Rose brought in a cat that the local louts were tormenting. You must have a word with Farmer Cooper about George. That boy is a menace."

"Yes, yes, I will." Irritation edged her father's tone. "Right now, I want you concentrating on Ophelia, not your confounded strays."

Portia didn't appear to be listening. It seemed to be a family trait.

Instead, she descended the stone steps, dogs trotting at her heels. As she climbed the stairs to the stage, she regarded Evesham with an open curiosity that contained none of Juliet's immediate bristling hostility. "We have a guest?"

"Yes, the Duke of Evesham is playing Romeo." Portdown gestured to his younger daughter. "May I present Juliet's sister Portia, Your Grace?"

Evesham took her hand and bowed over it. "Enchanted, Lady Portia."

"Your Grace." Giving him a broad smile, she curtsied. "I can see why Papa decided to make you Romeo."

"The minute I saw him, I knew," Portdown said. "I hope Evesham's presence on our stage will draw a large audience to our revels."

"Papa is planning to establish an annual Shakespeare festival here, where he does complete plays," Portia said. "But the neighbors don't find the prospect exciting. They're too used to seeing us all dress up and recite."

"Now people will come down from Town, if only to see a duke on the boards," Portdown said. "Once they witness the production's excellence, they'll come again."

Juliet clearly read Evesham's disgusted reaction to the idea of the ton observing his inept performance. A derisive smile appeared on her lovely face – how could anyone call a woman capable of such malicious glee a hidebound bore?

"It's quite possible that I'll be completely useless

on a stage, my lord," Evesham pointed out.

He'd relied on his lack of ability to rescue him from proceeding. But now, the last thing he wanted to do was return to London. Such a difference a snapping pair of blue eyes could make.

"I doubt it," Portdown said. "I have an instinct for talent. Anyway, I'm happy to coach you, and Juliet knows the play like the back of her hand."

"As a lady called Juliet would," Evesham said, directing a sly glance to where she stood beside her father. He approved of her coaching him.

"I knew you had something up your sleeve," Portia said to her father. "You've been so secretive, getting the Chinese room prepared and refusing to cast Henry Bell opposite Juliet as you always do."

"Henry has his qualities, but Juliet scares the life out of him. When they did Rosalind and Orlando, he looked ready to faint."

"Juliet can be terrifying," Portia said, fondness softening the remark.

"She can indeed, so be warned," Juliet muttered, and Evesham realized that she'd edged closer. Brave of her, under the circumstances.

He shifted to stand next to her, ignoring whatever Portia and Portdown were saying. "Only a foolish man would underestimate you, Lady Juliet."

"From what I hear, you *are* a foolish man, Your Grace."

He hid a smile. "Reckless, not foolish. There's a difference."

"Seeing both lead to certain disaster, I won't argue."

"Giving up the game already, my lady?"

"I can't see anything worth fighting for," she said with a sniff worthy of his grandmother, the late duchess, someone he'd liked a good deal better than he'd liked his sermonizing grandfather.

Evesham had a feeling that Grandmamma would have approved of Juliet, too. She'd appreciated an outspoken female. She'd completely cowed his mother, a bloodless little wraith who had faded away with a wasting illness when he was eight. But then his mother had never recovered from losing her husband to tetanus soon after Evesham was born.

"I have hidden qualities," he said, enjoying the cut and thrust.

He'd spent the last days cursing his inconvenient and rather inexplicable loss at cards. He didn't feel like that anymore. Right now, there was nowhere else that he'd rather be.

Juliet prickled just like the rose that he'd likened her to earlier. But then, he already knew that this bloom was beyond compare. "You've got that right, at least."

Shocked at her capitulation, he regarded her open-mouthed. "You don't think I'm a total villain?"

When another smile of pure wickedness curled her lips, a jolt of arousal slammed through him as powerful as a kick from a horse. Along with a warning that this was a formidable woman and he needed to watch his step.

"I do indeed think that. Just as I'm convinced that your qualities – if any – are very well hidden."

Not at all insulted, he burst into laughter. She was a champion. His knowledge of respectable females was limited. It turned out that he'd been missing out.

"Ahem."

At the sound of Portdown clearing his throat, Evesham sobered and reluctantly withdrew his attention from Juliet. It took an almighty effort. Desire pumped through him. Desire for the last woman that he'd ever imagined wanting. The last woman he should want.

Because a world of frustration loomed ahead. He

couldn't lure Lady Juliet into an affair. Even for a wrong 'un like him, that was a step too far. Not to mention that he'd accepted her father's hospitality. Some rules even the most dissolute gentleman didn't break.

About the best that he could hope for was a kiss or two to stop that smart mouth. And kissing her wasn't likely to ease his hunger, only feed it. Although right now, she looked more likely to bite him than kiss him.

"Perhaps I should have cast you two as Beatrice and Benedick, rather than Romeo and Juliet," Portdown said.

"I'm getting to know my leading lady," Evesham said.

Once more, Portdown wasn't listening. "All jokes aside, I could fit in a scene from *Much Ado*. It might add a nice edge of lightness to—"

Juliet and Evesham spoke in unison. "No!"

"If you insist." Portdown looked disappointed. "Let me know if you change your mind."

"We won't." Once again, Juliet's determination reminded Evesham of his daunting grandmamma.

"I'd like you two to go through your lines while I work with Portia."

"I told you not to cast me as Ophelia," Portia said with a hint of a whine. "Dying of unrequited love is just too feeble for words. Anyway, if I fell into a brook, I could get myself out."

Portdown looked so offended at this disrespectful attitude to Shakespeare that Evesham had to swallow a laugh, which made him choke.

As he caught his breath, Portdown looked worried. "Don't tell me you're coming down with a chill. That would be too bad, just when I need you to be in good voice."

"Perhaps he should rest his voice back at the

house, while I check how the maids are going with costumes," Juliet said with sudden cheerfulness.

Evesham shot her a knowing look and made sure his voice emerged steady and clear. "Only a week until the performance, Lady Juliet. No time to waste."

"Very well." He saw that she hadn't expected to prevail. She pointed halfway up the terraced slope. "Shall we, Your Grace?"

It wasn't anything like the privacy he craved, especially now that some rustics started hammering benches together from the lumber near the stage. But it was far enough away for Evesham to manage a quiet conversation.

He curled his hand around Juliet's slender arm under its pale green sleeve. "Let me assist you, my lady."

She stiffened. So did he, even as he told himself to settle down. He couldn't spend the next week at perpetual half-mast.

This strong reaction to Juliet Frain surprised Evesham. He was familiar with lust — too familiar, his critics would say. But he'd never before felt like a ninepin hit by a wooden ball. And every time he thought that he was ready to get up, Lady Juliet knocked him down again.

Through the pulse thundering in his head, he heard her catch her breath. Did the contact of skin on skin thrill her, too? Or was she just annoyed at his presumption?

Before she could think to pull away, he drew her off the stage and up the hillside. "Are you happy to sit on the ground?"

She snatched another shaky breath, although when she responded, her voice sounded as it usually did. "I'm not happy about any of this. What on earth prompted you to accept Papa's offer? I've never heard that you were interested in artistic matters."

He could imagine just what she'd heard. None of it to his credit, he knew. The scandal nine years ago had been bad enough, and retellings would only exaggerate it. Not to mention that he ran with a wild crowd on the Continent. "He challenged me to a game of cards at my club. If I won, he'd never mention Shakespeare to me again – which I now realize was unlikely, whoever came out ahead. If he won, I agreed to play Romeo." His voice flattened. "He won."

Juliet frowned. "He never loses when he's inveigling people into his schemes."

"Perhaps the Muses make sure he gets a good hand."

"That's one theory," Juliet said in a tone as dry as dust.

"Whatever the truth behind it, he trounced me. No Venetian card sharp could have done it better." Evesham released her arm and tugged off his dark blue coat to spread it on the ground for her to sit on.

She cast him a cynical look. "Very gallant."

He pretended to take her comment at face value, although they were both aware that he was no true gentleman. "Your dress is too pretty to spoil with grass stains."

That was true. The apple green muslin frock was in the first stare of fashion and made her skin look like fresh cream. She seemed to emerge from the spring greenery around her like a nymph.

The poetic atmosphere at Afton must be affecting his mind. He'd lost any impulse to romanticize his lovers well before he left Eton. He liked women. He liked them a lot. But he never suffered the smallest impulse to idealize them.

"Thank you," she said calmly.

How disappointing. For a moment there, he'd

wondered if Juliet found him as unsettling as he found her. And not just because he was a notorious rake.

Now she was back to sounding like her collected self. He much preferred her on edge. It was clear that he needed to do something to shake her composure. "May I assist you?"

Despite her wary sideways glance, she accepted his hand. Down on the stage area, Portdown put Portia through her paces, despite a chorus of barking from the canine audience.

"No, no, no, not like that," he complained. "You're meant to be ethereal."

Juliet smothered a laugh, as Evesham lowered himself to sit beside her. "Why on earth did Papa cast Portia in this particular part? She's a wonderful sister with a generous heart, but nobody in their right mind would call her delicate. I've seen her face down half a dozen bully boys to save a puppy from harm."

"Good for her. Although she ought to be careful. I suspect that so far, she's escaped unscathed more through good luck than good management."

Juliet looked at him in surprise. "You approve?"

"I approve of anyone willing to defend the weak against the strong. Robin Hood is my hero."

"Not Casanova?"

He met her steady blue gaze and was pleased when after a moment, her eyelids flickered down and she looked away. Yes, he could rattle her. He doubted many people – men – could say the same.

"You do like to lead with a challenge, don't you?" he said in a thoughtful tone. "Perhaps Portia isn't the only member of this family who lives dangerously."

Juliet had a lush mouth, created for kissing. A sharply defined upper lip and full pink lower lip perfect for a lover to nibble. That mouth firmed, as if she bit back a retort. "We should talk about the play."

If that kept her mind on him, he was happy to cooperate. "Very well."

"Where's your script?"

"I know my lines already. That was part of the infamous deal. I was to arrive word perfect and willing to work."

She'd returned to studying him, as if he was some exotic beast who had wandered onto her path. A beast that she feared would gobble her up. "You did what you were told?"

That had a deuced governessish ring, but he nodded. "A bet is sacred, don't you know?"

"Commendable." More of that sardonic tone.

Evesham didn't really blame her. He was renowned for flouting the codes of his class.

He sighed. She didn't trust him. Plenty of reasons why she shouldn't. But he wanted to find out more about her, and right now a wall of thorns discouraged genuine intimacy.

"You know, if we intend to make a half-decent fist of this performance, you'll have to stop treating me as if I have a contagious disease. We have to convince our audience that we're madly in love. You need to stop jumping every time I open my mouth."

"I don't jump."

"Yes, you do. I know that I'm not your choice of Romeo. It's not exactly my dearest wish either, to make an utter fool of myself in front of society."

"I don't know why you'd care. You can just go back to the Continent. Running away from your difficulties is nothing new for you, after all."

He winced theatrically. "You've been listening to too much gossip."

"I know who you are. I know what you did, and the damage it caused." She had a melodious voice. He imagined that she had a gift for speaking the

Bard's poetic language. But right now, her low contralto was as cold as ice, cold enough to make him shiver. "I can't help fearing that you'll end up doing damage here. I wish Papa hadn't invited you, however picturesque you are. Henry Bell may not be the world's greatest actor, but I've known him since we were children. He was my first dancing partner. He's kind and steady, and I can already tell you're neither."

"Your father is relying on me."

"If you leave, he'll get over the disappointment. The reality is you're far too old to play Romeo, just as I'm too old to play Juliet. Given all the rules that you've broken, Your Grace, what does it matter if you break one more by wriggling out of this bargain?"

"I gave your father my word." His answer emerged with uncharacteristic hauteur. "Whatever other sins I've committed, I've never broken an oath."

She didn't credit him with an ounce of honor. Usually he didn't give a rat's arse for what people thought, but half an hour in this girl's company and her opinion already mattered.

"Who will care about that when you're back chasing French courtesans or losing a fortune at some Italian casino?"

"You're mighty ready to exile me, my lady."

"You haven't seen your home in nine years. I can't imagine that you're pining for it."

There she was wrong. He'd been twenty-one when he left England, brimming with self-righteousness and a thirst for adventure. At thirty, he wasn't nearly so immune to the pointlessness of his current existence.

Over the last couple of years, memories of Lancers, his estate in Devon, had begun to nag. He wanted to come back to his country. To be an

Englishman at home, rather than an Englishman abroad.

When he discovered the unholy mess that his once-trusted bailiff had made of managing the estate, he found the perfect excuse to return.

"Perhaps I'm ready to settle down with a good woman and father the next generation. As you pointed out, I'm not as young as I once was."

She failed to hide her disbelief. "I suppose you'd like an apology for that remark."

He shrugged. "Your candor is refreshing – if a little bracing. Like standing outside in a winter gale. Definitely clears the head."

"And threatens to freeze one to death."

"All this honesty augurs well for our artistic enterprise. Now you just need to pretend that I've stolen your heart."

"You'd need to find a better actress," she said in a dark tone that made him burst out laughing once more.

"Juliet, some consideration please," Portdown shouted from the stage below. "Take His Grace to the summerhouse. The chatter is putting us off."

Juliet scrambled to her feet before Evesham could offer assistance. He caught an intriguing hint of snowy petticoats and two trim ankles in fine white stockings. She was a tall woman, built to match a big fellow like him. In his experience, tall, curvy women often had spectacular legs. And he had more experience than was good for him.

"Papa, it's not proper," she protested.

"You won't be alone. The gardeners are doing the flower beds. If you don't want to go to the summerhouse, take His Grace up to the house."

"Do you think he's trying to engineer a romance?" Evesham asked in a lazy voice.

It was possible. Despite Evesham's woeful

reputation, he was a rich man and a duke. Every girl dreamed of marrying a duke, in England at least, where the princes were boorish and spoiled.

Juliet's face betrayed her complete rejection of that idea. "Good heavens, I hope not."

"Don't spare my feelings, my lady."

She blushed, suddenly looking as young as the fictional Juliet. "You must think I'm a complete hobbledehoy."

"Haven't you worked it out yet, Lady Juliet?" He rose and bent to collect his coat. "I want you to be natural."

"I don't know why."

He tilted one eyebrow at her. "Yes, you do."

Again, her usually direct gaze avoided his. Interesting.

She was nervous, and nothing she said was complimentary. Nor was she acting like the doyenne of propriety that he'd been led to believe she was. But he was sure – *almost* – that dislike wasn't at the root of her prickliness. Much as she might wish that was the case.

No, Lady Juliet Frain found him of abiding interest. This immediate and powerful attraction was mutual. It was apparent in her barely controlled edginess and her attempts to keep him at a distance.

"Papa goes into a world of his own when he's working. I doubt that he's trying to maneuver you into proposing. Anyway, we both know that you've been caught in that trap before and you escaped, at the cost of the lady's reputation. There's no reason for things to be any different this time."

That dig went a little too deep. "You shouldn't believe everything you hear," he said sharply.

Her face flushed as red as a ripe strawberry. "I just wanted to reassure you that Papa is too involved in the production to worry about making me your duchess."

"Count me as reassured," he said dryly. "Anyway, the *on-dit* is that you've already got a duke dangling after you. By all reports, His Grace of Granville is smitten. You can't marry both of us."

It was her turn to look annoyed. "Nothing has been finalized. An eligible man just has to dance with a single female for rumors of an engagement to fly. It doesn't mean anything. You know how people love to talk."

"I do indeed."

She wasn't being entirely straight. Several reliable sources had told him that a betrothal was in the offing. His confidants had all pointed out that Granville and Lady Juliet were the ideal match. Both mature, well-intentioned, capable, principled. "I'm just letting you know that I've heard plenty about you since I returned to London."

Most of what he'd garnered about Lady Juliet had been positive. What hadn't been was grounded in jealousy, he'd soon realized. She was beautiful and rich and had a clear understanding of her duty. She also had a knack for attracting dukes. She'd been engaged to Bolton, another dry stick, before his unfortunate death. Now she'd captivated Granville. Why wouldn't people envy her?

"I'm sure most of it was twaddle."

"Perhaps if I give you the benefit of the doubt, you could return the favor."

That luscious mouth flattened again, as did her voice. "Perhaps we should concentrate on the play."

"Juliet, I've asked you once..." Her father sounded impatient.

Evesham couldn't blame him. The acoustics in this dell were excellent and while she and Evesham kept their voices low enough to hide the subject of their discussion, the constant murmur must be annoying.

Not to mention that Lady Portia was more interested in watching her sister fend off an encroaching duke than in her performance. Several times, Evesham had noticed her golden head turn in their direction.

"The summerhouse is this way," Juliet said in a subdued voice.

Eager to continue his tête-à-tête with this haughty beauty, Evesham followed her over the brow of the hill and onto a path leading through a woodland.

CHAPTER FOUR

What on earth are you doing?

As Juliet stomped through the woods, the critical voice that had taken up residence in her head over the years since her mother's death shrieked with bewildered rage.

So what indeed was she doing?

All her life, she'd strived to be a credit to her name and herself. She'd always known that her behavior provided a model for her younger sisters and that Papa, much as she loved him, wasn't fit to guide two young girls to take their place in society.

She had perfect manners, and she was famous for her poise and elegance. For goodness sake, both Portia and Viola had told her that she was so devoted to propriety that she was old before her time.

That was one reason why she was convinced that she and Granville would suit. He was a serious man, who knew that life wasn't for trifling with. They both had ambitions to make the world a better place, and she admired his clear-eyed view of the troubled state of the kingdom.

Even she had to admit that her assessment of her suitor sounded horribly sensible. But she was a horribly sensible person. Not for her the ecstasies of passion. From what she'd seen, passion only led to trouble. Look at Lady Caroline Lamb and Byron. Look at Viola and Renfrew. Look at Evesham and the disgraced Lady Vanessa Gould. Each had succumbed to their desires, and each had come to grief as a result.

Juliet's feet were firmly planted on the ground. She had no intention of throwing her bonnet over a windmill for the sake of a handsome rogue's smile. In fact, she was judged so cool and unemotional, some of society's crueler wits had dubbed her the icicle.

She'd been a mere eighteen when she first heard that, young enough to shed a few tears in the privacy of her bedroom. But these days, she relished her formidable and well-deserved reputation.

Except here she was with a rogue of surpassing handsomeness – and roguishness – and her idiot heart was skipping around and missing beats and lodging in her throat. She felt vividly alive in a way that she couldn't remember, and her manners seemed to have moved to the North Pole.

While she'd never reacted like this before, she had no doubt what it meant. Hadn't she just failed to save her younger sister from a scandal, precisely because Viola took one look at another handsome rogue and forgot every rule? When Viola was with Lord Renfrew, she looked like she dined on starlight.

Juliet had been sure that she was immune to such romantic silliness.

It turned out that she'd spoken too soon, confound it.

Because much as she wanted to despise Evesham, she couldn't control the fizz in her blood or the awareness of how tall and powerful he was. A masterpiece of virility like a hot-blooded stallion. He was everything that she abhorred, yet it seemed he was also everything that reminded her she was a woman with a woman's needs.

What in the name of heaven could she do?

Given that against all the odds, His naughty Grace seemed just as interested in her. Of course, it was likely that his eyes brightened when any nubile female appeared. This temporary madness didn't blind her to his dreadful reputation.

She tried her best to freeze him out, if only to mask his overwhelming effect on her. But even she could tell that every needling remark, every snub, betrayed that she was drawn to him like a cat to catnip. Or a drunkard to brandy, given how her mind reeled.

If she could summon her usual placid calmness, she suspected that she'd soon bore him to death. But placid calmness had also moved to the North Pole, the moment the Duke of Evesham appeared.

Honestly, she wanted to give this new and unfamiliar version of herself a good kick. Twenty-six years of prudence couldn't compete with an hour in a charming rake's company. It just wasn't fair.

A couple of paces of those long legs allowed His Grace to catch up. "Please stop fuming. You're spoiling a lovely day."

Juliet was tall for a woman. Evesham towered over her. He was imposing, whichever way she looked at him. But his extraordinary physical condition conveyed an impression of fitness and agility, rather than hulking size.

The gravel path through the copse had never before seemed too narrow. It seemed absurd now that it shrank to leave barely room for her and a far too impudent nobleman.

"A lovely day? It's a disaster," she bit out, then wanted to cut off her tongue.

All her life, her unruffled exterior had concealed a much less discreet inner conversation. Something about Evesham flushed every imprudent remark out into the open.

"I think you must accept my presence, my lady."

She sighed and stopped, as they emerged from the trees and onto a lawn leading up to a pretty wooden structure in the Chinese manner. This summerhouse by the lake had always been one of her favorite places on the estate. She could already tell that memories of His Grace's company would spoil that. "You must think every member of my family is a lunatic."

"So far, Lady Portia appears reasonable. But of course, I can only claim the most casual acquaintance with your sister."

"Actually she has her own eccentricities. Until today, I'd have said I had the steadiest head in the family."

"Oh, dear," he said with such exaggerated alarm that despite all her turmoil, she couldn't help laughing.

When Juliet caught her breath, she felt a little better. She was fretting herself into a decline when there was no need. Surely she could restrain herself from leaping on this picturesque scoundrel. He made her aware of her femininity in a way that she didn't appreciate. But he'd be gone in a week, and she could go back to being the even-tempered woman she'd always been.

Amusement played around his expressive mouth in a beguiling way that she struggled not to notice. She'd heard so much about the wicked Duke of Evesham. She'd imagined someone oily and worn out with lechery, not this vigorous, humorous man with laughing brown eyes and a smile that set her heart on fire.

She refused to burn for Evesham. She outright refused.

With luck, Granville still intended to propose and her golden future would unroll exactly as she'd planned. This unfortunate weakness for Evesham would prove a mere bump in the road, not a detour into uncharted wilderness.

Feeling more in charge of herself, she approached the summerhouse. She nodded to Haynes, the head gardener, who responded with a bow from where he supervised replanting the annuals around the gazebo.

"Papa wants us to run through our lines."

"Then by all means, let us start." Evesham pointed to the wooden steps. "Perhaps if you stand at the top to give the impression of the balcony? I'll stay on the path below."

"Good idea." She positioned herself in the summerhouse doorway and tried to place herself in the scene. A young girl in the throes of first love with an unsuitable young man. A girl trembling on the threshold between childhood and maturity.

Juliet Frain had been thrust too early into a mother's role. Perhaps she related so well to Juliet Capulet because the part offered her a chance to experience all the heady emotions denied to the real Juliet.

Heady emotions that led straight to a tragic end.

Much better to maintain control and follow the ton's rules and stick to the tried and true.

But wise counsel fell on deaf ears, when she stared down into an unforgettable face and met a gaze alight with desire.

He's just playacting. He's just playacting, she reminded herself in desperation, as her hands snagged in her filmy green skirts. Hands that ached to reach out and snatch forbidden pleasures.

Nor did it help when that infernally appealing baritone launched into the famous lines. "But, soft! What light through yonder window breaks? It is the east, and Juliet is the sun."

Somehow Juliet survived her rehearsal with Evesham and the afternoon's practice onstage under her father's direction. At first, she'd feared that she'd melt into a puddle under the ardor that the duke aimed her way. But reminding herself that it was pretense bolstered her defenses. She wouldn't let the Bard's magic sweep her away.

She'd been so guarded, in fact, that her father had criticized her portrayal as wooden. Whereas to her vexation, he'd gushed with praise over His Grace's Romeo.

It was almost a letdown that once they'd started their run-through, Evesham had behaved with perfect decorum. Granville himself couldn't have been more urbane.

Except...

Except attraction hummed beneath every word. She'd never been so aware of anyone's physical presence. It was as if the duke soaked up all the air in the world and left her breathless and giddy in his wake.

Now with the approach of evening, she trudged up to her bedroom. She was exhausted and in dire need of some solitude to soothe her shattered nerves. The day already felt like it had lasted for a year, and she still had to get through dinner.

So it was a blow to open her door and find Portia serving herself from the tea tray that Juliet had requested earlier.

Red the beagle and Scratch the lurcher observed their mistress with hopeful eyes, as she picked up a chicken sandwich. Ella, the old collie, had trouble with the stairs these days and would be hanging around the kitchen.

"So do tell all." Portia's avid curiosity made Juliet feel tarnished. Even though she told herself that she'd done nothing to be ashamed of.

"There is no all."

"Don't be mean. I nearly died of shock when I realized that Papa's mysterious Romeo was the infamous Duke of Evesham. Who looks like he's fallen like a bag of beans for your charms. Perhaps you'll go down in history as the lady who enchanted three dukes."

"Don't be a henwit, Porsh," Juliet said with a snap. "He's not enchanted."

"He looked it. I loathe Shakespeare, and even I felt a thrill when he said all those marvelous things to you at the rehearsal."

"That's the play."

"Henry Bell never looked like that."

"Well, the play, and His Grace proving that he's quite the actor." Evesham's skill with his lines had surprised her. And left her unwillingly impressed. She'd expected him to be tone-deaf to the poetry. "I suppose it goes along with a total disregard for morality. If one juggles a crowd of wanton ladies, it must pay to be a convincing liar."

"But what did you talk about on the hillside when I was with Papa? I tried to listen, but I had to keep rabbiting on about rue and rosemary. Honestly, that scene may as well be a page out of a recipe book. It would make more sense if it was."

"Nothing special." Juliet wandered close enough to pour herself a cup of tea and pick up a ham sandwich. Evesham had maintained his suave demeanor through lunch, but the knowledge that he was watching had stolen her appetite. Now she was hungry. "Will you undo me please?"

The day had been warm, and her dress was as tired as she was. Tonight she intended to wear something with plenty of starch.

"Turn around." Portia began to unhook the back of the gown then loosened the corset strings.

"You looked like you wanted to hit him," Portia said as Juliet finished her tea and moved toward the screen that hid the washstand.

"The person I really wanted to hit was Papa. He must know Evesham isn't good ton and that he and Granville have a long and nasty history."

"He mightn't, you know. He pays very little attention to tattle. And you can't argue that Evesham will make a much more dashing Romeo than poor Henry. Whatever else you may say about Papa, he has a great instinct for casting."

Juliet ground her teeth and scowled at the blowsy pink peonies painted on the screen that separated her from her cursed chatty sister. At least now she didn't have to guard her expression. "I wish he had a marvelous instinct for who was a proper person to invite to the house."

"Oh?" Portia said on a rising inflection. "So the duke did make unsuitable remarks? I was sure he did. He must make an exciting change from Granville."

Portia wasn't in favor of Juliet's marital plans. She thought Granville was the dullest man in England.

"Granville is always polite."

"Granville is always a first-rate bore. Honestly, don't you swoon when Evesham gives you that lazy smile that's all teeth and temptation, as if he could eat you up in one bite?"

Juliet was grateful that the screen hid her blush. Because the lamentable truth was that she knew exactly what Portia meant. And, yes, it did give her a frisson, confound the man's brilliant dark eyes.

"Portia Frain, you need to stop reading all those books from the Minerva Press."

"And you need to read a few more. They might help you to loosen up a bit. You need to convince an audience that you're in alt over Evesham."

"That's asking too much." Juliet's hands shook, as she tugged off her limp gown and undergarments. "He doesn't appeal to me at all. I admire men of principle, not silver-tongued cads who believe they leave a trail of swooning women behind them wherever they go."

Liar, liar, liar.

Because the unpalatable truth was that some hitherto unruly element in her nature thrived in Evesham's company. It was infuriating. It was unacceptable. It was terrifying.

Portia, drat her, responded with a disbelieving snort. "The lady doth protest too much, methinks."

Juliet poured warm water from the blue-and-white ewer into the bowl and began to wash. This was such an everyday action. It seemed mad that today, she couldn't help imagining Evesham's hands upon her skin instead of damp flannel.

Heaven save her. The man was like a contagious disease. She needed to get a grip on herself quick smart. "You're Papa's daughter, if you're quoting Shakespeare at me."

"I need to get something out of all these amateur dramatics. I wish Viola was here. It doesn't feel right to put on a show without her. I suppose if you marry Granville, I'll have to play all the female roles. It's enough to make me want to get married."

"You sound like that's a fate worse than death."

Juliet lifted the towel to dry herself.

"Papa puts up with my animals. I'm not sure a husband will."

Juliet wasn't sure either. "Evesham won't care enough about a wife to pull her into line. He might be your perfect match."

"You don't mean that."

No, she didn't. Which was as mad as everything else that had happened on this topsy-turvy day. "He might be just the neglectful spouse you need. If you could tolerate him straying."

"Evesham doesn't know I'm alive. He only has eyes for you."

"That's the play." She seemed to be blaming a lot on the play.

"That's all the time."

"I'm not his sort of woman." With unsteady hands, she tied her drawers at her waist and tugged a clean shift over her head.

"I'd say you're exactly his sort of woman."

She pulled a pink silk peignoir over her undergarments and emerged from behind the screen to see Portia sitting at the table with the dogs at her feet.

"Porsh, I told you not to feed them up here."

Portia looked up from the scraps of chicken that she was giving to Red. "Sorry."

She didn't sound sorry. Nor did she pause in her actions.

"I'm far too correct and dull and well-behaved for His Grace. He doesn't waste his time with respectable women. He's too aware that dallying with virtuous ladies can only lead to a trip down the aisle."

"It didn't with Vanessa Gould."

Something Juliet needed to remember when she found herself contemplating smiling dark eyes and the touch of a hard masculine hand. "No, it didn't. And it should have. That's warning enough to beware of his charm."

Portia observed her with an inquisitive expression. "So you do think he's charming?"

Juliet turned away to pick up another sandwich before her sister could give them all away. And to hide her reaction from someone who knew her far too well. "Of course he's charming. And handsome. But he's a man without substance or ethics. He isn't a man a woman can rely on."

"Perhaps not. But on the other hand, I suspect he could be very entertaining. You've devoted your life to duty, Juliet. Don't you want to enjoy yourself for once?"

She gave a sigh heavier than the question warranted and put down the sandwich that she was no longer interested in eating. "Not if it means losing everything that's important to me."

CHAPTER FIVE

When Juliet went downstairs to the drawing room before dinner, her father waited alone with a glass of champagne. At her arrival, his expression turned shifty and he surged to his feet.

Knowing him of old, she closed the door to the hall and planted herself in front of it. "Papa, I'm glad I caught you."

He edged toward the entrance to the dining room. "My dear, I must—"

"Don't you dare run away."

He sighed and sank back into his chair. "You mean to harangue me. I can already tell."

"I do indeed. You tricked the duke into coming to Afton. Release him from his obligation immediately."

"He's quite free to go."

"Not while he thinks you won that card game fair and square, he's not. A man might ruin women all over Christendom, but heaven forbid he welches on a gambling debt."

Her father glared at her. "I did win fair and square, and if you even mention card sharping to His

Grace, I'll disown you."

"I won't speak a word, if you allow him to go. I want Henry Bell to play Romeo. Can you imagine how tongues will wag, once the beau monde discovers that the greatest rake of the age is sleeping a few doors down from your unmarried daughters?"

"That ensures us an audience. The ton is agog to see His Grace, especially as he turns out to be quite the performer. Whereas you—"

"Don't try and distract me, Papa. Evesham goes or I do."

Her father studied her. "I won't believe that he's offered you insult."

"Why not? He's been seducing women since he left the schoolroom."

His eyes narrowed on her. "Juliet, has he exceeded the bounds of propriety?"

How she wished that she could provide a list as long as her arm of Evesham's sins at Afton Park. But she wasn't a liar. "Not yet."

"I didn't think he would." His shoulders lowered. "He strikes me as a good type of fellow."

Juliet stared aghast at her father, not sure where she could start. "Papa, he—"

Her father raised his hand. "We all know how stories get blown up."

"I've stated my position." Juliet drew herself up to her full height. "Excuse His Grace from his promise, or I'll tell him you cheated at cards."

Her father's jaw set in a stubborn line that she knew from past experience meant that he didn't intend to cooperate. "If you tell him that, you dishonor the family name."

"If he stays, the family name mightn't be the only thing dishonored."

"Can't we..."

Whatever her father was about to say, it faded to

silence as the door behind her opened. Juliet stepped aside as His Grace sauntered in.

Heaven help her. In evening wear, he was even more devastating than he'd been in a creased coat, spouting romantic nonsense to an unresponsive Miss Capulet. The stark black clothes made him more devilish than ever. Just so must he have strolled into hundreds of ballrooms on the Continent, sure of his impact on every foolish female present.

Juliet might be female, but she wasn't foolish. She told herself that her pulse kicked into a gallop because she despised his trashy attractions.

"Ah, Evesham, old man, have some champagne." Papa scampered forward and caught the duke's arm to coax him further into the room. "How do you like your apartments? Fine view of the lake from those rooms, what?"

"Indeed," Evesham said, but the gaze he leveled on Juliet was questioning.

Papa poured a glass. "Juliet, take His Grace his wine."

Juliet realized that she was staring at the duke in a most rag-mannered way. Bending her head to hide the heat in her cheeks – to Hades with him, nobody made her blush – she picked up the glass and carried it the short distance across to Evesham.

"Your Grace," she said under her breath.

Instead of accepting his drink, he regarded it with a thoughtful expression. "The play must be getting to me. I find myself awake to melodramatic possibilities. You haven't dropped any hemlock in this, perchance?"

Her father gave a nervous titter, as Juliet sent the duke a straight look. "Of course not."

He took the glass. "That's a relief."

"Although I'd be careful about eating too much of

the fish soup, if I were you."

She shouldn't like the way that his mouth quirked, as if he muffled a laugh. "Warning noted."

Juliet returned to the sideboard to pour herself some champagne. "My father wishes to speak to you."

"It can wait," Papa said.

She glowered at her parent. "No, it can't."

Her father sighed, as if he carried the weight of the world on his shoulders. He set down his glass with a despairing gesture, reminiscent of King Lear ruing his family's betrayal. As a man with three daughters, Portdown related to Lear.

"Juliet has made me see that I've been unfair on you, compelling you to leave London to join us in our great endeavor. She believes I should give you the chance to step aside from playing Romeo."

Juliet waited for the duke to leap at the offer. She didn't know why he'd left the fleshpots of France and Italy to return to England, but it certainly wasn't to rusticate in the wilds of Wiltshire playing at theatricals.

He stared into his champagne glass as the silence lengthened. By the time he spoke, her nerves were so stretched, they threatened to snap. "That's very…considerate of her."

They both knew that she wasn't considerate at all. She wanted him out of her life.

Evesham should be happy to go. London was packed with diversions for a man with deep pockets and no scruples. At Afton Park, the only game on offer was the pursuit of a virginal spinster. Why on earth was he hesitating?

Why on earth was he hesitating? Evesham had come down here most unwillingly. He had urgent plans to go to Lancers and sort out the havoc there. This week in Wiltshire had always been a dashed inconvenience.

Except he'd rather enjoyed playing Romeo this afternoon. If only because his Juliet eyed him as if she wasn't sure whether he was about to bite her.

When she'd told him that she'd poisoned his soup, he damn near kissed her. Which, given that he lacked suicidal impulses, was an odd reaction. She didn't much like him, or at least she didn't want to.

In all his wild days, he'd learned one thing. Women in general liked him. It was a novelty to meet one who didn't.

What a pity to bring the chase to an end so soon and in such an anticlimactic fashion.

"Surely you'd rather be in Town catching up with old friends," Juliet said in the tone that she would use to cajole a toddler into eating his carrots.

Evesham took a sip of wine. "My old friends have managed without me for nine years. Another few days won't make much difference."

The sad fact was that the majority of his cronies had dropped him like a hot potato when he'd fled to Berlin in Vanessa's company. Society's sticklers would still prefer him to stay on the other side of the English Channel.

Juliet looked sulky. Which made him want to kiss her even more. That pouting lower lip filled him with all sorts of depraved fancies.

Her father stopped looking like his dog had died and brightened up. "On the other hand, if you'd like to stay, I'd be most grateful. You showed such promise today, it would be a crime against art if you abandoned the project."

"Papa..." Juliet said in a warning voice, her hand

tightening around her wineglass.

Her father shot her an annoyed glance. "Well, if he wants to stay, I'm not going to throw him out."

"Pleased to hear it." Evesham really shouldn't revel in the way Juliet looked ready to explode.

It astonished him that everyone had described her as a cold fish. Instead, she was a still water that ran deep. All his instincts told him that those depths concealed a passion that would send a lover flying into the sun.

"So you'll stay?" Portdown looked so hopeful that Evesham nearly laughed.

"I'd hate to put you out, having to cast someone else."

"Capital."

"Capital," Juliet echoed in a completely different tone.

Lady Portia appeared, and looked around after a quick curtsy. "I always seem to come in on the tail end of things. You could cut the atmosphere in here with a knife. What's happened?"

"His Grace has agreed to stay to play Romeo." Portdown passed his younger daughter a filled glass. "Isn't that marvelous?"

The glance that Portia cast Juliet hinted that she knew of her sister's wish to banish Evesham. But the smile that she bestowed on him brimmed with approval. He couldn't imagine why, but he sensed that he had an ally in the younger Frain sister.

"Marvelous. You show real talent, Your Grace. Did you do theatricals at school?"

"No, I was too busy on the cricket pitch. And thank you for the kind words. I enjoyed it. Which is a surprise, as I thought I'd feel completely out of my element."

"It didn't show. You're a natural." Portia leveled an unfavorable glance on her sister. "You, on the other hand, Juliet, were as stiff as a board. I've never seen you like that. You'll have to warm up a bit before the performance, or people will think Romeo has fallen for a complete bore."

"I am a complete bore," Juliet said, for his benefit, Evesham knew.

"Usually not when you're on stage," her sister said with insulting frankness. "When you've done the part before, you've been lovely. Radiant with passion and ardor."

Now, that was something Evesham would like to see.

"That's true, Juliet," Portdown agreed, refilling his glass. "I don't know what's wrong with you."

The sidelong glance that Juliet directed at Evesham indicated that *he* was what was wrong with her. He lifted his glass to hide a smug smile.

"I'm not right for the part, Papa."

Portdown dismissed that remark with a wave that became very familiar. "Nonsense. You've brought me to tears playing Juliet in the past. You're just getting distracted. And of course, you have a new leading man. It will come right on the night."

"You always say that," Juliet said on a sour note.

"I'm always right, aren't I?"

"You know, he is," Portia said. "Remember when I was Desdemona and I always giggled when Papa tried to strangle me? Yet it was really powerful, the night we put *Othello* on for the neighbors."

"Everything mightn't be right this time," Juliet said, shooting her sister a look as if to ask, "Whose side are you on?"

"Of course it will be. You just need to rehearse a bit more," Portdown said in a comfortable voice. Evesham wanted to say "Hear, hear."

"We should swap the parts around. Portia will make a lovely Juliet, and she's younger than I am. I can play Ophelia. We both already know the roles."

Portdown frowned as if considering the plan, then shook his head. "No, you and His Grace look so right together. You'll get into the spirit of the part."

"Papa—"

"The matter is closed." He turned as the butler opened the door to the dining room. "Ah, dinner. All that work in the outdoors gives a man an appetite, don't you agree, Your Grace?"

"I do indeed," he said, but he wasn't looking at Portdown. He was looking at Portdown's eldest daughter.

With only four at dinner, Evesham didn't expect to speak to Juliet one-on-one. But as Portdown straightaway began to lecture Portia about the way she played Ophelia, that left Juliet and Evesham in a private bubble on the other side of the long mahogany table.

How fortuitous.

"I know you don't approve of me, my lady, but I believe the matter is settled," he said, as he eyed a bowl of lobster bisque with a frown. "It's only for a week."

"People will talk, and we're already trying to live down the scandal of Viola's wedding to Renfrew." She picked up her spoon and began to eat.

"You can't stop people talking. You certainly can't arrange your life around the fear of gossip."

"Perhaps *you* can't." She responded to his worried expression with a cool smile. "I wouldn't really poison you. The soup is quite safe. You have my word on it."

He picked up his spoon and tasted the bisque.

Delicious. "You want to get rid of me."

"But plotting an inconvenient duke's murder is too Shakespearean for words. And likely to overshadow Papa's gala."

"Not to mention that it would spoil the duke's enjoyment of the occasion."

Her modest silk dress sported a large ruff that covered her to just under her chin. The sleeves were long, and the gown merely skimmed her magnificent figure. She didn't need to tell him that she'd dressed to look as forbidding as possible. This austere gown conveyed no hint of glorious spring.

But if she meant to play down her looks, she failed utterly. The rich blue made her eyes as mysterious as a moonlit midnight, and the dress's severe cut couldn't hide the lush curves of her bosom. The severe knot that confined her golden hair emphasized her high cheekbones and the delicate strength of her jawbone.

"No, no, no, Portia!" Portdown said from the head of the table. "That's not the idea at all."

"He takes it all very seriously, doesn't he?" Evesham said.

"He does." To his surprise, Juliet's smile was fond as she looked at her father. So far, Evesham had only seen evidence of the differences between Portdown and his daughter. The principal difference of course being how they felt about Evesham. "He's a brilliant actor, as you'll see on the night of the show. I suspect if he'd had to make his living on the boards, he'd have managed very well."

"So you accept that I'll be here?"

She sighed in capitulation. At least that was how it sounded. "It seems I must."

He tried really hard to conceal his triumph. He doubted that he succeeded. "Thank you."

Juliet's disdainful glance sparked heat in his

unruly blood. "I won't say you're welcome."

"You'll like me when you get to know me."

"I doubt it. But everyone else in my family thinks you're marvelous. I refuse to fight a losing battle."

He responded with a gust of laughter. "You can yield with honor."

He suspected that Juliet did everything with honor. She was that sort of woman. His grandmother was the only person he'd ever known with anything like this gallant girl's courage and grit. Yet Juliet possessed a warmth that his grandmother had lacked.

No wonder Granville had set his marital hopes on her. She'd make a perfect duchess.

"I haven't yielded, Your Grace." Her direct stare told him that she knew exactly what he'd like to do with her.

No doubt she did. This was no wide-eyed debutante. This was a woman who understood the world and its dangers.

Right now, she counted the Duke of Evesham among those dangers.

To his regret. Not to mention to the credit of her good sense.

However, strategy hinted that he should change the subject. "Your father is an insightful director."

Juliet accepted the silent offer of a truce, thank heaven. "Yes, he is."

"And his daughters inherited his acting talent."

"Not really. Although Viola has a knack for comedy, which is a surprise because she's very self-effacing in real life."

"Yet she caused a scandal?"

"If it had been Portia, I'd be less surprised. But Viola always had her nose in a book, and she never showed the slightest interest in any of the local boys. Even if she fell head over heels for a young man, I imagined her choosing someone sweet and unworldly. A bit like Henry Bell, who you'll meet while you're here. But Renfrew is a wild young man with a reputation almost as bad as—"

"Mine?"

She didn't respond to that. She didn't need to. "Now that they're married, I hope he doesn't break my sister's heart. If he does, I may just poison *his* soup."

Viola Frain's hurried wedding had been the fresh tattle when Evesham arrived in London. Everybody forecast disaster for the cobbled-together match.

If Viola was anything like her older sister, perhaps Renfrew had found himself in the grip of overpowering attraction. After all, Evesham was, and nobody in their right mind would say that he and Lady Juliet had anything in common.

He regarded her in admiration. "How fierce you are."

She shrugged, as though strength of character in a female was nothing remarkable. He'd clearly associated with the wrong females. An admission with which most of the world would agree.

"I defend the people I love."

He dipped his head in acknowledgment as a footman slid the empty bowl out of the way. "Then they are privileged to earn your regard."

She frowned. More in confusion than disapproval, for once. "You sound sincere."

"I am occasionally," he said lightly. "Don't tell anyone."

Her bemusement lingered. "And we almost managed a sensible conversation."

"Along with a few slurs on my reputation."

"I'm sorry." Appealing humor flirted with that lush pink mouth. He wished to glory that she'd give him a genuine smile. "If I was as proper as everyone thinks I am, I'd pretend to be too refined to listen to gossip."

"How did Lady Portia describe you? Full of passion and ardor?"

Another pretty blush. "That's only when I'm playing a part."

"Or perhaps you reveal your true self when you're acting."

To his regret, her expression hardened. For a moment, she'd shown signs of warming up. "I don't think that's how it works. After all, you're earnest and romantic when you play Romeo, and we all know that has no relation to reality."

"Ouch." He gave an exaggerated wince. The atmosphere at Afton Park must be getting to him. Everything he did seemed exaggerated here, including how exciting he found his leading lady. "For a moment there, you treated me as a human being. I rather liked it."

A plate of Dover sole in butter sauce appeared before him. Lord Portdown kept a good table. This week in the country was replete with unexpected pleasures. The greatest and most unexpected of which turned out to be the woman sitting beside him.

Another of those direct looks warned him not to underestimate her. "I suspect you're all too human, Your Grace."

He accepted the silent message that he wasn't to trifle with her. Accepted the message but had no intention of heeding it.

Before Evesham could come up with an adequate response to her remark, Portdown stopped browbeating poor Portia and asked him about theater that he'd attended on the Continent. He bit back the urge to say that he mostly went to a performance to trawl for his next mistress. Juliet was so determined to cling to her composure that it was a pleasure to see her bristle and fume when he refused to succumb to her disapproval.

His accounts of Paris led to a general discussion on international styles of production that continued for the rest of dinner. There were no more thorny, thrilling, electric exchanges with Juliet.

But as Evesham lay awake in his luxurious chamber upstairs, it was his conversation with Juliet that lingered in his mind. Much had been said, but more had remained unspoken.

Even if she wasn't aware of it, she laid down a challenge. A challenge that he meant to meet.

CHAPTER SIX

"My bounty is as boundless as the sea, my love as deep. The more I give to thee, the more I have, for both are infinite."

A frustrated roar rose from her father. "No, for the last time, no! You're not talking to the housekeeper about the next coal delivery. You're confessing your forbidden love to an ardent admirer. Can we have just a touch of emotion, for pity's sake?"

Juliet gritted her teeth – not for the first time. Her jaw was aching.

She turned on her minuscule balcony to observe her father where he stood in front of the stage. Very deliberately, she didn't catch Evesham's eye.

The duke stood below, staring up at her as if he'd never seen anything as superb in his entire life, the lying toad. He had no trouble entering into the spirit of the play. But of course, he'd been born a deceiver.

"I'm trying, Papa."

"No, you're not. Do it again and inject a bit of passion this time."

Passion? That was just what she was worried about, heaven help her.

Despite all the urgings of good sense, she couldn't

control her traitorous senses. And her traitorous senses were convinced that the Duke of Evesham was the most attractive man she'd ever met. Three days of him wooing her in the person of Romeo undermined every scrap of her customary composure.

In her head, she knew that he was playing a part. So was she – however inadequate she might be. But when he focused all that heated attention on her, her body reacted as if the poetry promoted a genuine seduction. Of Juliet Frain. Not Juliet Capulet.

Even worse, Juliet Frain, despite all society's rules, couldn't help thinking that giving in to Evesham's blandishments might be heavenly.

What the devil was wrong with her? Since the wayward duke had crashed into her measured existence, she didn't recognize herself.

It didn't help that she had an unpleasant suspicion that His Dis-Grace was well aware of his unfortunate effect on her. How could he not be? He knew women, and he knew women had a soft spot for him. That roguish glint in his eyes must have turned sensible females silly since he met his first nursemaid.

At rehearsals, he, unlike her temperamental Papa, was endlessly patient with her. She wished to glory that this patience didn't convey his belief that resistance would soon melt and she'd tumble into his arms.

She wished to glory that she could say he was mistaken.

But half a week into his visit, and she wasn't sleeping, and she wasn't eating, and her nerves were stretched so taut that she jumped at the slightest sound. Even Portia had started avoiding her company because Juliet, always ready with a dry response, had become positively waspish.

Juliet straightened her backbone and told herself that she could withstand this tawdry temptation. She spoke her lines again, but faltered as Evesham, instead of keeping to a safe distance, began to climb the makeshift balcony.

"What on earth is this?" she hissed, as the wooden frame lurched under his weight.

"I'm doing what any halfway decent Romeo would."

His laughing response made her itch to push him off the balcony. She'd immediately noted and condemned his habit of treating life as a game.

"Get down." Her fists bunched at her sides. "Get down at once."

"No, don't stop," her father called. "I'm liking where this is going."

Where this was going was straight to disaster. Juliet backed away, but not fast enough. Evesham reached the top and caught her hand in his.

Juliet froze as those long fingers wrapped around hers. Froze, even as heat flared through her. The power of the contact stole her breath, set her heart tumbling, made her forget that they had an audience.

Unforgivably but unstoppably, she twined her fingers around his. For the first time in days, she stared into his eyes. Frantic warnings made no impact. Instead, she felt as though she plummeted deep into that velvety dark brown gaze.

Right now, Evesham didn't look like a double-dealing snake. He looked like a man half mad with wanting her. Even worse, he looked like a man she could trust.

Her shaky exhalation jammed in her throat, as her crazy heart set off on another wild gallop.

"Madam!"

Not even the sound of her father speaking the

Nurse's offstage line could break the moment.

For once, Juliet Capulet held sway over her actions. She spoke lines that she felt like she'd known in her cradle. "I hear some noise within. Dear love, adieu."

Rather than releasing her, Evesham brought her hand to his lips. She waited in a fever of suspense for him to kiss her hand. But he didn't close the inch that separated his mouth from her skin. The effect was almost more powerful than actual contact.

"You have a line," he murmured, still holding her hand, the devil.

She blinked at him as if she didn't speak English, then she snatched her hand back when she realized quite how she'd fallen under his spell.

Juliet swallowed to moisten a mouth as dry as the Sahara. But her voice emerged scratchy all the same. "Anon, good nurse."

Her skin tingled where he'd touched her, and she stretched out her fingers to banish the sensation. She didn't have the strength to break his gaze as she continued. "Sweet Montague, be true. Stay but a while. I will come again."

But her feet seemed glued to the rough pine boards of the floor. Her heart swelled until it filled her chest. Evesham smiled at her, a sweet smile that told her he found her as enchanting as she found him.

"Go," he said on a thread of sound.

Hectic color infusing her cheeks, she started. What in the name of all that was holy was she doing? Did she want to join the list of women the scoundrel duke had used and abandoned? At this rate, she'd be begging him to ruin her.

Blindly, she turned and stumbled through the door behind her that led to a rickety stairway. Her shaking hand clenched hard around the rail to save her from falling. The warmth of his touch lingered, God rot him.

Her heart still raced fast enough to make her dizzy, and now nausea churned in her stomach, soured her mouth. How had the duke managed to make time stand still? Her reaction to him had always troubled her, but only now was she absolutely terrified.

Did she have a hope of withstanding his charm? He was human opium.

Juliet trembled as if she was ill. Through the pounding in her head, she barely heard Evesham speak his next lines.

"O blessed, blessed night! I am afeard. Being in night, all this is but a dream, too flattering-sweet to be substantial."

Curse him, this wasn't a dream. It was a nightmare.

"Much, much better," she heard her father say. "Juliet, you're getting it at last."

She sucked in a shuddering breath, smoothed the skirts of her prim navy frock – they were yet to rehearse in costume – and made herself step back onto the balcony.

"Thank you, Papa." Her voice was too high, but her father had turned to talk to one of the workmen and wasn't paying her any attention.

She wished that counted for Evesham as well. But without looking at him, she knew he watched her with more of that steady concentration she felt in the pores of her skin.

"That was dashed wonderful, my lady," he said. "You came alive."

She shot him what she hoped was a dismissive glance. Although what power could her censure have, after she'd been staring at him as if he was a bowl of custard and she'd just found her spoon? "It always takes me a little while to find my way into a role. This time, it's been more difficult than usual because I didn't feel the emotion."

She'd hoped to squash his pretensions, but as usual, she failed. A slow smile curled that expressive mouth. "My apologies for putting you off your oats. You've found the part now. For a moment there, I forgot we were acting."

So had she, to blazes with him. She'd come back to herself enough to sound cool and collected as she responded. "That's the magic of the theater, isn't it? Although it would be a very foolish man indeed who read anything more into what just happened."

His eyes narrowed on her. "Be careful, Juliet. There's a hint of 'The lady doth protest too much, methinks,' in the air."

Portia had said the same thing to her. She was getting rather sick of the quotation.

Now Juliet steeled herself to meet that knowing gaze and summon an insouciant smile. "Wrong play, Your Grace. Papa and Portia are doing the scenes from *Hamlet*."

He dipped his tousled dark head, as if acknowledging a point in a fencing match. "I stand corrected."

He twisted his long, elegant body and leaped lightly back onto the stage. Juliet knew that it was unworthy of her, but she'd dearly love to see him fumble the landing. But of course, he didn't. She was the only one who had difficulty finding a firm footing in this ghastly situation.

"Let's go back to the beginning and get some of that feeling into your entrance, Juliet," her father said.

The idea of speaking reams of impassioned verse to her bugbear made her want to growl. But she squared her shoulders and told herself that she only had to survive another four days. Surely she had the strength to endure that.

Yet as her eyes inevitably fell on His Dis-Grace, a crushing weight of fear settled in her middle. Who knew what state she'd be in by the time the gala came around?

CHAPTER SEVEN

"See, how she leans her cheek upon her hand! Oh, that I were a glove upon that hand, that I might touch that cheek!"

The mellow baritone wrenched Juliet out of her preoccupation. From where she sat on the plinth that supported her balcony, she peered through the fading light.

Evesham stood about halfway up the rise where, in two days, their audience would gather. Despite wearing the elegant black coat that he'd sported at dinner, he still managed to look disheveled. And spectacular.

When she didn't respond straightaway, Evesham sprang down the hillside with the athletic ease that had stolen her breath the first day. And still did, confound him.

Without doubt, he made her mad, no matter how hard she fought to resist him. Even worse, she didn't like him. Or rather, she didn't want to.

She was a woman of principle. How could she yearn for a man with no principles at all?

It just wasn't fair.

Emotional turmoil was turning her life upside

down. It seemed ridiculous that physical attraction should dumbfound a woman of twenty-six, who had already been betrothed and was set to be betrothed again. But while she'd liked both of her suitors, nothing in those prosaic courtships set her blood bubbling like champagne shaken inside a bottle.

Juliet had no idea what to do about it. Telling herself to ignore Evesham had no effect whatsoever. It was as if her very skin listened for his footstep. Never in her life had she been so torn between what she knew she should do and what she wanted to do.

"You followed me." She kept her voice down, although they were well away from the house and the outdoor staff had finished work hours ago.

He didn't bother denying it. "You've been avoiding me."

She rose on shaky legs, as he climbed onto the stage. "I shouldn't be alone with you."

There wasn't much risk of discovery. After dinner, Papa had retired to his library to practice his soliloquies and Portia was busy in the stables with a new litter of kittens. None of the indoor servants would venture into the mansion's gardens to take their leisure.

Evesham prowled toward her. "'Shouldn't' is your favorite word."

She stiffened her backbone and told herself that under no circumstances would she succumb to the romantic atmosphere. "I'm frightfully dull."

A self-mocking smile teased his lips. Although it was possible that he mocked her instead. "No, you're sweet and charmingly unsure of yourself as a woman."

Her lips pursed. She hated that description. It made her seem weak and helpless. "That doesn't sound like someone who would appeal to the licentious Duke of Evesham."

"It doesn't." He ran his hand through his hair, causing a lock to tumble across his high forehead.

She bit back an irritated groan. For goodness sake, could he look any more inviting? She was doomed.

"Then why pursue me?" she said with more of the same irritation. "You're like a cat playing with a mouse."

His expression tightened, and he lunged forward to take her hand. "Juliet, no, sweetheart, never think that."

He'd touched her when they'd rehearsed. He'd taken her arm to escort her into dinner. Every time, the impact was like thunder.

But this? This was like an earthquake. Because this wasn't a polite gesture. This was skin meeting skin, heat flowing through the contact, a man claiming a woman he wanted.

Heaven forgive her, Juliet hungered for more. Even worse, she wanted him to call her sweetheart again, however little the endearment meant.

"You have no right to use my Christian name." She jerked free. Because she might be innocent, but she knew that holding his hand opened the door to further intimacies.

To her surprise, he let her go with another of those mocking smiles. "I call you Juliet all the time."

"In the play."

"And in my dreams."

She'd been on edge since he'd arrived. Not an altogether unpleasant sensation, although she wished it was. Now, fear chilled the wanton heat in her blood.

"Stop it." She retreated, bumping into the wooden frame under the balcony. "You don't have to act the lover now."

"I'm not playing."

"Neither am I." She sounded like she meant it, thank heaven. "I'm going back to the house, and I don't want to be alone with you ever again."

He bowed his head. "As you wish."

His show of cooperation, when she knew that he'd continue with this game infuriated her. Instead of leaving, she decided to stay to set him to rights. "This can go nowhere. Do you think I'll lie down with you, just for the sake of a wink? You've been away from England too long, if that's the case."

Her scolding didn't quash his impudence. Amusement sparked in his eyes. "Perhaps you should wait until I ask you."

Her temper spiked. "So you're saying this...this campaign you're waging is all in my imagination?"

"You know it's not." This time, when he took her hand, she didn't pull away. "Come and sit by me. We'll talk."

"Talk?" she repeated on a rising note. "You don't want to talk."

More of that dratted attractive self-derision twisted his lips. "Of course I do."

"You want to seduce me."

By now, she should know better than to try and shame him into retreat. He nodded. "That, too."

"You won't succeed." She winced at the false bravado in her voice.

"I'll take note," he said with a solemnity that made her want to kick him.

"You're wasting your time."

"It's my time." His voice turned to velvety inducement. "And haven't you, too, longed to be with me? What makes you so nervous isn't that I want you. I'm sure many men have wanted you. You're beautiful and precious and fine. No. What makes you so jumpy in my company is that, on this occasion, *you* want a man. You want me."

Evesham waited for a denial. But not for the first time, he'd underestimated her.

Juliet Frain was brave and forthright. Never coy. So instead of calling him a liar, her lips turned down in self-disgust. "Of course I do. You're irresistible. But then you know that, plague take you. You rely upon your charm never failing."

He knew that her anger was turned in on herself rather than on him, although she wasn't much in charity with him either. But despite the satisfaction of hearing her confess her attraction, something about her response stung.

His grip on her hand firmed. "You make everything sound so contrived."

While the look that she sent him might express aversion, desire smoldered beneath her hostility. "Isn't it?"

"It has been. In the past." He sighed and stepped closer, catching a hint of her floral scent. "Not with you."

Bitterness frayed her short laugh. "And I'm sure you've said that a hundred times before, too."

Devil take her, he had. But this time, he meant it. Although he already knew insisting would do no good. "How can I prove my sincerity?"

Another of those direct, devastating looks. "You can't."

"Then what are we to do?" he asked with a genuine despair that he knew she'd assume was just another act.

He'd relished his bad reputation as the wickedest duke alive. Now he cursed all the talk, because it placed a barrier between him and this woman he wanted.

To his regret, she tugged her hand from his. He missed the contact the moment that it ended. "Nothing."

"You don't mean that."

"I do." Her tone was decisive. "I'm not going to risk my reputation and my chance of making a good marriage, just because it turns out I'm as susceptible to your cheap tricks as every other woman you've ruined over the years."

That really did sting. Evesham drew himself up to his full height and replied in a supercilious drawl. "I may be disreputable, my dear, but I'm never cheap. I don't in general specialize in ruin, either. The ladies I pursue aren't breathless innocents."

"What about Vanessa Gould?"

The name stopped him in his tracks, evoked a whole cauldron of memories. "She was..."

"An innocent?"

Yes, she had been. "My friend."

The contempt in Juliet's exhalation made his skin itch. "I'm sure."

He'd sworn an oath that he'd never reveal the events of that summer nine years ago. He'd never broken that vow. It was one of the few shreds of honor still clinging to his stained soul.

When he didn't counter that jeering response, she went on. "And I'm an innocent, too."

He closed his eyes and sucked in a deep breath. "Of course you are."

Before he'd met Juliet, he'd wondered if she'd given her maidenhead to the late Duke of Bolton, who had died during their betrothal. But the moment he'd met her, proud virgin Athena, he'd known that she and her duke hadn't anticipated their vows.

Had she loved Bolton? Hell, did she love Granville?

The possibility smashed through him like a bullet fired from close range. Every muscle tightened in primitive denial. She couldn't love that self-important blowhard. He refused to accept the possibility.

And why the hell was he thinking about love? His affairs were pleasurable, but they never plumbed the more profound emotions.

"So there can be nothing between us," she said when the silence lengthened.

"There's already something between us."

"Physical attraction."

Evesham released a short laugh. "Don't speak of that with such contempt. A young man's hankering for a young woman is one of heaven's gifts to humanity."

Disapproval firmed her lips. Once, that critical look might have worked. But over the last few days, he'd learned that the formidable Lady Juliet wasn't nearly as stern as she liked to appear. "I don't think heaven has anything to do with it."

Perhaps not. Unless one referred to the very worldly heaven that one could find in a lover's arms. "Don't you ever want to have some fun?"

Then regretted his words when hurt flashed in her deep blue eyes. "Since Mamma's death, I've been responsible for my sisters. I've had no time for fun."

"Oh, Juliet…" His heart ached with compassion. Because he should have seen before this that duty had directed the entire course of her life.

This time, resentment lit those magnificent eyes. "Don't you dare feel sorry for me."

He spread his hands in apology. "I wouldn't be so bold."

Except he did feel sorry for her. He'd come to like Lord Portdown, almost despite himself, but his lordship's theatrical mania meant that he had no interest in filling a father's role. Someone had to take charge of Portia and Viola. And Juliet, with her strong principles, would step up without complaint.

She studied him with a suspicion that he knew he deserved. "I don't think a lack of boldness is your problem."

It wasn't. Perhaps it might even be his salvation. "How innocent?"

She frowned. "What?"

"How innocent are you?"

"I've never had a lover. You know that."

He did. Now. "Have you been kissed?"

Juliet wasn't someone who blushed often. Now even in the twilight, he watched color flood her cheeks. "I don't see that you have any right to ask that question," she spluttered.

He had his answer. What a tragic waste. "Not even Bolton?"

"His Grace was all that was correct," she said stiffly.

"And a great bore besides, I imagine."

Resentment darkened her expression. "A rapscallion like you has no right to criticize a good man who died too young."

A good man who didn't have the gumption to kiss the lady he meant to marry. How had the clodpoll resisted? Juliet, with all her banked fire, was born to be kissed. Surely Evesham wasn't the only fellow who itched to awaken this woman's passion.

"Perhaps not, but a rapscallion like me can show you what it's like to kiss a man. You're nearly twenty-six, Juliet. Don't you think it's time you discovered that life has pleasures as well as obligations?"

"You want to kiss me?" she asked shakily.

"You know I do." And the rest, even if he couldn't imagine that he'd ever fulfill that particular ambition.

But a kiss in the early summer twilight? That he might coax her into granting him.

"That would be wrong."

Interesting. Not an out-and-out refusal. He could tell that beneath the discouraging manner, she was intrigued. She'd always responded to him with a beguiling mixture of wariness and fascination.

"Why? You're not promised to another man, and I'm as free as a bird. We're both of age. Aren't you even a little curious to discover what it's like?"

"So an experiment?"

She still hadn't told him to go to blazes. Wonders would never cease. "If you like."

Juliet studied him, as if she could see right through to his ramshackle soul. She probably could. Juliet was no fool. "One kiss?"

Evesham shrugged. "Or several, if you decide that you'd like to venture further."

"Nothing else?"

He sighed. "Juliet, I'm not a ravening beast. I won't ask for more than you're willing to give. I'll stop when you ask me to."

He was renowned for his finesse with a lover. Here, he had more incentive than usual to do a good job.

"Do you promise?"

He was surprised that she was willing to accept his word. Perhaps she didn't despise him quite as much as he thought. The idea pleased him.

"Yes, I promise." He smiled. "Indeed, I'm rather overcome. I've never given a girl her first kiss. The responsibility is huge. If I don't do it right, I might put you off the pastime forever."

"I'm sure you'll rise to the occasion," she said drily.

He choked at the unwitting double entendre. "I'll do my best."

Actually, controlling the "rise" would be one of his difficulties. He wanted Juliet. He'd wanted her from the moment that he first saw her. Kissing her wouldn't appease his hunger. Yet he knew if he asked for too much, this bond that they forged, a bond that might even be trust, would snap forever.

"I can already tell that you're a man who knows how to kiss a woman. I'm sure I'll like it."

"That's a good thing," he said, noting her dark tone.

"If you say so."

"I jolly well do." He sent her a straight look. "Are we going to further your education?"

She was a delightful mixture of curiosity and trepidation. If he told her that he found her inexperience moving, she'd be offended. But he did. She was so supremely capable. And so unaccountably untouched.

For a long moment, a charged silence stretched between them, before she gave a nod. "Very well. You may kiss me."

CHAPTER EIGHT

*J*uliet closed her eyes and jutted her chin forward. Her heart raced so fast that she felt giddy. In a breathless hush, she waited trembling for the touch of Evesham's lips.

And waited.

Eventually exasperation replaced anticipation, and she opened her eyes. Evesham studied her as if she belonged to a species that he'd never before encountered.

"What?" she asked, puzzled.

"Haven't you ever seen a man and a woman kiss?"

She stiffened. No, she hadn't. Not a kiss of passion. "You're laughing at me."

He smiled. "Only a little."

She marched past him with a swish of blue skirts. "I won't stay to be mocked."

"Juliet, don't go." He caught her arm. As ever, immediate heat rushed under her skin. Her foolish heart skipped a beat before taking off on another reckless gallop.

"I changed my mind. I've lived all my life without playing silly flirtatious games. I can continue very well without you deigning to put me on the pathway to perdition."

"Hardly that. It's just a kiss."

"So why didn't you do it?"

"Because you caught me by surprise when you stood there, like a little girl waiting for her first dance partner to give her a peck on the cheek."

She was annoyed and uncomfortable. And she felt inadequate, as she often did when she thought of herself as a woman and not as a future duchess. Which made her even more annoyed.

"What should I have done? Hurled myself into your arms, panting for your attentions?"

His lips twitched. "You can if you like."

With a low growl deep in her throat, she pulled away. The fact that he let her go increased her irritation. Which made no sense. "This is all a joke to you, isn't it?"

Most annoying of all was admitting that she was hurt. She didn't want to acknowledge that he held such power over her emotions.

The amusement drained from his expression. She caught a glimpse of what, even in her innocence, she recognized as hunger. The summer twilight was fading, but she could see his face quite clearly. "No. On my soul, no."

"You don't have a soul," she said, knowing she was being unfair.

"You make me feel like I've got a soul," he muttered, and this time she saw more than hunger. She saw that this yearning that drew them together left him as bewildered as she was. Perhaps she wasn't alone in finding this attraction both inexplicable and invincible.

So she didn't resist when he caught her hand and drew her closer. God forgive her, she curved forward when he wound his arm around her waist.

Evesham released her hand and captured her

chin in a grip that felt both masterly and tender. Juliet caught the flare of heat in his dark eyes, before his face moved closer and his lips brushed hers.

Searing heat that lasted a second. An impression of fresh breath. A tingling aftermath.

His hand dropped away from her face. She made a brief murmur. Protest? Plea? Even she wasn't sure which.

Her eyelids felt heavy, as she lifted them to discover Evesham watching her with a steady interest that made her stomach clench in forbidden longing. Forbidden and unknowing, because while she understood the mechanics of what happened in bed between a man and a woman, she had an inkling that more was involved than a mere interlocking of bodies.

"What did you think?" he murmured.

Juliet licked her lips, expecting to taste him, but his kiss had been over too soon. His gaze fastened on the movement with feverish urgency.

"It was rather pleasant."

If only she didn't find his smile so inviting. "I've had better reviews."

She was conscious of the weight of his arm around her waist. His tangy scent teased her senses. He was so close that she felt his warmth, as alluring as a crackling fire on a bleak winter's day.

Juliet struggled to remind herself that fire could blister as well as comfort, but the warning had no power to break the enchantment. "I thought...I thought there might be more to it."

She recalled how vivid her sister Viola had looked after she was caught kissing the Earl of Renfrew in the Tierneys' garden. Disturbed and radiant, as if she'd glimpsed a dazzling new world.

Juliet didn't feel like that.

Evesham groaned and closed his eyes in brief torment. "I was trying not to frighten you."

"So there's more?"

"Much more," he said with fervor.

That should spur her into running back to the house. But instead, she stayed just where she was. Because shocking as it was, she wasn't satisfied with that single taste. Despite saying that he could kiss her only once. Despite all her common sense insisting that it was time to bring this encounter to an end. Insisting that she was all kinds of fool to start this in the first place.

"Will you show me?" Juliet was surprised that her question emerged steadily.

She didn't feel steady. Anything but. She felt like she'd swallowed a whole pond full of frogs who jumped around inside her. Her rubbery legs threatened to fold up at any moment.

Instead of seizing her – some wild part of her longed for him to sweep her up against that hard chest – he eyed her with a hint of suspicion. "Are you sure?"

"No," she said. Or rather squeaked. She was having difficulty drawing in enough breath to fill her lungs. Her hands opened and closed at her sides over and over.

"Well?"

She bit her lip and made herself meet his eyes. She expected to see mockery, but he was watching her as if he was willing to let her decide what happened next. "You're meant to be a rake. Why are you hesitating?"

He ran one hand through his hair. It was a characteristic gesture, she'd noticed. One that he made when he was frustrated or impatient. "Because I don't want you deciding that I took advantage of you. I don't want you deciding that you hate me again."

"I don't hate you." Before she could think to stop herself, she lifted her hand to cup the severe angle of his jaw. The skin beneath her palm was warm, and she felt the prickle of his whiskers. "I've never hated you."

She'd never touched a man like this. It was thrilling and strange. And addictive.

Briefly he closed his eyes, as if he, too, found the contact stirring. "You didn't like me much when we met."

No, she hadn't. In truth, she still wasn't sure why she did like him. He was everything that she disapproved of. A wastrel. A libertine. A man happy to expend his youth and talents in the aimless pursuit of sensual entertainment.

"I wouldn't let you kiss me if I held you in disdain."

Another of those self-derisive smiles that always made her silly heart cramp. "If you decide you hate me again after this, the play will suffer."

That surprised a laugh out of her. Then before she could reply, Evesham lashed his arms about her and hauled her up until his mouth crashed into hers.

There was nothing gentle or tentative about this kiss. This was desperate and passionate and all-encompassing. This was fire and darkness and insatiable demand. Juliet collapsed against him, looping her arms around his neck as his mouth plundered hers.

When he bit her lower lip, she parted on a gasp of astonishment. Then even more outlandish, his tongue slipped through to tangle with hers. The shocking unfamiliarity of what he did drowned in a wave of staggering pleasure. Her whole body, bones and all, melted into helpless and immediate cooperation.

Juliet was melting, and she was on fire. She was burning up, flaring into a column of flame. She found herself responding to him as the pleasure, already unprecedented, built to an inferno.

Without thought, she plastered herself to him. Her breasts swelled with longing, and the furious meeting of lips lit another fire in the pit of her stomach. She squirmed as the throbbing between her legs rose to drive her mad.

Vaguely through the pounding of her blood, she felt his hands slide down to catch her rump and lift her. He pressed her between his thighs. Something hard and long rubbed against her stomach.

The sudden intrusion of unmistakable masculine need sparked alarm in her dazed mind. She gave a troubled mutter against his seeking lips.

As abruptly as he'd snatched her up, she was free. He lurched back and regarded her with unconcealed horror that not even the advancing twilight could hide. She staggered to find her balance and struggled for breath, even as nausea knotted her innards.

"Juliet, forgive me," he grated out, his voice raw.

She touched a trembling hand to her lips and struggled to return to the real world after that flight into a new and alluring universe.

"So that's what a kiss is like," she said in a reedy voice. Her heart still banged like a drum, and she fought the urge to step back into his arms.

His face contorted with self-disgust. "It's what some kisses are like. I should have been gentler. I want you so much, I went too far."

She'd returned to herself enough by now to understand that she hadn't been alone in yielding to passion. This man, whose manner always conveyed endless self-assurance, was badly shaken.

"I like...I like that you forgot to be calculating."

Bewilderment sharpened his tone. "You don't

mind?"

She shrugged, although she didn't feel casual about any of this. "That the madness was mutual? Of course not. It makes me feel less like your dupe and more like your equal."

His lips twisted in derision. "Madness is precisely what overtook me."

"You stepped back. You kept your word."

He groaned again. "I almost lost control."

Juliet shouldn't like to hear this. After all, for one exhilarating moment, she'd been in genuine danger. She should be ashamed to admit that it wasn't she who had called a halt, but the man the world had dubbed His Dis-Grace. "Yet you didn't."

A charged silence fell before he spoke. "Shall we do it again?"

Despite everything, she almost said yes. She'd never felt so alive as she had in Evesham's arms. She suspected that he could kiss her to heaven and back.

But her native caution had revived. Despite wondering what other marvels Evesham could reveal to her, she shook her head. "I wanted to find out what it was like to be kissed. Now I know. The experiment is over, Your Grace."

His sigh was heavy with a regret that she shared – however shameless that might make her. Goodness, if Portia knew what she was up to, she'd never call her staid again.

"And you're happy to walk away from what that kiss promised?"

Happy? No. But she'd taken enough risks. The memory of that terrifying, intriguing moment when she'd felt his arousal shuddered through her. If followed through to its end, that wild kiss promised ruin. She had too much at stake to compromise her good name.

"I must." She sucked in a breath. "Thank you. I'll

remember that kiss forever."

"So will I."

She didn't believe him. He must have kissed hundreds of women and most − all − of them considerably more skilled in the art than inexperienced Juliet Frain. But she appreciated his gallantry. And also that he didn't insist she give him more.

"I must go. I've already been out here too long."

Or not long enough, a sly voice whispered in her head. Because while she might sound all primness and common sense, the duke had awakened a powerful sensuality. The sensations that had overpowered her in his embrace had been tempting indeed.

To her surprise, he took her hand. "I hope you dream of me," he murmured, lifting her fingers to his lips.

She battled to hide the effect of his lips brushing her knuckles. She'd managed to leash her wanton urges – just. That kiss of homage threatened her self-control in ways that she didn't want to consider. Because she'd loved his kiss. She'd loved touching him. And she'd loved the way that his lips had made her hot right to her toes.

That kiss had fed her famished senses. From his fresh, male scent to the tart, delicious taste of his mouth.

Turning away from the Duke of Evesham now was without doubt the right thing to do, even if at the most profound level, it felt unnatural. So her voice held a hint of acid as she jerked her hand back. "I never dream, Your Grace."

She dipped into a curtsy and marched away, while every beat of her heart begged her to return to Evesham for more of those spellbinding kisses.

Evesham fought the urge to chase after Juliet. Restraint proved astonishingly difficult.

She strode off into the trees at the top of the slope and disappeared from sight without a backward glance. How he loved to watch her in motion. In London, young ladies minced and pranced. Juliet moved with a countrywoman's purposeful glide.

He'd understood immediately that she was a woman who always knew where she was going. She still did – and where she was going was away from him. Which sparked an odd, unfamiliar twinge in his black heart. Because even though he knew it would tempt fate, not to mention his disreputable self, to kiss her again, it still felt wrong that she left him alone and longing like this.

He was in such a damned lather, he wouldn't sleep. His blood seethed like a volcano. One kiss from a complete beginner left the notorious rake as jumpy as a cat in a kennel.

One kiss. Devil take it. One kiss, and he was lost. So lost, he'd ignored her inexperience and devoured her as if he starved.

By heaven, he did starve.

For a proper spinster who would never give him what he craved.

As a rule, he didn't hanker after things that he couldn't have. That seemed a recipe for discontent, and why court unhappiness? But without doubt, he hankered after Lady Juliet Frain. Who guarded her maidenhead like a treasure in a tower.

Although however frustrated he was right now, part of him admired the self-respect that informed her every moment. This wasn't an airheaded light-skirt who spread her legs for the first man who gave her the eye.

Juliet was too good for him. He should turn away and seek out some lady who wasn't good at all to ease his frustration.

That was what he'd done on the very few occasions when his pursuit had proven unsuccessful. Disappointment hadn't lasted beyond bedding his next paramour. If one woman didn't want him, there were plenty more who did.

Already he could tell that this flirtation with the virtuous Lady Juliet shattered that pattern. No other woman could replace her.

She claimed not to dream. Lucky her. Because heaven knew that he'd dreamed of her and only her since the day that they met.

Juliet smiling. Juliet welcoming him into her arms. Juliet naked and willing, as she'd never be in life. Worst of all, Juliet casting him a blank glance, then flitting off to some other man. A faceless fellow, who Evesham very much feared was the Duke of Granville, may he burn in hell.

Evesham would dream of her again tonight. That sultry, unforgettable kiss demanded it.

And tomorrow there were more deuced rehearsals when, for Juliet's sake, he had to pretend to want her as Romeo, while pretending he didn't want her for himself. When right now, he wanted her as he'd never wanted another woman.

It was a sodding mess.

CHAPTER NINE

The next day, the Duke of Granville arrived.

Smith, the butler, found Juliet as she and the housekeeper discussed refreshments for tomorrow's performance.

She'd seen Evesham at breakfast, but Portia had been there as well, so the conversation had been general. Juliet had gobbled down her boiled eggs before scuttling away. She couldn't risk her perceptive sister noticing that something had changed between Juliet and their guest.

After those torrid moments in his arms, she didn't want to be alone with Evesham this morning. She hadn't lied about not dreaming. Last night at least. Because after that soul-shattering kiss, she hadn't slept a wink. Having to share his company with Portia had left her jumpy and snappy – and deflated.

Although what could she say to him after that kiss? "Pass the pepper, and did you dream of me last night?"

Nor did it help that he seemed as composed and urbane as ever. Or at least so she'd believed, until Portia had risen to select a second roll from the buffet and Evesham had shot Juliet a searing glance that told her he burned to get her alone again.

She couldn't allow that. If only because last night had revealed that she possessed no defenses against his wiles. Reminding herself that he'd seduced a line of women before her and no doubt would seduce a line of women after her didn't dampen her inconvenient lust.

Now she had the greatest difficulty concentrating on Mrs. Rose's questions about whether to serve lobster patties or vol-au-vents at the gala supper.

"We can do chicken sandwiches, can't we?" she asked.

"My lady, you already said you want egg and cress sandwiches." Mrs. Rose, who had worked for the late Lady Portdown and had known Juliet since she was a baby, looked puzzled at her infallibly efficient mistress's distraction. "Wouldn't a hot savory be a better choice, particularly if the night is cool?"

"Of course." Juliet blushed and struggled to remember when she'd given that order. The way things were going, society's brightest and best would be lucky to get stale crackers and cheese.

"Lady Juliet," Smith said, bursting into the library with uncharacteristic urgency. "You are required in the front hall."

Surprised, Juliet glanced up. "What is it?"

"His Grace, the Duke of Granville has arrived and says he intends to stay for the next week."

Juliet gaped at their usually unflappable butler. "Granville? Here?"

"Yes, my lady."

Since she'd left London to make hurried preparations for Viola's wedding, she hadn't heard a word from the man the ton had expected to propose to her. Yet here he was uninvited. And planning to remain until after the theatricals.

It seemed strange and out of character for a man who prided himself on always doing the correct thing. Strange and also high-handed. Annoyance nibbled at the edges of her surprise.

She was already on her feet and smoothing her skirts. There wasn't time to go upstairs and change. Her plain sprigged muslin would have to do. Nobody left one of the nation's premier noblemen kicking his heels in the entrance hall.

"Mrs. Rose, we'll need to prepare a room. The peacock apartments, I think."

The housekeeper was already on her feet. "Very good, my lady."

Juliet turned to the butler. "Smith, perhaps you could arrange refreshments in the morning room. If His Grace has traveled from London, he'll want a cup of tea." Or something stronger.

Smith bowed and stepped back for her to precede him out of the room. She rushed along the corridor but came to a stop before entering the hall. She sucked in a deep breath and drew her customary calmness around her like a veil.

She glided into the room with the air of authority that she'd cultivated all her life. "Your Grace, I apologize for keeping you waiting. What a pleasure to welcome you to Afton Park."

The duke was staring out of the tall windows that faced the turning circle in front of the house. He was dressed *comme il faut* in a bottle-green coat and buff breeches, and his fair hair was as neat as a pin. Juliet shoved away an unwelcome memory of another man with black, rumpled hair and a lazy smile.

Granville was very much admired for his classical fairness. Over recent days, Juliet had been distracted by the forthcoming performance, not to mention a Romeo who proved more compelling than she'd prefer. But seeing Granville again, she remembered that he'd always struck her as the perfect example of his sex. Competent, contained, prudent. Beautifully mannered. A pleasure to look at.

If he failed to move her emotions the way another much less well-behaved duke did, the fault lay with her, not Granville.

He turned to smile at her. As she curtsied, he bowed and stepped forward with the cool savoir faire that she'd liked from the first. "Lady Juliet, it seems I caught you unawares."

"We've been at sixes and sevens with my father's Shakespeare gala. I suspect there's been some confusion somewhere."

"I wrote to Portdown two days ago to say I planned to visit to see the production." Something in his voice, however steady, told her that more was going on here than a whim to take in some theater. "I'd have come sooner, but I was called away to Yorkshire a fortnight ago."

She gestured toward the morning room door. "I've arranged refreshments. Have you traveled from London?"

"Yes. I returned to Town this week. I gather you're expecting a large audience tomorrow night."

"We are." As her father had prophesied, the chance to see the Duke of Evesham on stage had created huge interest. "Papa is beside himself with excitement."

"I'm sure." Again, that hint of displeasure. She supposed he'd heard that Evesham was here. No wonder he wasn't in complete charity with the gala.

She was out of charity with her father. He could have told her that Granville was coming. She'd poured the duke his tea and watched him eat a couple of sandwiches before her father appeared.

"Your Grace, it's good to see you." He bowed before gravitating to the table where he chose a slice of cake. "It will be an honor to have you in the audience. What attention our little show will receive when we have not one, but two dukes in attendance. You know His Grace of Evesham is playing Romeo?"

Granville was sitting by the unlit fire. With the start of summer, the day was warm. He dipped his smooth golden head in acknowledgment, although Juliet caught a subtle flattening of his lips at the mention of Evesham. That confirmed her suspicion that his enemy's presence was behind this visit, not any particular yen for her company.

"My lord, I hope you'll pardon me for inviting myself to stay."

Her father made an expansive gesture. "No trouble at all, old man. No trouble at all. Juliet will make sure everything is right and tight."

Juliet wanted to kick her esteemed parent. She couldn't do much to make the duke comfortable, if she didn't know that he was coming. "I'll go and check on arrangements," she said, hiding her irritation under her accustomed composure. "If you'll excuse me, Your Grace?"

"Of course," he said. "There is a matter I wish to discuss with your father."

Granville sent her a meaningful glance, and astonishment made her falter on the way out. Good heavens, was she wrong about why he was here? Had he come down to Wiltshire, not just to check on his bugbear, but to propose?

A week ago, the prospect of becoming the Duchess of Granville would have fulfilled her dearest hopes. But a week ago, she hadn't met the troubling but fascinating Duke of Evesham. A week ago, she hadn't recognized how physical attraction could take over a life and lead even the most proper lady astray. A week ago, she hadn't been kissed.

Hiding a blush, she bent her head and left the

room. She cursed Evesham for causing such agitation and for distracting her from a future that gave her everything she'd always wanted.

Evesham spent the morning riding in the woods. Following a restless night haunted by memories of Juliet's kiss, what better way to clear the thickness from his brain?

After cleaning himself up so he was fit for the dining room, he came down for lunch with no idea that the household had increased by one. And one he had no wish to encounter at that.

He enjoyed the family's intimate mealtimes. Lord Portdown had become less grating as the acquaintance had developed. Perhaps because Evesham came to realize that his host harbored a genuine artistic ambition. More than that, Portdown had the talent and the drive to shepherd his aims to fruition.

Evesham was fond of Portia, who looked very much like Juliet, but wasn't nearly as self-contained. And Portia, also unlike her sister, appeared to have no reservations about the rakish Duke of Evesham.

Mealtimes offered him the chance to relish Juliet's company. He'd rather be alone with her, but he'd take what he could get. He was well aware that if she could avoid him, she would. But her role as hostess meant that she had to break bread with him, unless she wanted her family asking awkward questions.

So it was a nasty shock to enter the dining room and discover an addition to their little band. Not Henry Bell, who had visited for several rehearsals and proved to be an inoffensive young pup with an obvious penchant for Lady Portia.

Neither "inoffensive" nor "pup" described Alaric Dempster, Duke of Granville. Since his return to England a month ago, Evesham had managed to avoid the stuck-up prig. He'd be happy for that state of affairs to continue. Forever if possible.

Now the swine sat beside Juliet as if he owned the place.

"Granville," he said, baring his teeth.

Icy green eyes settled on him, and the response that emerged was no warmer. "Evesham."

Portdown, who was serving himself from a dish of cold roast beef, gave both dukes a beaming smile. "Oh, of course you know each other. How jolly."

Jolly wasn't how Evesham would describe the encounter. For once, he was sure that his antagonist would be in complete agreement with him.

"I hear you've taken up amateur dramatics, Evesham," Granville drawled in his superior way. "How...artistic of you. I don't recall you being part of that crowd at school."

Evesham shrugged and sat beside Portia who observed the interactions with an owlish look. Her father might be oblivious to the hostility in the room, but his younger daughter wasn't.

Juliet was picking at a salad and hadn't glanced up. Despite Evesham sitting straight across the table, she refused to meet his eyes.

Was she pleased that her suitor had arrived? He couldn't tell.

What he could tell was that she and Granville made a disgustingly striking pair, like two Norse gods. They'd produce beautiful babies, damn it.

Last night, she'd been in his arms, warm, vital, ardent. He saw no trace of that beguiling woman in today's reserved young lady.

Although he was still beguiled. She always

enthralled him, even when she did her best to imitate a glacier.

He remembered that Granville had asked him a question. A deuced insolent one, in tone if not in content. "I'm always open to a new experience. A narrow mind is an insult to the richness of creation."

Granville's glance, already frigid, cooled another ten degrees. He didn't miss the dig.

Portdown was cutting into his beef. "His Grace of Evesham has proven himself a fine actor. You'll be most impressed when you see him in action."

Granville had an untouched cheese savory in front of him. "I've come down to see just what His Grace is up to. There's been quite a flutter in Town about a man known for his cricketing feats suddenly turning thespian."

"You were no slouch on the sporting field either," Evesham said.

Although Granville had been involved in solitary pursuits like cross-country running rather than team sports. Because he was a couple of years older than Evesham, they'd had very little to do with each other at Eton. Their real enmity had begun once Evesham entered society after attending university.

"I had my moments," Granville said in a way that Evesham interpreted as smug.

"Your Grace, we're running a dress rehearsal this afternoon, if you'd care to observe," Portdown said.

Granville shook his head. "I'm content to wait until the performance. Although perhaps Lady Juliet could spare the time to show me the garden when she isn't involved in the play?"

Silence crashed down. Everyone except Juliet stared at Granville. Portdown looked approving. Portia's expression froze, which was interesting. Evesham had a feeling that Portia didn't like the duke.

Evesham had an excellent view of Granville and Juliet. He looked as stolid as ever. Juliet continued to toy with her salad and maintain her sphinx-like air.

It was clear that Granville meant to propose. Evesham shouldn't be surprised. The moment that he'd taken the trouble to listen, he'd heard rumors of a future engagement between the eldest Frain girl and His Grace.

The thought made bile surge up his throat. The salmon in aspic that he'd been eating formed a cold, indigestible lump in his belly.

Vanessa had been too good for this self-satisfied clod. Juliet was, too. The idea of her condemned to a passionless existence with Alaric Dempster made Evesham want to smash things.

Not just because he coveted her for himself. But also because he'd caught a glimpse of the vibrant woman she could be, and Granville would crush every ounce of spirit out of her.

Evesham hadn't let Vanessa sacrifice herself to worldly ambition. But he'd known Vanessa all his life, and she trusted him. Could he save Juliet? Even if he did, where did that leave them?

It really was none of his business who the formidable Lady Juliet married. Except every cell in his body insisted she was his and that dull dog Granville had no claim on her.

"I should be at leisure around three." Her voice was measured as if she, unlike everyone else here, hadn't guessed Granville's intentions. "If you can spare me then, Papa?"

Her father's gaze was surprisingly penetrating as it rested on Juliet. "Of course, my dear. We'll run through your scene with dear Evesham last, if you like."

Dear Evesham wanted to protest. Everything

would be finalized before he had a chance to talk her out of accepting Granville.

Although what could he say? He had no rights over Juliet.

CHAPTER TEN

On such a beautiful day, the rose garden was an enchanted space. The roses weren't yet at their best, but there were enough flowers open to perfume the air. A small marble fountain featuring leaping dolphins provided the pleasant burble of flowing water.

Granville appeared in the stone arch, then walked toward Juliet where she waited beside the graceful carving. "Lady Juliet, thank you for permitting me this interview."

She performed a quick curtsy. She knew what was coming. Five years ago, Bolton had proposed to her in this very place. He'd been a good man, and she'd been glad to accept his offer.

Granville was another good man. She should be equally glad to become his wife. Until these last unsettling days, she would have been. After all, it was something of a triumph to captivate two dukes to the point of offering marriage.

She didn't feel triumphant. She felt uncertain and beleaguered.

Juliet told herself not to be a fool. Granville was a catch, and they would deal well together. There wasn't another man in England she admired so much. He'd make a perfect husband.

"I always enjoy your company, Your Grace," she said with a calmness that didn't reflect her inner confusion.

He smiled and to her surprise, took her hand. Although why she should be surprised, she didn't know. After all, if she became his wife, he'd end up touching more than her hand. Thanks to what she and Evesham had got up to last night, she even had an inkling of what she might feel in his bed.

Yet this contact aroused no disturbing heat. She told herself that was a good thing. Marriage was too important a matter to be decided on whether a woman had an unfortunate physical weakness for her future husband.

"I always enjoy yours. I've missed you since you left London."

Her eyes widened with more surprise. It hadn't occurred to her that her absence might leave a hole in his life.

"There was Viola's wedding. Then Papa started work on the gala." She left her hand in his. She didn't mention the scandal. She didn't have to.

"And you're to play Juliet."

"Yes." He already knew this. Most of the talk at lunch had centered on tomorrow's performance. "At least I won't forget my character's name."

He responded with a smile. She realized that she'd never heard him laugh. Granville treated life with the earnestness that it deserved. Whereas Evesham wasn't earnest about anything at all.

As if her thoughts conjured up his name, Granville frowned. "I wish you had a different Romeo. Evesham's not respectable."

He wasn't. So why did Juliet feel the urge to defend him? "Papa wanted someone dark-haired to contrast with my fairness."

"I hope the fellow hasn't overstepped propriety. He isn't suitable company for you."

It was her turn to frown. "He's been quite the gentleman, Your Grace." It wasn't the full truth, but Granville made Evesham sound like a rampaging barbarian. "Surely Papa has the right to invite anyone he wishes to his own home."

"Alaric."

She needed a moment to realize that the duke was asking her to use his Christian name. His hold on her hand tightened. "I don't like the idea of you speaking romantic words to anyone but me."

Her stomach took such a swoop that it stole her breath. "Your Grace…"

He sighed. "I'm sure it will come as no surprise when I say that I admire you more than I've admired any other lady."

More than Vanessa Gould?

The thought popped up like a curse. She crammed it to the back of her mind.

"I am…" Usually she had no trouble finishing her sentences, but hearing that the duke saw her as more than a convenient match left her floundering.

He met her eyes, his green gaze warmer than usual. "You're beautiful and wise and a woman of character. You'll make a superb duchess. I thought so when I first met you, but my feelings toward you have only strengthened as our acquaintance has progressed. Now I can't imagine facing my future without you at my side. Juliet – I hope you'll allow me to call you Juliet – please make me the happiest of men and say that you'll become my wife."

For a horrified instant, she stared into his aristocratic features and wondered what in heaven's name she could say.

She slid her hand free of his. "I had no idea."

He looked puzzled. "It *has* come as a surprise. I'm so sorry. I imagined that you'd read my attentions to you as an expression of my hopes. I imagined – expected – that your acceptance of my company meant that you liked me in return."

Dear Lord, she made a complete botch of this. She'd done a better job with Bolton, all those years ago. But then Bolton's proposal had been short and prosaic. They'd both known that they intended to enter a practical partnership. She'd assumed that Granville had planned on a similar arrangement. Yet he spoke about emotions with more conviction than she'd thought he was capable of.

"Of course I like you," she said shakily. "You're everything that I admire, too."

"Yet you didn't expect a proposal?"

She linked her hands at her waist to hide their shaking. "I've always thought that we deal well together. We agree about so much. The importance of doing one's duty. The way great privilege comes with great responsibility. The need for political reform. I've always wanted to be in a position to do good."

"As my wife, you would be." He looked concerned. "Have you decided that you can't stomach me as a husband? If so, I'll go away and never trouble you again. You have my word on it."

His offer to withdraw his offer felt like someone poured a bucket of cold water over her head. For pity's sake, what was she doing? She'd always pictured herself as a duchess. She'd be brilliant in the role, as more than one person had told her.

The first time that they danced, she'd decided to accept Granville if he asked for her hand. So why was she hesitating?

He was everything that she'd always wanted. And it seemed that he wanted her in return. If she refused

Granville, the only other unmarried duke in England under the age of sixty was Evesham, and he wasn't husband material. She might have come to like him in the last few days, and he might make her blood sizzle. None of that blinded her to the truth that he was wild and unpredictable and far too ready to cause havoc.

Even if he wanted to marry her. When she'd lay good money that he didn't.

With his life of debauchery supplying such a banquet of pleasure, why the devil would he settle for one woman? And despite his current uncharacteristic yen for a chaste lady of sober habits, he was used to more excitement than sedate Juliet Frain could provide.

No, if she wanted to be a duchess – and she did – she needed to accept Granville, who was all that she esteemed, and forget Evesham, who was entertaining but unreliable.

"Your talk of affection took me unawares," she confessed in a low voice.

"You don't seek love in a match?" He sounded displeased. "You're still mourning Bolton?"

She shook her head. "We were friends. That seemed a good basis for a marriage."

Granville looked relieved to hear that she wasn't wearing the willow for her previous betrothed. She supposed that no man wanted a former suitor's ghost haunting the marriage bed.

"I thought we were friends."

"We are." How was it that she was so awkward? She was universally praised for her polished manners. "But are you speaking of...love?"

He looked a little uncomfortable. Hardly surprising when they'd never discussed intimate matters before. "My ideal is a loving union. My late parents were fond of each other. I hope to find a similar closeness with my wife."

She frowned, knowing she risked offending him, but this was a point that they had to clarify.

"I don't love you, Granville. Alaric." It felt odd using his Christian name. With reluctance, she shared the bleak truth that she'd recognized when she'd agreed to wed Bolton. "I'm not sure I'm capable of loving anyone."

"You love your sisters and your father. You'll love our children."

Her hands tightened to bruising. "That's not the love you're talking about."

"No, I'm talking about the bond between a man and a woman. While I appreciate your honesty, I still have grounds for optimism. We have so many other things on our side. I hope love will grow as we build our life together."

She sucked in a breath. He didn't love her. At least not yet. That pleased her. The prospect of starting a marriage on such an unequal footing had made her cringe. "So you're talking about a union based on respect and hard work and mutual aims?"

"If you like. And the possibility of children. I'd dearly love a family. I know what care you gave to your sisters. I soon realized that your father's attentions were focused elsewhere. You'll make a wonderful mother, Juliet. I pray that we'll find common cause in our offspring."

"Of course." She struggled to imagine sharing his bed. Whoever she married would claim the use of her body. She wasn't squeamish about that.

Or she hadn't been until now.

It was unsettling that when she pictured her children, they didn't have blond hair. They had ruffled dark curls and dark eyes.

Not useful, Juliet.

Granville eyed her, as if she presented an

unforeseen problem. She imagined that she did. Most girls would leap at the chance to wed such a paragon of breeding and character. "So, Juliet, will you be my wife?"

She tilted her chin and told herself to stop acting like a ninnyhammer. This was what she'd always planned, and Granville was the kind of man she'd always imagined marrying. She should be dancing with joy – if a sober creature like her would permit herself such frivolity.

She gave Granville the answer that she'd decided on the moment she met him in the Castellaines' ballroom back in April. "I'd be honored to accept your proposal, Alaric."

He smiled with such gladness that she felt guilty about her misgivings. He deserved a wholehearted commitment. She told herself that was what he'd get.

No more twilight kisses. No more succumbing to urges that threatened to sweep her out into dangerous oceans. She was a cautious, conservative woman, and she'd dedicate the rest of her life to paddling near the shore. The tempestuous seas of physical desire weren't for her.

"My dear, you make me so happy. Thank you. I know what a treasure you are and that I'm unworthy of this privilege. I promise you'll never regret accepting my proposal."

"I'll do my best to be a good wife."

"May I kiss you?"

"If you like." This time, she didn't have to struggle to sound like her levelheaded self.

The hand she extended was quite steady. Alaric's hand closed around hers. He drew her closer. His head lowered, and his lips touched hers.

It was like Evesham's first kiss. Over in a second. Undemanding.

Except that while the contact was pleasant, she

felt no thrill. No craving to take things further. She couldn't imagine giving in to an open-mouthed voracious invasion like Evesham's kiss last night. Although she suspected that once Alaric had her in his bed, he'd ask more of her than this passionless tribute.

Or perhaps like her, he wasn't someone who sought passion as an essential part of life. Perhaps the consummation of their union would require only her cool cooperation.

She would *not* regret that.

Juliet smiled at her future husband and told herself that she was content with how events turned out.

She intended to be a wonderful duchess, by heaven. Or die trying.

CHAPTER ELEVEN

*E*vesham didn't manage a private word with Juliet during the final run-through for the gala. With everyone involved in the show, including neighbors and family and servants, creating bedlam onstage, there were too many people around.

The lack of ardor in her performance had her father scolding her. She'd reverted to the lifeless, unconvincing portrayal that she'd given at the start. Over the last few days as she'd grown more comfortable in Evesham's company, she'd shown flashes of brilliance to rival her father's talent. But not today. Today, she had all the animation of a cricket bat.

Evesham wasn't much better. His mind wasn't on playing Romeo. His mind was on what had happened when Granville joined Juliet in the garden.

Had the bastard proposed? If he had, had Juliet accepted? He couldn't tell from her expression. She didn't look rapturous, but then, she liked to be inscrutable.

The thought of her marrying Granville stoked the volcanic rage that had given him indigestion at lunch. The idea of a woman as exceptional as Juliet Frain throwing herself away on Alaric Dempster, however rich and distinguished he was, made Evesham feel sick.

He was also burningly aware that his time at Afton Park was running out. Once the gala was over, he had no excuse to stay. How ironic that he'd dreaded this visit, yet now he couldn't bear the thought of leaving.

Hoping to catch Juliet alone, he came down to dinner early. But this once, she was tardy, appearing in the drawing room just before everyone went through to the dining room. He studied her as discreetly as he could, but be damned if he could discern any excitement.

Yet if she'd refused Granville, surely she'd be awkward in the pompous ass's company. He saw no sign of that either.

Had Granville's nerve failed at the crucial moment? Had he avoided asking the question?

Portia seemed as curious as he was. If Juliet was engaged, her sister didn't know about it.

When they moved through to the dining room, the seating was exactly as it had been at lunch. He was next to Portia, facing Juliet and Granville on the other side. Portdown as ever occupied the head of the table. His host's taste in virulent colors continued. Today's coat was the unappealing shade of bread mold.

They'd settled into their places when everything went to hell.

Smith the butler brought in a bottle of champagne. No, no, no. It couldn't be. This was wrong. The anger inside Evesham coagulated into a hot mass of refusal, even as the butler filled their glasses with golden bubbling wine.

Portdown stood, his face wreathed in smiles. Why

not? His daughter had just secured her second proposal from a duke. Sod it all.

"Before we begin our meal tonight, I have a very happy announcement to make." Portdown glanced at Granville and Juliet. "His Grace, the Duke of Granville, has requested the hand of my beloved daughter Juliet. I'm delighted to say that Juliet has accepted his proposal. We'll have another wedding at Afton Park before the end of summer. I'd like to propose a toast to the happy couple. To Juliet and Granville."

As if from a mile away, Evesham listened to Portia express her congratulations. It might be something wrong with his hearing, but she sounded rather flat.

"Congratulations," he muttered, not meaning it, but in such a small group, his silence would be noted. The champagne tasted like wormwood on his tongue.

"Thank you," Granville said, his smile missing Evesham. Of course it did. The oaf loathed him almost as much as Evesham loathed him back. "I'm the luckiest man in the world."

He had that right, Evesham couldn't help thinking.

Juliet kept her eyes lowered. Perhaps it was maidenly shyness, but Evesham didn't think so. She avoided his gaze because she feared what her expression might betray. That she wanted him and not the smug jackanapes beside her.

Because Evesham mightn't know much. But he knew that the woman who had kissed him last night as if she'd die if she stopped hadn't switched her allegiance in the last twenty-four hours.

Portdown took another sip of champagne and sat, nodding to Smith to serve the meal. "For the moment, we're going to keep the engagement between us. Once the gala is over, we can announce it to the world. I don't want anything to distract from our performance."

"The news that Juliet is to be a duchess will set society buzzing," Portia said. "It would steal your thunder."

Evesham had regained enough control over his revulsion to realize that he hadn't imagined Portia's unenthusiastic reaction. It seemed that he'd guessed right about her not liking Granville.

Smart girl.

If only her older sister was half as smart. Although he couldn't deny that Granville and Juliet made a gorgeous couple. Even if she looked like a beautiful ghost. Evesham feared that in a cold marriage, she'd fade away altogether.

Her father didn't react to the jibe in Portia's remark. Nothing was going to erode his jubilation. "Exactly, my dear. They're coming to see Evesham. After all our hard work, I'd hate another duke to divert their attention."

"Actually," Granville said with an uncharacteristic hint of diffidence. "That's something I would like to raise."

"Oh?" Portdown said, as the footman removed his empty soup bowl.

Granville placed one hand over Juliet's where it lay on the polished mahogany table. She hadn't spoken, nor had she touched her soup. If she was happy about her betrothal, it didn't show.

Which begged the question of why the hell she took Granville, if she didn't want to marry the blackguard.

"I realize that my request may seem very last minute, but I only discovered the nature of the gala a few days ago. Nonetheless I believe it's imperative that I speak out on this matter. I don't believe it's appropriate for my future wife to act in public.

Particularly when the scene is of a romantic nature. Given that it's only one part among many, would it be a problem to cut the excerpt from *Romeo and Juliet*? It wouldn't affect the rest of the entertainment."

Portdown choked on his champagne.

"Papa, are you all right?" Portia rose and caught his glass before he splashed wine everywhere. "Take a breath."

Red-faced and watery-eyed, Portdown glared at Granville. "I cannot have heard you correctly, Your Grace."

Evesham knew it wasn't the acting that Granville objected to. It was the person playing Romeo. The clod abhorred the idea of Juliet proclaiming her affections to his worst enemy.

Granville looked uncomfortable, and a muscle jerked in his cheek as he toyed with his glass. "I don't want malicious gossip to tarnish my betrothal."

"Gossip?" Portia asked in a dangerous tone. "What are you trying to say? Amateur theatricals in a family setting aren't considered outré, even by the sticklers."

Granville cast her a hostile glance. It appeared that he wasn't overly fond of his prospective sister-in-law either. "But this isn't really a family setting, is it? Half of ruddy Mayfair is arriving tomorrow night. To witness my future duchess declare her love to a man who's unfit to wipe her boots."

"Please don't spare my feelings," Evesham murmured.

"Well, it's true." Granville didn't bother to hide his contempt as he glowered back. "The Frains have already flirted with scandal this season, and you trail destruction after you, wherever you go."

"There has been no impropriety." Juliet at last joined the conversation. Evesham commended her conviction, when both of them knew that she was lying. Nobody would doubt her. "But if you're determined to see wickedness where no wickedness exists, perhaps we should reconsider our future."

The festive atmosphere had deteriorated with notable speed. Granville turned to his prospective bride with an appalled expression. He'd clearly underestimated the family dedication to the stage. "You mistake me, my lady. I'm only trying to protect you. I don't want this man's toxic reputation to cause you any harm. If you take time to consider the situation, I'm sure you'll see my point."

What Evesham did see was that the timing of this engagement was no accident. He should even have expected it. Granville had rushed down to Afton Park to snatch Juliet out of his rival's reach.

Juliet regarded Granville down her imperious nose. She'd never looked more like a duchess. Ice edged her voice. "I've played a part in my father's productions since I could walk. Nobody has ever raised an eyebrow. If you doubt my character, I must ask myself whether you trust me as you should trust your future wife. You clearly have no faith in my judgment."

"I don't doubt your character or your intelligence," Granville started.

Evesham had never seen the coxcomb caught on the wrong foot like this before. He enjoyed it in a way that he hadn't enjoyed anything else on this pestilential day.

"Juliet and Evesham are performing Shakespeare." Portdown regained his voice at last. "Where the art is so great, there can be no impropriety."

Evesham wasn't sure that he agreed, and he could tell that Granville didn't either. But the duke seemed to recognize that he had no power to prevent Juliet's appearance tomorrow night.

"We've all worked so hard," Portia said. "When you see the show, you'll understand that there's no harm in what we do."

"I did invite Your Grace to attend the rehearsal," Portdown added. "If you had, I'm sure that would have allayed your misgivings."

"I'm only trying to ensure no untoward talk mars our nuptials," Granville said, lips thin with annoyance.

Untoward talk had marred his first engagement. It must burn like acid that the man who had brought that match to an end was also on the scene this time around.

"I appreciate your care for my daughter, Your Grace. Your concern for her reputation does you credit," Portdown said.

Evesham knew he was lying through his teeth. He didn't appreciate it at all, the old trickster.

Portdown went on. "But Juliet has been in my care all her life. She doesn't become your responsibility until the day of the wedding. If I say no dishonor attaches to her name by performing a quarter hour on the stage, my word prevails."

Both Granville and Juliet looked annoyed at that. Evesham hid a smile behind his wineglass. This was a strong, independent woman who chose her own path. She wouldn't appreciate her father's patronizing tone. Especially when Evesham was well aware that most of the day-to-day management at Afton, not to mention her sisters' upbringing, had been left to her.

"I'd like to play the part," Juliet said firmly. "If, as Duchess of Granville, I must forsake something I've always enjoyed, it would be nice to finish on a high note."

Her tone brooked no argument. Granville nodded

that glossy head in agreement, however grudging. "As you wish. I'm sorry to cause our first argument. It seems a pity to spoil the celebratory atmosphere. I'll hold my peace."

The door opened to footmen bearing the fish course. Silence fell until the servants had left. Portdown glanced around the table and lifted his glass of claret. "We've toasted Juliet's wonderful news. Let's now toast the success of my Shakespeare gala."

Portia and Evesham readily held up their glasses. If Juliet and Granville were a little slower to respond, only a man as observant as Evesham would notice.

After dinner, Portia accompanied Juliet to her bedroom. Juliet rather wished that she wouldn't. Her sister didn't like Granville, and after that awful scene at dinner, she wasn't sure that she was up to more nagging. That awful scene, and her desperation to avoid any contact with Evesham.

She knew that Granville mistrusted and disliked her Romeo. Even more, she was smart enough to guess that more than a little jealousy lurked beneath his concern for her reputation.

The last thing she wanted was her fiancé suspecting that despite her self-righteous assertions, she and Evesham weren't quite as lily-white as they liked to appear.

She shouldn't have kissed Evesham. If Granville found out, she feared that blood might be spilled. When there was more than enough fake blood on the stage already.

Even more mortifying, for a moment tonight, she'd wondered if Granville meant to cry off. And instead of dismay, her strongest reaction had been relief.

"So you've caught your second duke," Portia said tartly, once they'd sent Juliet's maid off to her bed. "Well done."

Juliet sat at the dressing table, removing her pearl necklace and earrings. She met troubled blue eyes in the mirror. "Please be happy for me, sis. I know you don't like Granville, but I hope you'll respect my choice. He and I will make a formidable team, when it comes to doing good in the world."

She braced for an argument. An argument that right now, she was ill-equipped to win. But after shooting her a probing look, Portia wandered across. "Stand up, and I'll help you get out of this frock."

Juliet rose and presented her back to her sister. "Is that all you're going to say?"

"Yes." Portia began releasing the back of the azure silk gown. It was one of Juliet's favorites. She'd chosen it to lift her morale. It hadn't worked.

She met Portia's eyes, blue like hers, in the mirror. "Really?"

"I'm entitled to my opinion, but you've made your decision. Everybody always said you'd make the perfect duchess. I suppose now we'll see if that's true."

"He's a good man." Juliet hid a wince at the plea for affirmation contained in her statement.

"Yes, even I can see that. And you're a good woman." Portia moved onto loosening Juliet's stays. "Goodness shall rule."

"There's nothing wrong with goodness."

"No, there's not." Portia spoke with such careful neutrality that Juliet gave a short laugh as she stepped away from her sister.

"Very tactful."

She tugged at the pins holding her elaborate

hairstyle, until thick blond waves cascaded around her shoulders. She hoped that letting her hair down might ease the pounding pressure at her temples.

It didn't.

"That's me. Tactful all over." Portia studied Juliet with a puzzled frown. "Do you want me to talk you out of your engagement?"

Heat prickled Juliet's cheeks. To hide her flush, she stepped behind the screen to undress. "Of course not. I told you at the start of the season that I admired Granville and that if he proposed, I intended to accept him."

It was a relief to escape that perceptive gaze. Portia knew her too well.

"Yes, you did," Portia said thoughtfully. "But you're not acting as if it's all a dream come true."

"I'm not a demonstrative person. You know that."

"Even a reserved individual like you is allowed a little sparkle when she announces her engagement. You're looking morose."

"Nonsense." Except it wasn't nonsense.

"Yet you seemed willing to sacrifice your chances to be a duchess in favor of Papa's gala."

"I could hardly leave Papa in the lurch. So many people are coming down from London to see Evesham."

"It still speaks to priorities. Few women would risk a wedding to a duke to play at amateur theatricals."

Juliet lifted the ewer to pour warm water into the bowl and started to sponge her skin. "Granville will take charge of me in a few weeks. Until then, I can make my own decisions."

"Are you afraid he means to bully you?"

Juliet ran the damp cloth down her arms, as she considered Portia's question. "He seems to respect me. I don't think he'll be a tyrant. But who can tell?"

Portia moved closer to the screen. "Jules, is that why you're hesitant? You fear losing all your freedom?"

This time she didn't even try to conceal the heaviness of her sigh. "I must marry. It's the way of the world."

"You could stay with Papa. You've been mistress here most of your life. You could wait until you meet a man you like."

She had met a man she liked, but he wasn't marriage material, unfortunately. "I'm twenty-six. I've seen most of the eligible gentlemen. And I do like Granville. He's everything I admire."

All true, although she still couldn't work out why after planning this match all year, now it eventuated, she found herself hesitating. She had no patience with vacillation. Yet no doubt, she was vacillating. She wanted to kick herself.

"You won't much like bowing your head in obedience."

"The duke and I will work out how to go on. I don't fancy fading into a lonely spinster, and I'd like children. It's something to become the Duchess of Granville."

"It is, if that's what you want from life." Portia sounded unconvinced. Juliet couldn't blame her.

A silence fell, punctuated by the soft splash of water as Juliet washed.

"You haven't mentioned...love," Portia said with uncharacteristic diffidence.

Juliet finished drying herself and hung the towel on the rail. "I like the duke. I respect him. We have a great deal in common. I think we can be friends."

"That's not love."

No, it wasn't. "He believes love will grow."

"So he doesn't love you either?"

"We see ourselves creating a successful

partnership."

"That's so cold-blooded," Portia said in such a sad voice that Juliet couldn't find it in herself to be annoyed.

She pulled her cotton nightdress over her head and bundled her hair into a ribbon. "I'm a cold-blooded person."

Portia's snort expressed her contempt for that remark. "Don't be ridiculous, sis. Just because you don't wear your heart on your sleeve doesn't mean you're lacking a heart altogether. You feel things deeply. You know you do. You couldn't love Viola and me more than you do. You even love Papa, despite him driving you to distraction."

Juliet sighed again, well aware that her manner ill-suited a girl who had just accepted a duke's hand in marriage. She wrapped a silk peignoir around herself and tying the belt, stepped around the screen to see Portia sitting on the bed, looking unhappy.

Portia was a romantic. She always had been.

"Of course I love my family. I mean that I'm not a woman of strong physical passions." She shoved away the unwelcome memory of kissing Evesham. She'd suffered a fit of lunacy. She certainly hadn't been herself. A brief flash of insanity wasn't enough to change the path of a lifetime. "No man has ever aroused powerful feelings. At my age, I doubt any man will."

Portia looked puzzled. "I thought you loved Bolton."

Juliet shook her head. "I liked him. I was sad when he died. But it wasn't a grand passion."

"Don't you want to fall in love?"

"Not if it means a life of chaos and misery. Look at Viola and Toby. They hardly know each other, but a lack of control over their desires means that they're now shackled together for life."

"I'm hoping they might find their way," Portia said.

"I'm hoping, too," Juliet said, and heard the doubt in her voice.

Her shy, bookish sister and the roguish Earl of Renfrew had nothing in common. It was like pairing Juliet with the Duke of Evesham. A recipe for disaster.

"You deserve everything wonderful that the world has to offer," her sister said in a somber tone. "You're a remarkable person, and you have so much love to give."

As sisters will, she and Portia spent a lot of time squabbling. Juliet's role as a mother figure only complicated the relationship. Her sister's sincere tribute touched her.

Portia went on. "I hate to think that you're settling for Granville, just because people say you'll be the perfect duchess and he's the only marriageable duke left in England."

"But I'm going to be the perfect duchess." Juliet willed away tears. "Just you wait and see."

Portia stood and hugged Juliet with a fervor that made her heart ache. "Of course you will. But remember you're a woman, too."

Juliet returned the hug with a hint of clumsiness. "I love you, Porsh."

"And I love you, Juliet." When Portia drew back, she wiped her eyes. "That stiff-necked blockhead Granville had better make you happy, or he'll have me to deal with."

CHAPTER TWELVE

*E*vesham tossed away the butt of his cheroot and glowered into the gathering dark. He wasn't a habitual smoker, but occasionally he indulged when he was troubled in mind. Tonight, he was more troubled than he could ever remember.

He didn't much like it. Over recent years, he'd skated across life's surface in a haze of pleasure. So much effortless pleasure, that it all became a bit interchangeable. Nine years of purposeless amusement had begun to pall, even before he came to Afton Park.

This time last night, he'd been kissing Juliet and he'd been as happy as a dog in a butcher shop. Now, he wandered the gardens, hoping to settle to a point where he might sleep. He was tired. Craving for Juliet Frain had chased away sleep since he'd arrived in Wiltshire.

Right now, he felt like a mongrel cur kicked into the gutter. He didn't specialize in emotions, particularly the bleaker kind. But as he surveyed the idyllic landscape from the terrace outside the morning room, he felt as low as he could remember.

Restless, he drifted further around the house.

Everybody except him had retired early in preparation for tomorrow's performance. If Granville had expected late-night carousing to celebrate his engagement, he was to be disappointed.

On the other hand, the fellow probably didn't mind. He'd always struck Evesham as a man of middle-aged habits. Early to bed. Early to rise. Evesham doubted that the milksop had ever downed a tankard too many in all his measured, virtuous life.

Granville should be sodding perfect for Juliet, who took life seriously and believed in following the rules. Evesham suspected that the only time Juliet had ever overstepped propriety's line was when she'd kissed him.

Since then, she'd decided to return to the straight and narrow. Granville was certainly straight – and narrow-minded.

What a waste. What a tragic waste.

When Juliet lost herself in acting, Evesham saw a woman a world away from the genteel cipher she preferred to present in public. That scintillating woman wouldn't be allowed out to play, once she became the Duchess of Granville.

Her inevitable fate made him angry and regretful. More, it made his gut revolt in denial. And something that felt very like despair.

His Dis-Grace, the Duke of Evesham, didn't deal in despair, God damn it.

Almost inevitably, he found himself under Juliet's window. He shouldn't even know which room was hers, but of course he'd found out. She had apartments at the end of the north wing. Portia and his lordship were in the south wing, along with the guest room that he'd been assigned. Granville slept a few doors up from him.

To his surprise, a light shone through the

casement window above. He'd been slouching around outside for a couple of hours, so he'd assumed that the rest of the household must be asleep.

It seemed that Juliet, like him, found repose elusive.

He eyed the gothic exterior of the house, as an outrageous thought crept into his mind.

By Jericho, she'd never forgive him. She'd scream. She'd have him banished from the estate, gala or no gala.

He couldn't. He really couldn't.

But he was already striding toward the building, and his heart was racing with anticipation.

Juliet was in bed, pretending to read *Emma*, when she heard muffled scraping outside. It startled her out of a brown study, where she stared into space, telling herself over and over that she'd done the right thing today.

She put aside the book and scrambled out of bed. Curious, she stuck her head through the open window to an airless night. Whatever caused the odd sounds, it wasn't the wind.

"But, soft! What light from yonder window breaks?"

She squeaked with shock and looked down to find Evesham poised on a stone parapet about ten feet below. As usual, his soft black hair was mussed. He'd discarded his coat, and his loose shirt made a white patch in the darkness.

The unwelcome insight struck her that he looked more like Romeo now than he did when he wore the doublet and hose of his costume. Not that he didn't look dashing then either.

She'd long ago recognized that the Duke of Evesham looked dashing in everything that he wore. Curse him.

"What the devil are you doing there?" She sounded irritable, mostly because the surge of joy that greeted his arrival wasn't permissible in a newly engaged woman.

"I want to talk to you," he said in a low voice.

"It's late," she hissed. "I'll see you at breakfast."

"Everyone else is there at breakfast."

"You don't need to see me privately."

The lamplight spilling from inside her room revealed the stubborn set of his jaw. "Yes, I do."

She lowered her voice even further, although nobody had a bedroom nearby. "I would like you to forget last night's unfortunate...encounter."

He stared up, as if intent on memorizing every inch of her features. "I'll be a dead man before I forget what happened, Juliet."

Confound him, he sounded as if he meant it. Even worse, he sounded as if he suffered.

Juliet kept enough grip on reality to know that neither could be true. In a lifetime of carnal encounters, one kiss wouldn't make a lasting impression. Especially when she was such a rank beginner at the activity.

To her chagrin, she had a sick feeling that he'd scarred her for life. He'd never think of her once he left, while she'd dream about that fleeting taste of sin forever. Which was a wicked thing to admit when she'd just agreed to marry another man. A man worthy of her undiluted loyalty.

"You must forget. Now leave me be." She started to turn away.

"Don't marry him, Juliet. He won't make you happy." This time, he didn't keep his voice down.

She rushed back to the window in a panic. "Shh. Somebody will hear you."

"I'll say I'm practicing for the play. That's what gave me the idea of climbing up to you."

Her hands closed hard on the stone sill. "It's a stupid idea. Go away."

He didn't shift. "I will, if you tell me you won't marry Granville."

"I won't discuss this with you," she said in a furious whisper. "It's nothing to do with you. *I'm* nothing to do with you. I'm shutting this window and going to bed."

"Then I'm not going anywhere."

"You'll get sick of perching on that ledge."

"That's true. I may find I need to sing to keep awake. Or perhaps yell, so that you can hear me through the glass. There's a thought."

Rage filled her, mainly at herself. The hussy who had replaced sensible Juliet Frain would dearly love to invite Evesham into her bedroom. "You're blackmailing me. You should be ashamed of yourself."

"Shame isn't part of my vocabulary."

"That's nothing to be proud of." She straightened and folded her arms over her bosom. "Leave me alone, Evesham. I've got nothing to say to you."

A smile lightened his features. "That's good. Gives me more chance to talk to you. And I've got plenty to say."

"None of it relevant," she snapped.

"We'll see about that." He reached for the carved gable around the top of the darkened window below her.

"Don't!" She forgot to be angry and leaned as far forward as she dared. "You'll fall."

Now he was closer to the light, she caught the laughter in his eyes. It was cruel that he was so beautiful. She'd always thought Granville was good-looking, but he was like a plaster saint compared to Evesham's masculine appeal.

"So you do care."

It alarmed her quite how much she cared. It took an almighty effort to sound hard-hearted, but she managed it. "I care that if you come to grief, I'll have to explain why there's a body on the flagstones under my window."

"Stray corpses are so untidy," he responded, with the humor that had undermined all her defenses from the first.

Her heart pounded with fear and unwilling excitement. "Yes. That's exactly it." She leaned further out. "Really, Evesham, it isn't safe."

She watched him dig his fingers in, as he clambered up the walls. "I sneer at safety." His breathlessness hinted that the climb was more strenuous than he'd expected.

"I don't. I've already had one dead duke in my life. I don't want another."

"Even if this one is no great loss."

"I didn't say that. Oh!"

Boots scrabbled across stone, as Evesham lost his footing. The hand hooked around the drainpipe was all that kept him from plummeting to the ground.

"Please...please don't do this." Her heart was lodged in her throat. "You'll get hurt."

By now, she couldn't hide her genuine distress. She only started breathing again, once he found purchase and stretched up to grip the windowsill in front of her. A heavy gold signet ring on his little finger caught the light from her lamp.

"Me? I'm indestructible," he said. "Now don't distract me while I climb in. To blazes with Romeo. He makes the whole thing look so easy."

Irate and still jumpy from watching him come

close to falling, Juliet stepped back to watch him haul himself up. He paused as he straddled the ledge and took a long look at her. His unabashed appreciation made her flush and tighten the belt on her pink robe.

"You shouldn't be here," she said stiffly.

That devil-may-care smile lifted his lips, as he hoisted one long leg over the sill. Once he was inside, he leaned against the window ledge with a casual air that stoked her temper.

He shouldn't be in here. He definitely shouldn't be looking so at home.

"With love's wings did I o'er-perch these walls, for stony limits cannot hold love out."

Her lips flattened. Even though he quoted the play, it stung to hear him speak of love, when love had nothing to do with the forbidden attraction raging between them.

"Don't try to be charming. I want you out of here this instant. You know the price the world will extract from us, if anyone guesses that you've been in my bedroom." She wrapped her arms around herself. Her tone, already firm, turned acerbic. "Although you've already avoided taking the honorable path with one woman you've ruined, haven't you? So I suppose if any price is to be paid, I'll have to pay it."

She waited for him to defend himself. When he didn't, she wondered why she'd bothered. Instead, he directed a searching regard at her. "I was going to tell you not to be afraid. But you're not, are you?"

She met his question with a pointed look. "Do you intend to harm me?"

"No."

"Then all I'm afraid of is someone turning up."

Satisfaction lit his eyes. "You trust me."

"I wouldn't say that," she said in a dangerous

voice. "But do I think you'll force yourself on me? Certainly not."

Perhaps she was so confident that he'd never take her against her will, because she feared that if he exerted himself to seduce her, she'd surrender anyway.

Get a hold of yourself, Juliet.

He straightened and began to wander the room with unhidden curiosity. "Do you have any brandy?"

She stayed where she was and folded her arms again. "No, I don't."

"Pity."

His presence made the spacious room feel small and suffocating. She'd never had a man in here before, apart from her father, who used to come up to kiss her good night when she was a little girl. She had a horrible premonition that after tonight, Evesham's presence would haunt these chambers.

"If you need brandy, perhaps you should go downstairs to the library."

"Actually, I thought you needed some. You looked rather green around the gills at dinner. Did the halibut disagree with you?" He paused. "Or perhaps it was that cold fish, Granville. He always puts me off my soup, too. You don't want to spend the rest of your life looking at him across a dinner table, do you? You'll go into a decline."

"As if you give a fig for that." Her lips pressed together. She refused to enter into a quarrel about her engagement. In part, for the mortifying reason that she feared Evesham might win the argument. "If I don't get some sleep, I'll look like I've gone into a decline anyway. In case you've forgotten, I'm standing in front of half the beau monde, playing a radiant adolescent tomorrow. This isn't fair, Evesham."

He halted his restless pacing beside her dressing

table and sent her a questioning look. "I'm trying to save you from making a terrible mistake."

Juliet squared her shoulders and glared at him as if she hated him. Right now, she suspected she might. While she'd been mulling over her future this evening, she'd come to a few stark realizations about the man who played her Romeo.

"No, you're acting out of nothing but spite." Her voice dripped with acid. "I wonder now whether spite has been behind everything you've done here at Afton."

He looked innocent. Another warning sign. "I don't understand."

"And you so clever, too," she said in a jeering tone. "If you were any sharper, you'd cut yourself."

"Juliet, I'm thinking of you."

"No, you're not. You're thinking that this is another chance to wreck the Duke of Granville's wedding plans. Why else would an acknowledged rake like you waste his time pursuing a spinster as dull as ditchwater?"

"Juliet, don't." He stepped forward and reached for her hand, but she jerked away.

"Don't touch me. You make my skin crawl."

He obeyed, but the way his eyes narrowed on her made her nervous. Not that he'd assault her, but that he'd use her weakness for him to prove her last reckless statement false. "I didn't make your skin crawl last night."

"Last night, I was a fool."

"Last night you weren't thinking of Granville either."

"You were."

He spread his hands in a lying show of innocence. "I could hardly guess that the ass would hare down here to propose."

"Well, you should have. So should I. He wasn't

going to leave you free to subvert another potential duchess."

"I do want to stop you marrying him."

"Destroying his hopes is worth dredging my good name through the mud?"

"I don't care about his hopes." He made a sweeping gesture. "I care about you. He'll never make you happy."

"Just as he'd never have made Vanessa Gould happy."

His voice turned cold, as it always did when she mentioned his former lover. "You're very different from Vanessa, but, no, he wouldn't have made her happy either."

She gazed up at Evesham, blinking away scalding tears. The week had been full of strain, and tonight just made everything worse. "You're such a benefactor to wayward gentlewomen, I'm surprised they haven't set up a statue in your honor."

"Stop it, Juliet." Her sarcasm made his expression harden. He stepped up to tower over her. "You'll make yourself mad."

"Go away," she said, even as her shaking hands closed around the unyielding muscles of his upper arms.

By heaven, she shouldn't be touching him. She was angry with him.

She should be pushing him out of her room or screaming for help. If only he wasn't so big and so stubborn and so blasted appealing.

If only he wasn't so warm and standing so close. If only every breath she took wasn't tinged with his evocative male scent.

If only she didn't want him so much...

"God forgive me, I can't go away." He stared down at her, as if he was the one going mad. "It's too much to ask of a mere mortal."

Juliet caught irate bewilderment in his answer. Then all she heard was the rush of her blood, as he lowered his head toward hers.

CHAPTER THIRTEEN

Evesham took Juliet's lips in a kiss unlike any that he'd ever experienced. She'd made him furious. Everything about this God-awful day made him furious. Yet the moment his lips met the softness of hers, the rage drained away, leaving agonizing yearning behind.

Because he wanted her. He wanted her more than he'd ever wanted anything in his reckless, aimless, shallow life.

While wanting her, he also cherished her. He adored her spirit and her strength and her defiance. He even admired the way that she didn't fall for his tired old lines.

When she fought him, it was exciting. Even more exciting when she melted into helpless participation. She was too fine for him, but that didn't stop him lashing his arms around her and hauling her against his body.

Instead of demanding her response, he teased her, taking his time to let her come to him. Which given how exasperated she was with him, might be a mistake. Except he tasted a desire on her lips as inescapable as his own, and she parted for him almost immediately. Soon she was using her tongue to seduce him.

Heaven help him, he was seduced to the depths of his soul. Heat pulsed in his blood, and he was hard and ready.

Panting, he lifted his head and struggled to clear his vision. The innocent had kissed him into a storm of passion.

Juliet curved against him, as if she swooned with the intoxicating bliss of it all. Her eyelids drooped over her eyes, and a flush brightened her face. A wealth of golden hair had escaped its ribbon and cascaded down her back. She'd never been so beautiful.

She was all warm, enticing woman, lost in the pleasure roaring between them. But even Evesham recognized that only a despicable cad would take things any further. And while he'd broken most of the world's rules, he continued to abide by one or two principles.

Nevertheless, it hurt his tight throat to say what he must. "Juliet, we can't."

"No, we can't." To his regret, the sensual rapture faded from her expression. Now she regarded him with frantic eyes, and her hands kneaded the flesh of his arms. "We must stop."

"We must," he agreed. Wishing to hell that he meant it. But the dreadful truth was that he ached to claim her for his own.

Evesham wasn't sure whether she rose to meet him or he leaned down to her. But they were kissing again, and gentleness became a mere memory. This was raw passion, such as he'd never shared before. This was as desperate as life and death.

When she stumbled backward, tugging him with her, he went. Right now, if she kept kissing him, he'd jump off a cliff into a rough ocean and wouldn't say one word of protest as he drowned.

They toppled onto the bed together. For one extravagant moment, he luxuriated in her luscious softness beneath him. Her loose nightclothes flowed around him, and he found himself poised between her parted legs. When he raised his head, he snatched a breath laden with delicious female arousal.

He still couldn't see straight, and his heart threatened to leap out of his chest with excitement. When he cupped one voluptuous breast in his hand, she cried out and arched up in an incoherent entreaty for more. Her robe had parted to reveal the flimsy lawn of her night rail. So flimsy, he could see the dark pink jut of her nipples.

Temptation spiked to take this encounter to its end. Lying cradled between her thighs, he was on the brink of reaching paradise.

"Dear Lord, you're so beautiful," he grated out, as he pulled at the loose knot that held the top of her nightdress closed. If he didn't see her now, he'd shatter into a million pieces.

Sheer white material parted to reveal perfect breasts. White. Generous. Tight pointed nipples. A jolt of overpowering arousal gripped him, as he drew one beaded crest between his lips.

Her husky moan built his agony. As he tongued the sensitive tip, her hands, which had been running up and down his back in a fever of touching, raked through his hair, pressing him closer.

Evesham nuzzled the creamy flesh, relishing the piquant taste. Then he shifted to kiss her other breast. One hand lowered to lift the hem of her nightdress.

His hand trailed along her thigh to tangle in the feathery nest of curls. When she shifted under his caresses, more of that earthy female essence tinged the air. His fingers dipped between her legs to seek out her satiny heat.

Juliet cried out and bowed upward. "Evesham..."

He must stop. He would stop.

Soon...

Juliet shuddered as he stroked the hot, swollen folds. She wasn't far off a climax. Her hands dug into his shoulders, as she quivered beneath his wanton caresses. He loved her lavish response to his touch.

He returned to kissing her, nipping and sucking at her lips. When his hand found the center of her pleasure, he built her responses into a frenzy. Her body tensed with rising excitement. Before on a rasping exhalation, she crashed into an orgasm that sent liquid heat flooding over his seeking hand.

"Evesham..." She clung to him as she trembled through her peak.

Desperate to have her, he rose onto his elbows and settled between her legs. Her eyes were closed, her lips were parted in rapture, and her body lay defenseless beneath his.

A couple of quick fumbling tugs opened his breeches. His throbbing cock sprang free. He drew in a deep breath and prepared to thrust.

She was made for him. Joining his body to hers would hurl him higher than heaven.

He gazed down into Juliet's beautiful, spellbound face. Her hair spread around her face like a golden halo. Her breasts spilled free of her disheveled nightdress. Her hands clutched his shoulders, as if she never wanted to let him go.

She was everything that he craved. She lay ready for him. He could take her now.

Yet he paused.

Slowly, Juliet's eyes opened. He stared into dark blue irises, stormy with need. Confusion drew her pale brows together. "What is it?"

Berating himself as all kinds of fool – because this chance would never come again – he rolled off her and out of the bed. He couldn't risk remaining within touching distance. His shaking hands took an age to fasten his breeches.

Juliet remained splayed across the sheets like his wildest fantasies made real. He already knew that this image would torment him for too many nights to come.

"Juliet, we can't do this." His voice emerged raw and shaking. Because the vile truth was that they could do this. They were two healthy young animals in a fever to mate. Taking her maidenhead would be the easiest thing in the world. And a transgression even an irredeemable sinner like him couldn't countenance. "You deserve better."

Resentment flashed in her eyes, and a sexual frustration that he understood far too well. Then he watched her pale in horror, as the afterglow of pleasure dispersed and she realized how close they'd edged to consummation. "Dear Lord above, how could I?"

She propped herself against the pillows and dragged her nightdress across to cover herself. Despite everything, he regretted losing sight of her breasts.

"What have you done to me?" she asked in a cracked voice. "I've never…"

He closed his eyes and bunched his fists at his sides so tight that they hurt. But not as much as his balls did.

Evesham braced for what he must say. The only thing he could say.

He opened his eyes and forced out the inevitable words. "Lady Juliet, will you marry me?"

Juliet was too upset to listen to him. "What did you say?"

Evesham looked sick. She was sure that she didn't look much better. Her stomach revolted with another wave of nausea. And shame. Shame worst of all. She'd almost...

He straightened, and that impressive masculine jaw set like granite. "I'd be honored if you would become my wife."

"No, you wouldn't." She clutched her robe to her throat like a despoiled virgin in a play.

Except that she'd flung herself headlong into ruin, hadn't she? Evesham just had to smile at her, and she forgot everything except desire. Bile flooded her mouth with rancid self-hatred.

Her blunt response surprised him, she could see. "I would, you know."

He didn't sound quite as overcome as he had at first. She was used to him being assured and ironically amused. When he'd first proposed, he looked as if he was about to step up onto the gallows.

Juliet heaved herself out of the bed and straightened her disordered clothing with clumsy hands. Nightmare images invaded her mind of how close she'd come to taking Evesham into her body. He'd been on top of her. Dear God above, he'd had his mouth all over her breasts.

She hadn't uttered one single denial. Heaven forgive her, she'd goaded him on.

As the waves of sexual response receded, leaving her feeling queasier than ever, her gaze sharpened on him. His always rumpled hair was more chaotic than usual. Because she'd threaded her hands through it, begging him for more. At the first touch of a rake's lips, the word "no" had vanished from her vocabulary.

Heaven might forgive her. She'd never – *never* – forgive herself.

"After what just happened, no man would be honored to marry me," she said bitterly, knotting her hands at her waist and telling herself that she would not be sick.

His gesture rejected her remark. "What we did proves that you're human, Juliet. Nothing worse than that. People are designed to succumb to sexual attraction. That's how the race continues."

"I have morals. Or at least I believed I did."

"Of course you have morals," he said with a hint of impatience. "But you're also a woman with natural urges. Why else do you think society works so hard to protect young girls from finding out what fun they can have with a man?"

Her temper kindled, although her anger remained turned on herself. She knew better, but that hadn't saved her from losing her head. Evesham had just done what Evesham did when a willing woman came within reach.

"Blast you," she snapped. "I don't care about deuced society. I care that instead of throwing you out the moment you climbed through my window, I kissed you and touched you and dragged you into my bed."

His lips turned down. "You didn't have to drag too hard. Any madness was entirely mutual, darling."

The endearment didn't soothe her outrage. It only emphasized how close she'd come to forgetting every code she lived by. Forgetting everything that she owed herself. "Except I didn't tell you to stop."

"You would have."

"Would I?" She sank her teeth into her lip, then confessed the worst of her sins. "I didn't pull back from what we were doing, Evesham. You did."

Juliet watched him heft in a huge breath, as strong emotion darkened his eyes. She sincerely hoped that it wasn't pity. "I'm much more experienced than you are. You were taken unawares."

She turned away on wobbly knees, blinking hard to keep the tears from falling. Her self-respect had taken so many blows tonight. Bursting into tears in front of Evesham would be the last straw. His understanding just made her feel worse. "I'm not fit for civilized company."

"Juliet, sweetheart, stop torturing yourself." He came up behind her and slid his arms around her, drawing her against his body.

She managed a fragmented breath and allowed herself to rest against him. He was so big and strong and warm. And right now, she felt alone and broken.

Pride goeth before a fall. She'd always imagined that she was immune to the foibles that led weaker women to their downfall. It turned out that given adequate temptation, she was just as fallible as everyone else. She should have been kinder to Viola after the scandal broke.

When Evesham cuddled her closer, she couldn't muster the will to pull away. The embrace was comforting rather than sexual. After tonight, she knew enough to tell the difference.

This care for her shouldn't be so potent. But his nearness relieved some of her lacerating distress. Which was ludicrous, when he was the cause of her trouble.

They stood together in silence. He buried his face in her tousled mass of hair. The heat of his body seeped through her, and despite everything, she started to feel better.

"You must go," she murmured, after a long while.

He shifted against her back, and the hand splayed over her stomach stroked her through the thin layers of her robe and nightdress. Despite everything, her unruly nerve ends stirred with interest.

How could she want him after what had just happened? It made no sense. She'd veered so close to disaster, yet still ruin lured her.

"I'll speak to your father in the morning," he murmured.

She frowned, not following what he meant. "You'll tell him what we did?"

He grunted with amusement. "No, you delightful goose. I need to get his permission to wed you."

All Juliet's brief serenity disintegrated to dust. She wrenched out of Evesham's arms. Curse her, she shouldn't be in his arms at all.

She lurched around to face him. "We can't marry."

"Of course we can." He looked puzzled. "After tonight, I think we must."

She waved away his answer and used his own arguments against him. "Nothing happened."

"Yes, it did." He looked determined to do the right thing in a way that a dedicated debauchee never should.

"Nothing irrevocable."

His gaze hardened. "I've touched your bosom. I've had my hand between your legs. I've been in your bed. I'd say all of that makes it imperative to step up to marry you."

She scowled, wanting to clout him for not acting like the careless philanderer that she knew him to be. "Why are you pretending to be an honorable man? Just because we were unwise doesn't mean we should sign up for a lifetime of misery."

A muscle jerked in his cheek and if she hadn't known him to be impervious, she might think her response injured his feelings. "Then you've mistaken me, my lady. The liberties I've taken require me to make an honest woman of you."

Her fists closed at her sides. Boxing his ears became more appealing by the second. "I am an honest woman."

"Too honest," he retorted. "You may not like me. But you like what we do together. A wedding is the price of things getting out of control."

Things? No, it wasn't things. It was Juliet Frain who had lost control. Painful as it was to face that truth.

Evesham had been excited, but he'd kept his head enough to stop in time. For a few unhinged moments, she'd been ready to welcome his possession. A rake and a libertine. An unrepentant seducer. The last man she'd ever imagined herself wanting.

She wrapped her arms around herself to contain her shivering. It was a betrayal of everything that she wanted to feel, but she missed the clasp of those strong masculine arms.

Juliet strove to sound determined and rational. Like the woman she'd been before Evesham lumbered into her life, laying everything to waste. "I appreciate your chivalry, Evesham, but I won't marry you."

His lips flattened. "After what happened, won't you at least call me Lucas? Evesham is too formal when we've stretched out on a bed together."

She flinched. "I wish you'd stop saying that."

"Whether I say it or not doesn't stop it being true."

Damn his eyes. He was right. "I'd like you to go," she said in a voice calmer than she felt.

He didn't shift. It was an odd moment to realize that he was at least as obstinate as she was. "So shall

I speak to your father tomorrow?"

"No, a marriage between us will be a disaster."

"And of course you've got Granville," he said with a hint of malice.

Granville? In all this mess, she hadn't remembered her fiancé. How could she be so remiss? Today, she'd promised to become another man's wife. Yet she'd dived straight into Evesham's arms as if she belonged there. What sort of woman was she?

She gaped at Evesham in shock. "You..."

He growled and turned away, raking one hand through his hair. "That was shabby. I'm sorry."

Juliet knew that the only really shabby person here was her. She'd betrayed Granville twice over. Once when she'd yielded to Evesham's caresses. Twice when she only now realized that she hadn't spared him a thought. "I want you out of here."

Despite her best efforts, her voice cracked. Because she was tired and heartsick and disgusted with herself. And Evesham's presence in her bedroom only reminded her of her lapses.

He glanced at her. "We still need to talk."

"No, we don't. Let's get the gala out of the way. Then you can disappear from my life."

"It's not going to be that easy, my dear."

"I'm not your dear," she bit out. "If I'm anything, I'm your fool."

His expression stern, he bent his head in a short bow. "Think about my proposal."

"I won't." Although of course she would. Memories of this dreadful night would persecute her forever. "The subject is closed."

"You'll still be a duchess if you wed me."

The snideness provoked a heated response. "That may be true. But I don't want to be *your* duchess."

"I'll make you happier than Granville."

"I doubt it."

Evesham cast a telling glance at the jumbled bed. Juliet waited for him to point out that at least if she married him, she'd know passion.

He failed to meet her low expectations, which didn't make her feel any better. They both knew what he'd been thinking. "My offer stands."

"So does my refusal."

Please go. Please go. I can't bear much more of this.

"That's your right." When she didn't reply, he strode toward the window. At last. "Better I leave as I came in. I'd hate to encounter your betrothed in the corridor."

His sarcastic reference to Granville bounced off her. She was so close to splintering, all she wanted was for Evesham to leave her in peace.

After that devastating encounter, Juliet felt like she'd barely withstood a tidal wave. God help her tomorrow, having to pretend to be an innocent young girl euphoric with first love. Right now, she felt about a hundred years old. And love seemed nothing but a cruel farce.

"It doesn't matter," she said in a dull voice.

"Chin up, Juliet." He cast her a sharp glance over his shoulder. "It's not the end of the world."

It felt like the end of the world. But he was right. She was acting like a wet hen. And Juliet Frain would never be so feeble.

She corrected her drooping posture and flashed him a glare of real dislike. By now, she was almost as angry with him as she was with herself. "If you say parting is such sweet sorrow, I'll dig out Papa's pistol and shoot you."

He turned to gape at her, as if he'd been struck by lightning. "By Jupiter, you're a splendid woman. Granville doesn't deserve you."

The compliment only fueled her rage. "And you do?"

"No, but at least I understand your value. He doesn't. He thinks that he's doing you a favor when he asked you to marry him." He crossed the floor to grab her around the waist. "Whereas that's anything but the truth."

His touch crashed through her. She should push Evesham away. If she did, he'd let her go. But her traitorous body arched closer and when he pressed his lips to hers, she answered with unrestrained need, spiced with sparking animosity.

Rancor set the kiss on fire. Volcanic heat engulfed her, overpowering even her acrid humiliation. Then, so abruptly that she staggered, he was gone.

She remained where she was, shaking and distressed, yet longing for more kisses. For more than kisses.

Because while she might remain a virgin, she was no longer an innocent. A man's weight had crushed her into a mattress. Masculine hands had explored the secret hollows of her body. Most of all, she now knew how lust could overcome every scruple in one steamy instant.

More than angry, she was afraid. Not that Evesham would force her into his clutches, but that she'd throw herself at him of her own accord.

CHAPTER FOURTEEN

The next morning, Juliet waited to meet the Duke of Granville in the summerhouse by the lake. It was early, and mist lay across the water as the sun appeared over the hill.

Granville stepped through the doorway. "Lady Juliet, you asked to see me?"

She rose and performed a quick curtsy. "Thank you for coming, Your Grace."

She'd been here since dawn, although she hadn't expected Granville to be out quite that early. After a horrid night of admonishing herself for what had happened with Evesham, it had almost been a relief to dress and come outside.

"Your note said it was urgent." He looked curious, but not overly concerned. Why would he be? Much as she hated to agree with Evesham, she knew that he was right about one thing. Granville believed that he'd bestowed inestimable favor upon her when he asked her to be his wife.

"It is." She'd asked a footman to deliver her message to His Grace the moment that he stirred. Luckily for her twanging nerves, the Duke of Granville woke early, as befitted a man noted for his regular habits. She wasn't sure that she could survive waiting too much longer to do what she must.

"Is there some trouble?" He'd picked up the strain in her tone. Or perhaps he'd noticed that she was yet to call him Alaric rather than Your Grace.

She straightened her spine and made herself meet his eyes. Her hands twisted together, until she forced herself to bring them to her sides. "Yes, there is."

He stepped up beside her, catching her arm. "Juliet, tell me. Whatever it is, I'll help. Your troubles are mine."

Oh, he was a good man. A tad self-important, perhaps, but then he was an undoubted power in the kingdom. All her life, she'd imagined marrying someone just like him. Someone clearheaded and purposeful, who would work with her to make the world a better place. Someone she could respect and like and support.

She sucked in a shaky breath and reminded herself that there was no other way. "You're too kind, Your Grace. But I've asked to see you because I'd like to withdraw from our arrangement."

He frowned in confusion. "Our arrangement?"

Juliet bit her lip. He wasn't usually slow on the uptake. But then it wouldn't occur to him that any woman would reject his proposal. Especially after she'd already accepted it.

"I'm asking you to release me from the betrothal that we entered into yesterday."

He lurched back as if she hit him. "You don't want to marry me?"

His tone suggested that she wasn't making sense. She supposed from his point of view, she wasn't. He was the most eligible bachelor in the land. Rich. Handsome. Highly principled. More, he'd devoted the season to wooing her and she'd given him every encouragement.

"I've reconsidered my future," she said

unsteadily. She hated how inadequate she sounded.

Anger flowed in to replace shock, and his hands fisted at his sides. "I'll bloody kill him."

His belligerence startled her. It was widely assumed that the Duke of Granville didn't possess any of the stronger emotions. But hadn't gossip said the same thing about her? In the right circumstances, anyone was capable of a powerful reaction.

Her hands had gone back to twining together at her waist. "You mistake me, Your Grace. I assume you refer to the Duke of Evesham. This decision concerns nobody but you and me."

His eyes glittered with fury. "Horseshit."

Juliet flinched. She hadn't expected such a volatile reaction. Granville didn't love her. He'd told her so. "When you accept my decision, you'll come to see—"

"This is that noxious bastard Evesham's doing. I should have shot the swine nine years ago."

"This has nothing to do with the Duke of Evesham," Juliet protested.

Granville cast her a disbelieving glance. She couldn't blame him. After all, she was lying.

Although the humiliating truth was that she broke her engagement because of her own behavior, not her bugbear's. After permitting Evesham such liberties, she couldn't in good conscience go to Granville's bed.

"Yes, it has. I should have known he was sniffing around your skirts, the minute I heard the ridiculous rumor that he was down here playing at Shakespeare. That maggot wouldn't know Shakespeare from a blasted cricket ball. He couldn't resist breaking up my engagement."

Juliet stiffened and spoke with the voice that had allowed her to play mistress of Afton Park at fifteen.

"Your Grace, I'll thank you to credit me with the character and intelligence to reach this conclusion, free of outside influence. I've spent all night reflecting upon this matter. I believe we will not suit. There's no point seeking someone else to blame. I regret if my actions have caused you pain. At least the engagement wasn't yet public, so no adverse gossip should attach to your name."

He eyed her, as if what she said annoyed rather than appeased him. "Gossip will attach to you. Society's been waiting for me to propose. You'll be derided as the woman I rejected. That makes two dukes you've missed out on, my lady. If you aim to become a duchess, you're running out of candidates. Good luck squeezing a proposal out of Evesham. He has a habit of seducing my fiancées, then leaving them high and dry."

Juliet hid a wince, although he had a right to his resentment. "I don't believe I'm suited to marriage. I'll retire to a quiet life in the country."

She'd be a laughingstock. She knew it. And Granville wouldn't be the only one who blamed her spinsterhood on Evesham. She'd feared gossip from the moment that her father produced a rogue to be her Romeo.

Granville regarded her the way that he'd look at a cockroach on his path. If any cockroach would have the gall to inconvenience such an exalted personage as the Duke of Granville. "You disappoint me, Lady Juliet."

She made an apologetic gesture. "There are plenty of other girls who—"

He shook his head. "No, you mistake me. From the first, I admired your strength and your virtue. You struck me as my perfect duchess. A paragon among women."

"I'm no paragon," she said through tight lips.

"Apparently."

"I know you want to shout and insult me," she said in a toneless voice. "I deserve it for dashing your hopes. But I also know that you're a good man, who will regret losing his temper. Are you willing to release me from our engagement, sir?"

He surveyed her down his ducal nose, making her feel more like a cockroach than ever. "If I must."

She sucked in a relieved breath. "I hope we can part as friends and without acrimony."

"I wouldn't go quite that far," he muttered.

She braced her shoulders. "I assume you'll have breakfast before you return to London this morning. I'll let the staff know."

His expression remained haughty. "I have no intention of returning to London just yet."

"But surely—"

"I'm going to stay for the performance tonight. The rest of the world's agog to see Evesham play Romeo. Why should I forgo the pleasure?"

"But what purpose..."

One hand cut through her faltering protest. "For my own satisfaction, I want to see the two of you together."

"There's nothing to see."

"I'd have laid money that if anyone could withstand Evesham's vulgar charms, it was the pure and wise Lady Juliet Frain. I should have known better."

She hoped that the duke blamed the heat in her cheeks on irritation, not cringing humiliation. "I told you – my choices have nothing to do with His Grace of Evesham."

The glance Granville gave her burned with contempt. "And I reserve the right not to believe you."

After a brief bow, he strode away. Juliet collapsed

onto a wooden bench under the window and cursed long and loudly, and with a fluency that would have surprised her society acquaintances.

Evesham spent all day trying to talk to Juliet, but she kept herself busy with preparations for the night's entertainment. The house was packed with guests, down from London to witness his theatrical debut. He'd also discovered that every inn within ten miles of Afton was full.

He wished to hell that he gave a rat's arse about his performance.

All he cared about was finding Juliet and making amends for the damage that he'd done last night. Since coming to Wiltshire, he'd spent many an hour imagining touching her as he'd touched her last night. Now all he could think of was the desolation in her expression when she sent him off.

At least that miserable cur, Granville, also stayed out of his way. Right now, knowing that Juliet had accepted the prig's proposal and refused his made him contemplate murder.

Evesham watched most of the show from the trees at the top of the terraced slope. The long benches between him and the stage were packed with aristocratic rumps. Curiosity and expectation hummed in the air, sparked by a scandalous duke's involvement in the entertainment.

The hum built to a crescendo when Granville took his place in the front row. The antipathy between the two dukes was well known. The ton had traveled all the way from London, hoping Evesham would make a complete fool of himself. That prospect became even more enticing, when there was the added spice of a possible confrontation between two sworn enemies.

Portdown, a showman to his fingertips, had scheduled the scene from *Romeo and Juliet* as the second-last item on the program. This ensured that his audience remained to the end. The gala would close with his delivery of Prospero's final speech from *The Tempest*.

Until then, there were a sequence of monologues from Portdown and staged scenes, including a surprisingly touching Ophelia from Portia. All her father's coaching had paid off.

The sophisticated audience may have come to scoff, but Evesham soon realized that the quality of the production won them over. Portdown was a magnetic actor, even more so now that he had an audience, and the neighbors, while perhaps not up to his standard, managed their parts with credit.

By the time interval arrived and the servants laid on an extravagant feast, the dell rang with unstinting praise. Evesham made himself scarce during supper. Since his return to England, he'd avoided society events. He had no wish to undergo a barrage of prying questions before his stage debut.

The performance had started in the late afternoon, progressing into twilight, so the balcony scene took place soon after nightfall. In the beautiful gardens of Afton Park, the effect of the changing light was genuinely magical. Portdown had engaged a small orchestra, and the music added to the atmosphere.

When Evesham first met Portdown, he'd derided the fellow as a deluded windbag. Over the last week, he'd grown to admire his lordship. But seeing the gala come together like this and engross a jaded, sophisticated crowd made Evesham want to applaud his host. The audience felt the same way. Tentative clapping at the start had become an enthusiastic ovation by interval.

A couple of scenes into the second half, Evesham slipped away to change into Romeo's doublet and hose. When he'd first put on the costume, he felt like a mountebank. Now he was so used to the garments, they felt like a second skin.

By the time he stepped into the makeshift wings, the stage was lit with flaming braziers, creating a dramatic effect. Portdown stood in front of a piece of painted scenery. He was dressed in black and delivering a couple of soliloquies from *Hamlet*.

Behind the flat, servants in slippers crept around setting up scenery for the balcony scene. Evesham had been impressed at the staff's professionalism in ensuring that everything went without a hitch. The gala was almost over and so far, it had been a triumph.

Evesham was grimly aware that the coming scene might bring that triumph crashing down to earth. When Juliet was self-conscious, she was more wooden than the scenery, and he feared that his acting inexperience might show, now that he was in front of a crowd.

"Are you nervous?" Juliet asked from beside him. She kept her voice to a whisper.

He turned, surprised that she'd sneaked up on him. This attraction had caught him by surprise in so many ways, not least because of his preternatural awareness of her. When she was nearby, his skin prickled and heat ignited in his blood.

But not tonight.

"A little," he said, which was an understatement. Like her, he kept his voice low. "Are you?"

"Yes. This is the largest audience I've ever played to. And the neighbors aren't the most critical crowd."

He permitted himself a quick glance at her. He'd

seen her costume at the dress rehearsal, a rose-pink high-wasted gown in some gauzy material cut low across her opulent breasts.

For rehearsals, she'd kept her hair confined. Now it flowed about her shoulders in a shining golden fall.

He briefly closed his eyes, as he recalled tangling his hands in that lustrous mane last night. The medieval dress was close enough to a nightgown to offer an inevitable reminder of having her in his arms, passionate, eager, willing.

More than once today, he'd damned himself for being clodpoll enough to hesitate when he'd been so close to possessing her.

"You'll be superb," he said, then wished he'd chosen a different word. He'd called her superb last night and roused her ire.

This was the first time they'd crossed paths since they'd quarreled in her room. So far, she didn't sound hostile. By heaven, having her speak to him at all seemed like a victory.

"Wasn't Portia marvelous?"

"Yes, she was." Although he'd never before thought of Ophelia having a pet beagle. Red's mournful expression as he observed his mistress's deranged meanderings had deepened the scene's pathos.

"We can't let Papa down. This is a dream come true for him. Especially when it's all going off with a bang." Juliet's voice lowered even further. "I'd hate our…differences to spoil everything."

Evesham realized with a shock that she fretted about him wrecking the performance as a way of getting back at her. She really didn't have much confidence in him.

It shouldn't sting. But it did.

He quashed the momentary pique. "For the next twenty minutes, I'm Romeo and you're Juliet, and we're trapped in helpless enchantment."

The sad truth was that, at least as far as he was concerned, it was true. She'd bewitched him at first sight just as powerfully as the fictional Juliet had bewitched his alter ego. Seeing her looking so lovely and so bloody approachable right now only dragged him deeper under her thrall.

Her tentative smile made his susceptible heart flip over. "Thank you." Then even more surprising, she moved closer and caught his hand in a quick clasp under cover of her floaty skirts. "Good luck, Your Grace."

He started to tell her to call him Lucas, but she'd already left him to skitter behind the scenery and climb up onto her balcony.

The applause was warm for Portdown's recital, then warmer still as two footmen slid the painted flat away to reveal a balcony above a moonlit orchard in Verona. A lilting violin solo established a mood of romance.

Evesham sucked in a deep breath and stepped onto the stage. To his surprise, when he spoke the words that he'd said so often in rehearsal, his voice emerged steady and resonant. "But soft, what light from yonder window breaks?"

"Good night, good night! Parting is such sweet sorrow, that I shall say good night till it be morrow."

Juliet blew her watching suitor below a couple of final kisses before melting away from the balcony to her bedroom, which was in reality the flimsy stairway. Romeo kept watch, as if he couldn't bear to lose sight of her. The curtain rigged up between a pair of wooden columns descended upon him standing alone in the moonlight.

For a moment, the hush extended before a thunderstorm of applause broke out.

Juliet felt like she'd held her breath for the entire scene. Her father had had her playing at amateur theatricals since she could lisp a line. Most of the time, she was a competent, if not inspired actress. Very occasionally, something lifted her out of the everyday into a realm where she didn't play a part, she became a character.

Tonight for the wondrous interlude of the balcony scene, she'd been a young girl desperately in love for the first time. She'd felt all of Juliet's bubbling joy and aching longing and crippling fear.

Evesham had taken the journey with her. His skills as an actor had blossomed with every day, but tonight he'd been extraordinary. She'd believed every vow of adoration. She'd recognized him as her soulmate. Her heart had broken a little, when she had to leave him to return to her chaste bed.

She stopped at the base of the stairs and struggled to shake off the overwhelming effect of the past few minutes. Because she was most certainly not that innocent young girl, and Evesham was as far from ardent, romantic Romeo as a man could be.

"Juliet, you were miraculous." Her father rushed up and drew her into a heartfelt hug. "I've never seen you light up the stage like that."

"Thank you," she stammered, still floating somewhere between Verona and Afton Park. In front of the crimson velvet curtain, the cacophony of shouts and clapping continued.

"You'll have to take a bow," her father said, releasing her. He turned to Evesham, who approached from the other side of the stage. "Your Grace, you were a revelation. I had high hopes, but even I am awed. Well done. Very well done."

Evesham looked as lost as she felt. Like her, he'd been caught up in the spell. If he hadn't been, she couldn't have dissolved mundane Juliet Frain into Shakespeare's glorious words as she had.

When his eyes met hers, the warmth that she read there had her heart performing somersaults. She battled to remind herself that it was just the play, but it was impossible to get a grip on reality just yet.

"Juliet, you were wonderful," he said. "I couldn't look away from you."

When he extended his hand, it seemed natural to take it. His fingers closed around hers and sent heat surging up her arm.

Her father gave them both a push forward as the curtain rose. The roar of approval was deafening. Dazed, Juliet looked out over the audience, who were on their feet and cheering with no hint of genteel irony.

"Bow, bow," her father urged from the wings.

Evesham laughed and sent her a glittering look. "We've done it."

Still holding her hand, he gave a low bow. When he straightened, Juliet dipped into a deep curtsy. As she rose, his hand firmed around hers. When she turned to him, he lifted her fingers to his lips.

For a moment, the boisterous crowd disappeared and she stared into his dark gaze. Then she recalled that every eye was focused on them. She jerked her hand back and made herself smile at the audience, as the curtain fell once again.

But the crowd wanted more. Half a dozen curtain calls before Juliet and Evesham retired to the wings and her father took his place at the front of the stage to deliver Prospero's immortal farewell to sorcery. For this, he wore conventional evening dress so that he was ready to mingle with the spectators after the show.

"Our revels now are ended. These, our actors, as I foretold you, were all spirits and are melted into air, into thin air."

Evesham was holding Juliet's hand again. Around them, the wings were empty. There were no more scene changes, so the staff had disappeared to set out the refreshments at the end of the gala.

What had just happened so entranced her, that it didn't occur to her to let him go. For once, nobody was observing them, so she didn't have to pretend that her longing for Evesham wasn't irresistible.

When he drew her toward the trees, she didn't pull back. He didn't speak. Nor did she.

But when he stopped in a small clearing in the woods, well out of the audience's earshot, she stepped into his embrace without hesitation.

CHAPTER FIFTEEN

*E*vesham gathered Juliet up in his arms and kissed her as if the world was about to end. The embrace was the only possible end to the extraordinary bond that they'd forged on the stage.

She sighed in rapture and parted her lips. Blazing heat shuddered through him, but the powerful wave of desire only expressed his soul's longing to possess this glorious woman. He'd never felt like this before, battered between devastating emotion and carnal hunger.

In the distance, a storm of applause broke out. Old Portdown must have done a good job of the finale. The noise seemed to come from a different universe.

Evesham tangled his shaking hand in Juliet's silky hair and angled her head closer. She twined her arms around him, until he felt every curve of that long, lissom body against him. Her scent drowned his reeling senses. Flowers. A hint of perspiration. The delicious drift of female arousal.

He groaned against her lips, fighting the lure of pleasure. Every masculine instinct urged him to pull her down onto the grass and take events to their proper conclusion. But even lost in a kiss as he'd never been lost before, he couldn't forget that half the beau monde was sitting only a few yards away.

The applause and cheering continued. Rose in volume.

Evesham had to let Juliet go. Return to the stage to take a bow.

But he was only human. How could he abandon this paradise?

"Good God, what on earth are you doing?"

Portdown's furious question pierced Evesham's haze like a sword pierced flesh. Juliet went rigid, then struggled free of his embrace.

"Papa!"

The full moon and the light filtering through the trees from the stage allowed Evesham to see her horrified expression. He almost wished that he couldn't. She looked as brittle as overcooked toffee, and she wrapped her arms around herself as if she was cold. Her father stood a couple of feet away, breathing in audible gusts and looking like he was about to explode.

There was no hiding that Evesham and Juliet had been in the middle of a passionate embrace. Guilt and self-castigation congealed in his gut. What in blazes had he thought he was doing?

He cursed his recklessness. He should have kept his head. More than that, he should have kept his hands to himself.

"Juliet, are you all right?" Evesham stepped closer.

She jerked away, as if he carried a disease. "What do you think?" she choked out.

Evesham turned to her father. "Lord Portdown, I know what you saw, but Juliet bears no blame. The fault is mine."

"We can't go into that now. They want you both to

take a bow." There was enough light for Evesham to read his host's expression. Portdown looked completely overturned. Seething. Confused. Upset. "You'll have to—"

"I damn well knew it!"

Granville burst out of the surrounding trees and strode up to them. He grabbed Evesham by the shoulder and wrenched him around until they were face to face. "You sodding bastard. You won't get away with this shabby trick twice. Name your seconds."

"Get your hands off me," Evesham snarled.

"With pleasure. After this." Granville surged forward and planted a punch on Evesham's chin that had him staggering.

Pain rocketed through him, and bells clanged in his skull. Seeing double, he struggled to keep his feet.

"What the hell..." Evesham placed a hand over his jaw to make sure it wasn't broken. He blinked to clear his vision. By Jupiter, he'd have to stop calling Granville a milksop. That blow was worthy of Gentleman Jackson.

Juliet stepped up to her betrothed. "Your Grace, there's no call to—"

Granville overrode her interruption with a lordly sweep of his hand. His searing fury remained focused on Evesham. "Name your seconds, you sneaking weasel. And this time when we duel, I'll do better than wing you."

"Your Grace, let's not be too hasty. The scandal..."

Granville ignored Portdown's bleating and bared his teeth at Evesham. "You're poison, Evesham. They should have drowned you at birth. But by heaven, you won't ruin another woman, if I have anything to say about it."

"You have no right to defend my honor," Juliet said in a voice sharp as a knife. "You have no rights over me at all, Your Grace."

Shock swamped Evesham. He stared at Juliet. "He doesn't?"

Juliet's hands dropped to her sides, and she raised her chin. Despite everything, he wanted to applaud her spirit. She must be cringing with humiliation, but right now, she looked like a queen. "I ended my engagement to His Grace this morning."

Evesham shouldn't be happy about that. They were in the midst of a full-scale catastrophe. But he wanted to hug her, even if that was how they'd got into this almighty mess in the first place.

"You broke your engagement?" Portdown turned on Juliet, sounding more flustered than ever. "You didn't say anything."

He looked as if he weathered a hurricane. Poor bugger, he'd just mounted a brilliant entertainment and achieved success beyond his wildest dreams. Now that accomplishment would disappear beneath a deluge of gossip and recrimination.

"I thought the news could wait until after the gala, Papa." She sounded like she was fighting tears, blast it. This public exposure of a private moment would scald her to the soul.

"But why would you jilt Granville?" Portdown asked in confusion.

"Because the silly widgeon has fallen victim to Evesham's wiles," Granville said through his teeth. "Can't you see what's going on?"

"I'll thank you to address Lady Juliet with respect," Evesham said with matching heat.

Behind them, the applause petered out over a murmur of curiosity from the audience. With the thunderous ovation fading, the sound of the orchestra drifted through the air. They were playing something jolly that created a sickening clash with the tension in the glade.

"All I want to hear from you is that you accept my challenge," Granville sniped back, rubbing the knuckles of his right hand. Evesham, whose face ached like the very devil, was glad that he wasn't the only one in pain after that massive thump.

"Can't you see that will only plunge us further into scandal?" Desperation honed Juliet's voice. "If you ever cared a whit for me, Your Grace, please forget what you saw and go back to London."

Granville's chiseled features set in obstinate lines. "The world will be a better place without this human fungus causing misery wherever he goes."

"There's no need for this to go any further," Portdown protested, his hands fluttering with distress. "Juliet is right. High jinks after a performance are regrettable, but nothing out of the ordinary."

"I'm taking Juliet back up to the house. If anyone wants to say more, they can say it in private, not where every rumor-monger in society can interrupt us," Evesham announced. "And somebody needs to go back to the stage and keep the audience busy, or else they'll all be here, sticking their noses in our business. Lady Juliet, will you accompany me?"

"Don't you dare run away, you slimy toad," Granville bit out before she could answer. He was so livid, he, too, had forgotten discretion. "Do you accept my challenge?"

"I'm not going to fight you, Granville," Evesham growled. "As Lady Juliet said, that will only make everything worse. Have some sense, man."

"I want you dead." Granville bit out every word as if it cut him. "I should have bloody well killed you nine years ago."

"Stop it, both of you," Juliet said, inserting herself between them. "I will not tolerate either of you turning me into a laughingstock, just because of stupid male pride."

Evesham straightened to his full height and leveled his shoulders. "Lady Juliet, I would consider it an honor if you would marry me."

He'd proposed last night, and she'd refused him. Surely now, when they were all about to become the talk of London, she'd take him.

"At least this time, you have some idea of doing the right thing," Granville sneered.

Evesham ignored the pompous numbskull. All his attention remained fixed on Juliet. From what the fitful light revealed of her face when she turned to him, the outcome wasn't promising.

"Juliet, my dear, you must agree," Portdown said in a placating voice.

Evesham bit back the urge to tell the man to shut up. Didn't the old fool know that the last word anyone should say to Juliet was "must?"

Juliet's jaw set at an angle even more obstinate than Granville's. With a sinking feeling, Evesham knew what she was going to say before she opened her mouth.

"Thank you, Your Grace, but we would not suit."

No uncertainty in her answer. He couldn't doubt that she meant it. Evesham's lips tightened, as he stifled crushing regret. And a hurt deep enough to crack his heart.

Granville permitted himself a satisfied smile. "It's clear that the lady has your measure, Evesham."

"Juliet, I'm afraid it's gone too far now. You need to marry someone," Portdown said, wringing his hands. "I'm sure no harm was done. Just a kiss or two in the moonlight. High spirits after all that poetry. Nobody would blame you. Perhaps if you won't have Evesham, Granville will offer again."

Despite the fraught circumstances, Evesham almost laughed. As if that puffed-up peacock would take his leavings.

Because that was how Granville would view Juliet. Even if she remained a million times too good for him. Lord above, she could swive half the Grenadier Guards, and she'd still be too good for him.

But Granville proved him wrong. Even, much as he hated to admit it, impressed him. The man didn't hesitate, and his answer betrayed no misgivings. "I'd count it a privilege to make Lady Juliet my duchess. I hold her in the highest esteem. I always have."

Juliet looked as amazed as Evesham. Damn it, the glance that she cast Granville was almost warm.

Evesham started to move toward her, then stopped. She'd made it clear that she didn't want him touching her. But dear God above, don't let her accept the oaf.

Something bone-deep inside Evesham howled denial. Because Juliet was his. She belonged with him. Even if, right now, he was the only person who recognized that.

He looked back on his chaotic, pointless existence, and he knew he wasn't worthy of her either. But how could he bear to see her march out of his life with her purposeful walk and her unshakable determination?

"That's...very generous of you, Your Grace," she said, and for the life of him, Evesham had no idea whether she meant to take the blockhead.

"There, Juliet," Portdown said, taking her arm. "That will put an end to all this nonsense. Once you're the Duchess of Granville, nobody will dare to—"

She shook her father off. "It won't do, Papa. I appreciate Granville's gallantry, but I won't marry him either."

She was refusing Granville's offer? Evesham

sucked in a huge breath of relief. "My offer stands, my lady."

"That's very kind," she said, sounding as if she didn't mean it.

"You have to choose one of them," Portdown said, bouncing from one foot to the other in his distress.

Juliet looked strong and resolute – and lonely. He feared that if she didn't bend, she'd break. His hands itched to touch her, to hold her together through this harrowing ordeal.

"No, I don't." She'd sounded like this, likely to snap in two, last night when she'd refused his first proposal. She couldn't make her opinion any clearer that Evesham was good enough to kiss, but not good enough to wed. The pain in his heart, already crippling, sharpened beyond agony.

"Lady Juliet, whatever your decision, I believe we need to return to the house," Evesham said, even as he struggled to come to terms with yet another categorical refusal. "Nothing can be gained from an argument here."

But it was too late. A muffled titter rose from the shrubbery. All four people in the center of the glade stiffened and exchanged horrified glances.

Evesham bit back a savage curse. Poor Juliet. Poor Portdown. Scandal was now unavoidable.

Granville turned and spoke with his usual imperiousness. "Show yourselves."

Despite some rustling, nobody appeared. But it was clear that the vile little scene had an audience. In the dell behind them, the musicians continued to play. The jaunty music grated on Evesham's nerves and made him want to skewer them all with a sharpened violin bow.

"What on earth is happening?" Portia burst onto the scene. As usual, her dogs raced after her, leaping and running around in circles. "Half of London seems to be heading in this direction."

Unsettled by the tense atmosphere, the dogs started to bark and growl and snuffle through the bushes. With varying degrees of protest, a dozen fashionably dressed people tumbled out into the clearing.

Evesham ground his teeth and wondered if things could get any worse. Portdown glanced around in alarm. "My lords and ladies, this is not well done."

The dogs added to the cacophony, turning the bristling confrontation into pure farce. Aristocratic eavesdroppers shouted and swore and squealed, as they fought off Portia's curious pets.

"Juliet, what is it?" Portia ignored her overexcited dogs. Instead, she stepped up to put her arm around her trembling sister. "You look like you're about to throw yourself into the lake."

Juliet sagged against Portia as if she couldn't have remained upright for another minute. "That might solve a lot of problems," she said in a reedy voice.

How Evesham loathed Juliet's suffering. It made his very skin sting, he loathed it so much. He burned to sweep her into his arms and carry her away. But to his infinite regret, he was the last person she'd look to for rescue.

Portia looked bewildered. "Juliet, what—"

"Lady Portia, kindly assume control of your mongrels," Granville demanded.

Portia's response conveyed scorching dislike. "They're good dogs."

"Oh! Oh! Oh, my. Oh, dear. Nice doggy. Nice doggy," Celia Edgecombe twittered in a hysterical tone only likely to work the dogs up while she tried to dance clear. "I fear for my life! Get off! Get off!"

Evesham had been away from England for a long time, but he recalled that she used to be one of the worst gossips in London. He couldn't imagine that had changed.

"Don't be such a dashed ninny, Celia," her husband said wearily from beside her, pushing Red away from where he'd jumped up on her. "He's just playing."

"His Grace is right, Portia," Portdown said with an attempt at regaining his authority. "Call your dogs."

Heaving an impatient sigh, Portia moved away from Juliet and clicked her fingers. "Red. Scratch. Bella. Heel."

The dogs obeyed straightaway and retreated to sit panting behind their mistress. At the same moment, the musicians ceased to play.

Abrupt silence descended like the crack of doom. For a prickly moment, the crowd of people, swollen now with the horde who had rushed up the path to see what all the fuss was about, eyed one another.

Evesham had reached the end of his tolerance for all these dramatics. The beau monde had enjoyed quite enough entertainment for one evening, both planned and unplanned.

He turned to Juliet with a bow and presented his arm. "My lady, allow me to escort you up to the house."

"I'll come, too," Portia said, as if afraid that her sister might make a scene.

But he knew that Juliet had reached a point where all she wanted to do was hide. To his surprise, she accepted his arm.

"Thank you," she said in a muffled voice. The frantic grip of her fingers betrayed how close she verged to the limits of endurance.

Evesham drew on five hundred years of ducal ancestors and summoned up a tone worthy of Granville at his loftiest. "Make way for her ladyship."

It worked. Without a word, the crowd parted for

him to lead Juliet through.

Sadly, the quiet didn't last. He heard chatter crescendo behind them, as he reached the torchlit path that led up to the house. Juliet lost her footing, but found her balance before he could help her.

"Juliet..." He'd give anything to make everything right. But it was too late for that.

"Please, no more." Unshed tears thickened her voice. "I beg you, if you have a shred of kindness for me, don't say anything."

Another stab of hurt. Much more piercing than the pain that radiated from his jaw. He couldn't recall the last time a woman – anyone – had possessed the ability to affect his emotions, but Juliet did. "Very well. I'll leave you in peace tonight, but we need to talk tomorrow."

Her stricken look left him feeling like he'd kicked a puppy. "I don't think I want to talk to anyone ever again."

He faltered and reached for her hand. "My darling..."

But Portia and her dogs rushed up behind them, and the moment was lost.

CHAPTER SIXTEEN

*J*uliet's knees were so unsteady that she needed to cling to Evesham until they reached the house. Even if right now, she'd give up her hope of heaven in return for never having to see him again.

Despite a few stumbles, she managed to walk the distance. The thought of collapsing in a heap and him carrying her the rest of the way made her want to vomit.

Thank goodness, he didn't say anything. What was there to say?

Standing in the middle of that repulsive brouhaha tonight had been the worst experience of her life. She'd wanted to shrivel up and die. Every lewd snicker and knowing glance had felt like someone peeling off her skin an inch at a time.

In the hall, Evesham consigned her to Portia's care, still with the gentleness and concern that she should appreciate. But gratitude couldn't pierce the haze of misery enveloping her. As the two women climbed the stairs away from him, he remained below with the dogs.

Once they'd turned into the corridor leading to her room, Portia put her arm around Juliet. "What in heaven's name happened? I've never seen Papa so furious. Granville was seething, too. Not to mention Evesham looks like his best friend just died. And he's got a bruise on his chin. Did you hit him?"

Juliet fixed her gaze on the door to her bedroom like it was the gate to the promised land. Right now, she wanted to lock herself inside and never come out again. "Can I tell you tomorrow?"

"Not even a hint?" Portia was nothing if not persistent. It was one of the qualities that made her an effective advocate for her animals.

Juliet set her jaw and pushed the door open. Without invitation, Portia followed her inside.

Juliet slumped in front of her dressing table to remove the gold locket and earbobs that she'd worn for the play. The gala felt like a million years ago.

That radiant girl on a balcony was someone else entirely.

Her image in the mirror turned misty, and her shaking hands couldn't manage the intricate catch on the necklace. She bit back a curse and lowered her hands to her lap.

"Do you need help with your gown?" Portia asked, her tone solicitous.

Juliet blinked away the moisture stinging her eyes and shook her head. "No. Once I unfasten the sash, it's loose enough to pull over my head."

"You were wonderful as Juliet. I've never seen you like that before. It was like someone lit a candle inside you."

Evesham had lit a candle inside her. For the love of God, he'd lit an inferno inside her. But consuming fires burned out too fast. Now all that was left was ashes.

"Thank you. You were a lovely Ophelia, too." She met tired eyes in the mirror. She looked haggard and strained. Not enough sleep, even before her life turned into a spectacle to rival Astley's Circus.

Portia ventured up behind her, her worry reflected in the glass. "What changed everything from triumph to tragedy?"

Portia's question made it impossible for Juliet to maintain even a shred of her famous control. This was why she'd wanted to be alone, so that when she crumbled, there wouldn't be any witnesses. She wouldn't have to explain or excuse.

Although what excuse could she make?

To Juliet's mortification, tears flooded her eyes. Blinking hard, she fumbled to open a drawer to locate a handkerchief.

Portia shoved one into her shaking hand. "Here."

Juliet held the practical cotton square to her face and gave in to a storm of tears.

"Jules. Sis. Don't take on so." Portia dropped to her knees beside Juliet and put her arms around her. "It can't be that bad."

To her eternal regret, Portia was wrong. It was that bad.

It was worse.

The situation was beyond salvage. Everywhere she turned, she only saw complete devastation.

"I've made such an awful mess of everything," she forced out, turning into her sister's embrace and burying her face in Portia's shoulder.

"I'm sure you haven't." Portia's arms tightened. "You always do the right thing."

"Not anymore." Juliet hiccupped. "Papa caught me kissing Evesham."

Papa. Granville. And every nasty gossip in London. She cringed at being the object of general ridicule. Nobody would say that she'd make a perfect duchess now.

"Evesham?" Portia pulled far enough away to see her face. "Aren't you engaged to Granville?"

Juliet gulped for air and wiped her eyes. Through her tears, she saw Portia's astonishment. "I told him this morning that I couldn't marry him," she said unevenly.

She waited for Portia to exult. Her sister had never liked Granville. But she'd underestimated her. Portia's concern was all for her distraught sister. "Oh, Jules, I'm so very sorry. That must have been difficult."

She hadn't wanted Portia to stay, but right now, she was grateful to realize that her younger sister was on her side, right or wrong. In this case, definitely wrong. "It was hideous. But nowhere near as hideous as that scene tonight."

Juliet watched Portia think through the implications of what she heard. "So are you going to marry Evesham instead?"

With a dismissive grunt, Juliet dropped the sodden handkerchief onto the dressing table. "Of course not."

The crippling shock of the world discovering that she was no better than she should be was wearing off. However the humiliation and anguish remained as blistering as ever. She still felt as if she'd swallowed a cauldron full of snakes.

"Why not? You liked him enough to kiss him, and honestly when I watched you two onstage, my heart skipped a beat."

"That doesn't mean anything." Her crying fit subsided, but tears clogged her voice.

Portia frowned. "Don't tell me he didn't propose? There's all that nasty gossip about him, but he's very likeable in person. He must have stepped up to save your reputation."

Juliet tried for her usual wry smile, but her lips crumpled at the last minute. "He did the right thing."

"I'm so relieved. I'd hate to take another duke in

dislike."

That did elicit a shaky smile. "We're rather overrun with dukes, aren't we?"

"We are. I trip over a duke at every turn. So why did you say no?"

Wasn't it obvious? It was to her. "He's a rogue and a rake."

"Not as much as we thought, if he asked you to marry him. Don't you like him?"

"Of course I like him." She would not cry again. She would not cry again. "I told you I kissed him. I'm not in the habit of kissing men I don't like."

"I didn't think you were in the habit of kissing anyone."

A shamed flush mottled her cheeks. "I seem to have got into the habit of kissing Evesham."

To her surprise, instead of reacting with appropriate horror, Portia laughed. "Well, three cheers for you. And three cheers for Evesham."

Puzzled, Juliet regarded her sister. "You should be appalled. I'm meant to set an example for you and Viola. Lately, I've been a complete failure."

A wave rejected that woebegone assessment. "If you encourage me to kiss a handsome rascal, I think that's an excellent example. Was it nice?"

Juliet's lips tightened in self-disgust. Something in her wanted her sister to scold and criticize, not treat her like a heroine. She deserved to be a pariah. Right from the start, she'd recognized Evesham as trouble, but that hadn't stopped her from running hotfoot to damnation. She was the architect of her own downfall.

"Portia, you're not seeing the full picture. I'm the second Frain sister to spark a scandal in the space of a month. Half the ton was hiding in the bushes when Papa was ranting about my misbehavior. How on earth will you make a good marriage with such ramshackle connections?"

Her sister shrugged. "I told you I don't care about making a good marriage. I'm a little too eccentric – and I like having the freedom to do what I wish. I can't imagine any husband would want to take on me and my menagerie. Nor do I want to marry a man who objects to my love of animals."

As if it had happened a hundred years ago, Juliet remembered back to her conversation with her sister, the night Evesham arrived. On that occasion, she hadn't taken Portia's lack of interest in marriage seriously. Maybe she should have. "I always assumed you wanted what I wanted."

Portia shook her head. "No. You were born to be a duchess. I wasn't."

"I wish people would stop saying that."

Portia rolled her eyes. "But it's clearly true. Three dukes have proposed to you."

Juliet didn't want to talk about that. The memory of Evesham's devastated reaction to her refusal haunted her. Although common sense told her that she'd only injured his pride, not any deeper feelings. "You enjoyed your season. At least until Viola brought it to an abrupt end."

"Society lining up to treat me like a goddess? Of course I enjoyed it. But it's nothing to do with my real life. My real life is looking out for creatures who need my help."

Right now, Juliet had a sick feeling that those creatures included Portia's older sister. "What about a family?"

It seemed an odd moment to have a heart-to-heart conversation about her sister's future. But it saved her from having to confess the true extent of her transgressions over the last days. She didn't even want to think about those.

"I've got a family. I've got you and Viola and Papa,

for what he's worth. I'll be the dotty aunt with a house full of dogs and cats, the lady the nieces and nephews love to visit. Grandmamma left all three of us provided for, even if Papa cuts up rough about our future plans. I'll be more than all right."

"You will," Juliet said in dawning realization. "Perhaps she left us her fortune to give us a choice. I gather that she wanted to marry the village vicar instead of Lord Plunkett. But the bishop got involved, and the vicar was sent to Africa."

"I never knew that."

"Years ago, I overheard Mamma talking to Papa about Grandmamma's girlish infatuation with an impoverished suitor."

"You never told me." When Portia took Juliet's hand, Juliet's fingers closed hard over her sister's.

Juliet had never sought Portia's support before, even after Bolton's death. She'd always been the strong one, the one in charge. That was her role in this family.

Until now. Tonight, she wasn't strong at all.

"I never thought to." She'd always underestimated Portia, she realized. Portia was twenty-four, and Juliet still treated her like a child. Only now did she see Portia as an adult equal to herself.

Equal? Portia was a million times her superior. Portia, for all her eccentricity, would never kick over the traces, the way her supposedly wiser older sister had this evening. Juliet swallowed and reminded herself that she wouldn't cry again.

Portia's gaze was steady, as she stared into Juliet's eyes. "Don't forget those choices, Juliet. I have a feeling they're going to bully you into accepting Evesham tomorrow."

"Or Granville."

Portia's pale brows contracted in puzzlement.

"Didn't you say you'd jilted him?"

"I did."

"He looked like murder when I found you all. He'd loathe that you kissed Evesham."

"I thought he'd despise me, but he proposed again to save my reputation."

Portia looked thunderstruck. "Good heavens, I thought he'd be too bloated with pride to offer you the time of day, given that the man you dallied with is his worst enemy."

Juliet released Portia's hand and turned back to her dressing table. Guilt and trepidation coagulated into a rancid lump in her stomach. What on earth was she going to do? Because Portia was right. Tomorrow, she'd face the full force of parental disapproval. A prelude to public disgrace.

If she didn't marry someone, she'd no longer be welcome in the beau monde. And that would bring all her plans for her future crashing down to the ground. Her whole life, she'd looked forward to becoming a person of influence in the wider world.

"You always misjudged Granville." The words emerged in an exhausted monotone. "He's a good man. A better man than I deserve."

"Perhaps." Portia didn't sound convinced. She stood and came up to stand behind Juliet. In a few seconds, she unfastened the necklace and deposited it on the dressing table. "You didn't tell me – was it nice kissing Evesham? I'll wager it was."

In the mirror, Juliet watched dejection flood back into her eyes. She might have cried enough, but she had a nasty feeling that she was going to cry again. And again. "Yes, it was nice."

It had been more than nice. It had been transcendent, glorious, stupendous. The clouds had parted to reveal golden arcs of light. The angels had sung hosannas. Heaven itself had seemed within reach.

"So why can't you marry him?"

Juliet's shoulders sagged. "I told you. Because he's a philanderer and a wastrel."

Portia cast her a sharp look. "You brought up two sisters when you weren't much more than a child yourself. You can handle one obstreperous duke and turn him into the husband you want."

Right now, Juliet wasn't sure that she could handle the next five minutes, but she appreciated her sister's vote of confidence. "I'm glad you think so."

"Evesham might be worth a shot. You'd still be a duchess if you accept him."

Her hand closed hard on the locket. "But how can I take the man who ruined Vanessa Gould and didn't lift a finger to save her? That's not a passing peccadillo. That's a sin of the deepest black. That was the act of a man who at his most essential level is irredeemable. If I entrust my future to Evesham knowing that, I'm inviting disaster. However beautifully he might kiss me."

Portia's brief cheerfulness faded. "I know you think you're being pragmatic rejecting Evesham, but I'm not sure that's true. Marrying him still seems the best solution."

Juliet stared unseeing at the heavy silver brush set on top of her dressing table. Bleakness invaded her like a cold frost. She didn't think that she'd ever be warm again.

The endless grimness of what awaited her, not just tomorrow but for years to come, weighted her reply. "It might solve my current problems. But marriage is a lifelong commitment, and I will not spend the rest of my days with a man I don't respect."

Juliet woke late. She'd stayed up most of the night, fretting and scrambling to devise a way to restore her reputation. A way that didn't involve marrying either of the gentlemen who had proposed over the last few days. It was dawn before sheer exhaustion sent her into a fitful doze.

So when at ten, her father sent a note requesting her presence in the library, she was heavy-eyed and wrung-out. Only after a quick wash and her maid helping her into a dark blue muslin gown of modest cut did she think of anything beyond her own troubles.

"Goodness, we've got a house full of guests. Who's been looking after our visitors?" Juliet's duties as hostess had completely fled her mind. The people lucky enough to be invited to stay at Afton were supposed to remain for a short house party after the gala.

Mary finished fastening her gown and started arranging Juliet's hair. "Everyone left after breakfast, my lady, apart from the Edgecombes, and they're away after lunch."

They'd probably stayed to see if they could ferret out more gossip, Juliet thought uncharitably. She winced when Mary began to work at a knot. Her troubled night meant that her hair was a complete bird's nest this morning.

Her life was a complete bird's nest, too.

"We have no more guests?"

"The two dukes have stayed on, my lady."

Of course they had. Her torments were far from over. "I suspect they'll be away today, too."

Mary began to arrange Juliet's hair in a soft chignon. For a moment, she almost told her maid to do something more severe. Then she stopped herself. She refused to go to this interview in sackcloth and ashes. That would give her father too much advantage.

"I don't think so, my lady. They'll both be here tonight at least. Not that the staff mind. They're considerate, easygoing gentlemen who do most of their own organizing. Unlike some who don't bear nearly such lofty titles. We've all been honored to serve the two His Graces. Nice, appreciative, polite guests."

That was unexpected enough to penetrate Juliet's gloom. She'd imagined that Evesham would be a nightmare of untidiness and disorganization and that Granville would be cold and distant and demanding.

Mary must know by now that Juliet had kissed Evesham, yet one would never guess it from her respectful manner. But then most of the staff here had known her all her life. They would be slower to judge her unfit for company than society would. As Afton Park was to be her lair for the foreseeable future, that mightn't be a bad thing.

Finally, both too late and too soon, she was ready. She checked her appearance in the mirror. She almost looked her capable, composed self, if one ignored the purple shadows under her eyes and the strained line of her lips.

"Would you like a morsel to eat before you go downstairs, madam?"

A breakfast tray had arrived as she'd left her bed. So far, it remained untouched. To prove that her calm was only on the surface, the thought of food made her gorge rise. "No, thank you. Although a cup of tea would be nice."

"It will be cold by now. Shall I order some more?"

Juliet could imagine her father, never the most

patient of men, fuming if she delayed any further. "I'll drink it cold."

After a mouthful of unpleasantly stewed tea, she stood and trudged toward the door. She almost didn't feel frightened, until she caught Mary's reflection in the mirror. Now that her maid didn't have to pretend to tactful ignorance, she looked sick with anxiety.

The tea threatened to come up again. Because last night, Juliet had broken too many rules to find quick redemption.

Most of all because she refused to contemplate an uncongenial marriage, which was the shortest road to restoring her good name.

CHAPTER SEVENTEEN

*E*vesham sat in Portdown's library, as an increasingly awkward silence built. His lordship did his best to pretend that the two dukes who shared this room with him didn't detest each other, but it was a losing battle.

Evesham also suspected that, right now, Portdown would dearly like to punch him in the nose for destroying his daughter's formerly untarnished reputation. But he couldn't risk sending any of Juliet's suitors away in a huff before a wedding could be arranged.

A punch in the nose would give him a bruise to match the mottled purple and green extravaganza on his jaw. He'd spent more time than usual dressing this morning, but his marked face rather counteracted the effect of combed hair, a snowy neckcloth, and a fashionable navy blue coat.

When he'd entered the library, Evesham had been surprised – and displeased – to see Granville present as well. He'd hoped that the sod would scuttle back to London with the other guests, who had taken off in a flying hurry to spread word of Lady Juliet Frain's fall.

It was apparent that Portdown hoped that if Juliet wouldn't take on his disreputable self, Granville could persuade her to accept him as an alternative.

Evesham remained astounded that Granville was willing to stand by Juliet. Even more astounded that she hadn't leaped at the offer.

They'd all sparked a gigantic scandal last night, but if Juliet became a duchess, she'd come out ahead. There might be a few whispers about her flirtation with Evesham. More than a few, given his tricky history with her new husband. But whatever her reputation, the Duchess of Granville would be accepted everywhere.

The unexpected generosity of Granville's response made Evesham question the low opinion that he'd always held of the fellow. Vanessa had hated the man, but she'd had her reasons. And if Evesham was honest, he'd accepted her assessment of her betrothed without too much analysis. Now, he wondered if perhaps His Grace mightn't be quite the sink of irredeemable dreariness that Evesham had always judged him to be.

Which didn't stop Granville despising him with every atom in his body. Last night, the man had wanted to commit murder. Evesham knew that hadn't changed. It said something for the swine's affection for Juliet that he could stomach Evesham's company this morning.

The door opened, and Juliet appeared on the threshold. As Evesham rose to bow, he studied her. Last night in the play, she'd been incandescent. Even more incandescent in his arms afterward.

The woman who stepped into the library now was elegant and self-possessed. Her dress was unadorned, and her curtain of golden hair was drawn back from a face that was grave and composed. She didn't look like she'd had much more sleep than Evesham had.

She returned to her role as the unruffled chatelaine of Afton Park. It was a pity that her severe demeanor summoned to mind a march to the guillotine. This was someone prepared to face her fate, but there was no joy in her.

How could there be? His dashed irresponsibility had inveigled her into a scandal. He'd wager that she'd spent the night cursing his name. He'd spent quite a bit of the night doing the same. And struggling to come to terms with how low he felt because she wouldn't marry him, even when a wedding was the only thing that would save her from disaster.

Without looking at either him or Granville, she curtsied. She was wan and determined. The line of her jaw told him that she meant to hold her own.

Bugger it. That meant that, this morning, his chances of changing her mind about marrying him were slim. He'd hoped against hope that a night of reflection would bring her around to accepting him, if only to restore her good name. What a moment to realize that claiming this exquisite woman would be his crowning achievement.

"Good morning, Juliet." Portdown's coldness surprised Evesham. He was usually the jolliest of fellows.

"Good morning, Papa," she said with a hint of wariness.

Evesham couldn't blame her. She must feel like she'd entered an ambush. An ambush where she was severely outnumbered.

As he greeted her, he fought the urge to stand up and tell her that he was going to whisk her away from all this misery. There had been quite enough histrionics last night. And anyway, she'd say no. The way that she always said no to him.

"Good morning, Lady Juliet," Granville said, rising and bowing.

"I've invited Granville and Evesham to join us, as they have a stake in this matter," Portdown said with a dignity that he'd lacked last night.

Juliet's lips firmed, but she didn't protest. "Good morning, Your Grace and Your Grace."

"Please sit down. Because of last night's events, we need to settle your future before the scandal engulfs all of us."

Looking more like a doomed French aristo than ever, Juliet took a chair opposite Portdown. At least her father had resisted the impulse to berate her from behind his desk, as if she was a naughty schoolgirl.

Evesham waited for her to speak up, but she remained silent. Her graceful hands twisted in her lap, the only sign that she was more nervous than she appeared.

Granville cast him a lethal glance and sat beside her. Evesham took the place on the other side of her. He only realized his mistake when she shot him a resentful glare. Sitting between her two suitors would make her feel like a besieged castle.

Something that had puzzled him last night niggled at his mind. He knew why his proposal was unwelcome, however physically attractive she found him.

But why in hell had she broken her engagement to Granville?

"I'm appalled at your behavior, Juliet," Portdown said. "Appalled and astounded. You've always been such a proper young lady. I'm ashamed of you."

Evesham watched Juliet closely enough to see her hide a wince. This dressing-down in front of outsiders would humiliate her, he knew.

His "Any blame in this matter is entirely mine" clashed with Granville's "My lord, chastising Lady Juliet serves no purpose."

Juliet sent Granville a grateful glance. "Thank you, Your Grace."

Evesham tried not to mind that she ignored him.

Portdown went on. "What's important is that we act to scotch any talk as soon as possible."

Juliet looked directly at her father. "Papa, I can't tell you how sorry I am that I spoiled your Shakespeare gala."

Her father scowled at her. "That's not the worst of it. It was bad enough when Viola decided to kick over the traces. I never imagined that I needed to worry about you. You've never set a foot wrong. Damn it, Juliet, what on earth got into you?"

Faint color marked her cheekbones, and the hands in her lap clasped each other so tightly, her knuckles gleamed white. "Midsummer madness. I can only apologize again."

Her father's scowl intensified. "You can do more than that."

He meant a wedding. Evesham spoke up. "Lady Juliet, please say you'll be my wife. I swear I'll do my best to be worthy of you."

Blistering looks from Juliet and Granville told him that they found his statement unpersuasive.

"I'm also willing to overlook last night's misconduct, my lady," Granville said. "I'd count it a privilege if you'd change your mind about becoming my bride."

Get away from her, you encroaching bastard. She's mine.

A hunted expression crossed Juliet's face. "I thank both of you for asking, but it won't do."

"Juliet, don't be a fool," Portdown snarled. With each minute, his paterfamilias act descended further into uncomprehending anger. "You have to marry one of them."

Her lush lips flattened. "I'm willing to pay the price of my misdeeds and retire from society. I'll live quietly here at Afton Park. After all, it's what I've done since the Duke of Bolton's unfortunate accident."

"But you were born to rule society, my lady," Granville protested. "If you forsake the world, the world will be the poorer."

Another grateful smile to Granville, blast his eyes. If she liked the blackguard so much, why didn't she jolly well marry him?

"Thank you, Your Grace. But after last night, whispers will always follow me."

"The Duchess of Granville is above the ton's petty spite."

"Perhaps. But if I accept your proposal, it won't be a match of equals. My gratitude for your extraordinary condescension would poison our marriage."

"I will never say a word of reproach, my lady. You have my word on it."

Her smile this time was regretful. Not that any of them were real smiles. Right now, she looked like she'd never smile properly again. Which made Evesham sick with guilt.

"You're a good man, Your Grace. Far too good for me. Thank you for asking me to marry you, but I must decline."

Her refusal left Granville looking shocked. "I hate to think of you throwing yourself away on this wastrel. I'd still like to shoot him."

Juliet looked weary. "That won't improve matters."

"It would make me feel better."

Evesham's eyes narrowed on his rival. "I don't

know why you're so convinced that if it comes to a duel, I'll miss, old man."

"You fired into the air last time. Honor requires you to do the same this time."

"Your Grace, there will not be a this time," Juliet said sharply. "When I released you from our engagement, you lost any right to interfere in my life."

A muscle flickered in the duke's cheek. "If I shoot the villain, it's purely for my own pleasure."

"Stop it," Juliet said. "Nobody is getting shot. My...mistakes aren't worth the loss of life."

Granville rose and gave her a bow that expressed chilly politeness. Much as Evesham wanted to despise the jackanapes, he understood the man's umbrage. Granville had rushed onto the scene ready to play Sir Galahad and rescue the fair damsel, only to find that the fair damsel preferred to stay with the dragon.

Or at least, given Evesham played the dragon in this particular fairy tale, he hoped that was the case.

"In that case, my lady, I believe I should leave Afton Park." Granville's voice was crisp and unemotional, but something told Evesham that he wasn't as unaffected as he wished to appear. "I wish you well."

"Thank you." Juliet's gaze was sad, as it dwelled on her former betrothed. "You leave here with my deepest admiration and gratitude."

Evesham wanted to smash something. Perhaps the pair of blue Sèvres vases on the mantel with their smug cupids who seemed to sit in judgment on him. And found him inadequate, just like Juliet did. Juliet, who was so confoundedly grateful to Granville, but wouldn't give Evesham the time of day.

Portdown leaped to his feet and caught

Granville's arm. "Your Grace, don't be too hasty. She may change her mind. She's just being a willful, reckless fool. She'll think better of her refusal, if I have anything to say about it."

Granville shook Portdown off with an elegantly spare movement. "I'm not sure I want a willful, reckless bride, my lord."

Portdown's face fell, as he realized that he was taking the wrong tack. "She's a good girl. It's just that right now—"

"Papa, let him go. I won't marry him. He can ask me until doomsday."

"I won't ask again," Granville said with a hint of a snap. "I've suffered enough humiliation at this family's hands."

Juliet flinched. "I can only beg your forgiveness."

"One day, I might even bestow it." He was back to sounding like his usual high-and-mighty self.

Granville had lost a hell of a woman in Juliet, and Evesham suspected that the clod knew it.

Did the man love her? He couldn't tell. Once he'd have said that his fellow duke was incapable of the emotion, but recent events had made him realize that he'd misjudged his enemy. Granville turned out to be a lot more human than he'd ever given him credit for.

With insulting brevity, Granville bowed to Portdown. "Your servant, my lord."

Once he was gone, the straight line of Juliet's shoulders drooped. She'd looked tired when she came in. Now she looked beyond exhausted.

Portdown turned on Juliet with bewildered fury. "What in Hades did you do that for? Heaven knows why, but he was ready to take you. Even after what you've done. The man's a saint. Why in God's name won't you marry him? You liked the fellow well enough to accept him two days ago."

Juliet's shoulders braced again. "He is a saint to offer for me. He deserves better than a woman of besmirched reputation."

"So you'll take Evesham?"

"No." Implacable as ever. "I told you I don't wish to marry."

"That's too bad, given you've been such a hussy."

"Stop it," Evesham said in his ducal voice. "A few kisses in the moonlight don't turn your daughter into Lady Macbeth."

"We know that's all it was," she said in a voice weighted with desolation. "But the tattle they're spreading in London will tell a different story."

"The talk will say it was more than kisses," Portdown said in a grim tone.

"Bugger the talk. Stop haranguing the girl. If you're going to harangue someone, harangue me. Everything is my fault."

"That's not true," Juliet said in a stony voice. "You just behaved as you always do. I'm the one in the wrong. I knew I should stay away from you, yet I couldn't."

Evesham kneeled beside her chair and took her hand. "My dear, I'd love to marry you. Say you'll make me the happiest man in the world."

Blue eyes full of turmoil met his. For a moment, her fingers closed around his hand, as if he offered her a lifeline when she was drowning. "You sound like you mean that."

"On my life, I do."

For a tremulous instant, he wondered if he might have succeeded. Instead of uttering the instant denial that she'd given him before, she studied his face. It was as if she probed his soul. Hope surged with a strength that shook him to the foundations.

Then Portdown ruined it all. "There, you'll marry Evesham. We'll have the banns called on Sunday and the wedding in three weeks. A special license will only fan the rumors. A long wedding trip abroad, a baby in nine months, then by the time you come back, all this nonsense will be forgotten."

Evesham cursed silently, as horror wiped the softness from her expression. She wrenched her hand from his and lurched to her feet. "I've given His Grace my answer and that's an end to it."

Evesham rose more slowly. "I hate to think of you hiding down here like a dirty secret."

"Don't worry. I'll let it be known that you did the right thing. *This time.*"

Her tone held a hint of a jeer. He ground his teeth in frustration. She referred to Vanessa, damn it. And on that subject, he couldn't speak in his own defense.

Portdown settled behind his desk and glared at her. "Juliet, if you refuse to take Evesham, you will no longer be my daughter."

She went as white as paper, and her balance wavered. Evesham caught her arm to keep her upright, although he doubted that she even knew he was there. "Papa, you don't mean that."

"I do." Lord Portdown's face set in lines that indicated Juliet wasn't the only stubborn Frain. "It was bad enough when Viola brought the family name into disrepute. At least she had the sense to marry the reprobate. I will not countenance a second daughter ignoring common morality, and moreover refusing to do what she can to fix the problem. You have my word on it."

Evesham was already angry with Portdown. Now he wanted to kill the blockhead. Every word that the callous ass said landed on Juliet like a bullet. How dare he treat his daughter like this after all she'd done for the family?

The man went on. "Unless you rethink this disastrous conduct, I have no choice. I have one unsullied daughter left, and I will not allow you to destroy her prospects. If you won't marry Evesham, you're dead to me."

"But you love Juliet," Evesham protested. "Think again, man. She might have a chance of coming through this, if you offer her your support."

"Yes, I love her." Evesham had never thought the ebullient Portdown could sound so bleak. "Which is why I must make this difficult decision."

"Don't make me call your bluff, Papa," Juliet said in a voice like iron.

"It's no bluff."

A militant light entered her eyes as she straightened. "In that case, I'll arrange my departure. I'll let you know my address, once I've set up a household."

Portdown bore no resemblance to last night's exuberant impresario. "Don't bother. If you won't marry Evesham, you're nothing to me."

She angled her chin up, and her expression set. "Very well. I bid you good day, sir."

Juliet strutted out of the room with a superior air that under other circumstances would make Evesham want to applaud. This wasn't Juliet Capulet. This was Cleopatra.

"Juliet..." Portdown began as she went through the door, but she didn't turn back.

Evesham shot Portdown a contemptuous look. "You're an infernal fool, my lord."

Portdown didn't answer, merely stared after his daughter with a distraught expression.

Evesham swore under his breath and dashed out after Juliet. "He doesn't mean it."

"Yes, he does," she said in a choked voice.

She stood on the bottom step, clinging to the pineapple carved into the newel post, as if that alone kept her upright. She didn't look up, and he realized that she struggled against bursting into tears.

The show of proud defiance had been exactly that. A show. Thanks to her involvement with Evesham, Juliet had lost her home and her family, as well as a respected place in society. Her life was in ruins.

Self-hatred soured his gut, as he admitted that she'd been right to want to send him away when he arrived. A mere week in his company had turned her life into a barren waste.

"But what will you do?"

Juliet sucked in a shuddering breath and faced him. She'd gathered her control around her with staggering swiftness. Now she looked as pale and perfect as if she was carved from ice. "Don't worry. I won't go on the streets."

He didn't laugh, if indeed it was intended as a grim joke. "Of course you won't. You have family and friends."

Her mouth twisted with a bitterness that made him flinch. "I do. Or at least I did, until I lost my reputation. I doubt that I'm quite as in demand on the social scene as I was before last night."

"I won't let you go without."

More bitterness. "So I'll become *your* kept woman?"

"I won't ask anything in return. This debacle is my doing."

She squared her shoulders. He'd thought that she looked lonely before, but now she looked like the loneliest girl in England. "That's kind of you."

His hand cut through the air. "I'm not bloody kind. I refuse to see you destitute."

"I won't be destitute. My grandmother left me a substantial fortune that became mine to use as I wish, once I turned twenty-five. I'll be more than all right. If Papa imagines he's going to starve me into submission, he'll soon realize how wrong he is."

One part of Evesham was grateful that Juliet had resources. Another much more unworthy part was sorry that she wouldn't need to turn to him for help. This Sir Galahad stuff was deuced addictive. He felt a pang of unexpected sympathy for Granville.

But of course, Juliet was no helpless waif. Even now, with her world a wreck, she remained self-reliant and strong. So strong, he feared yet again that she might crack under the unrelenting pressure.

"He's drunk with pride and pique and vinegar. He'll get over it."

Juliet directed a hard look at him. "Papa might, but I'm not sure I will. If his daughters run amok, perhaps he should consider his role in their upbringing. After Mamma's death, he left Viola and Portia to me. I wasn't much past fifteen. He consigned the management of the house and estate to me, too, while he chased dreams of theatrical acclaim. Once I leave, he'll face a rude awakening."

Perhaps Lord Portdown would see the error of his ways and take Juliet back. But Evesham still couldn't help thinking that it would be easier on everyone for her to marry him.

He drew himself up to his full height and told himself that he couldn't take her into his arms. Nor would he propose again. Or at least not until Juliet realized the full price she'd pay for defying the world's mores. Even for someone so brash, he'd endured enough rebuffs to be going on with.

Last night had been vile for her. Humiliating. Confronting. But he had a feeling that when she experienced the weight of society's opprobrium, last night would seem like a summer holiday.

Even if she didn't need his money, he could still do something for her. "Allow me to escort you to where you want to go and help you find suitable lodgings, while you decide what you're going to do next."

He prepared for another refusal, but after a tense second, she nodded. "Thank you. I'd appreciate your help."

CHAPTER EIGHTEEN

*E*vesham waited in front of the manor in his luxurious traveling coach. Yesterday's fine weather had deteriorated to wind and rain. He couldn't help seeing that as symbolic of the way his whole life was headed.

He was glad that he'd chosen to travel from London in the larger vehicle. He'd originally intended to drive his new curricle to Wiltshire. But the curricle wasn't built for large amounts of baggage or the presence of a maid. And the coach would provide Juliet with privacy on the road. Not to mention more comfort on a cold, stormy day.

Inevitably, his present circumstances reminded him of running off with Vanessa, although his emotions in that case had been very different. But there was the same havey-cavey element. The same odd, portentous feeling that he'd burned bridges, and that the path ahead took an unknown direction.

When a maid came around the side of the house, he got out and looked toward the imposing front doors above the sweep of stone staircase. They remained shut.

No Juliet.

Disappointment cramped his heart. She must have changed her mind about leaving with him. He hadn't realized how much he'd been looking forward to traveling with her.

He was piercingly aware that once they reached Town, he no longer had any reason to be in her company. What a comedown for that infamous debauchee, the Duke of Evesham, to be sick with yearning for a woman's presence. And a woman who would never share his bed, at that.

He was well aware that he'd caused Juliet an ocean of trouble. Did she have the tiniest inkling of the trouble that she'd caused him?

"Your Grace." The girl curtsied and held out a folded paper. "Her ladyship asked me to give you this."

"Thank you," he said, taking the note.

After the maid left, he broke the seal and read the few words written there. He only just contained a shout of triumph, his pulses started to race, and he called to his coachman to go as he leaped back into the vehicle.

Juliet emerged onto the drive from the trees near the summerhouse. The place was several bends of the road away from the main house and out of view if anyone was watching.

She wore a dark gray traveling ensemble, and she carried a valise in her hand. As the coach stopped, Evesham opened the door.

"Is that all you're bringing?" His experiences with numerous mistresses had led him to expect piles of luggage.

"Yes." She looked serious, but not overcome with wretchedness. Which didn't mean that she was reconciled with her father's decision. Evesham knew her well enough now to understand that she always did her best to hide her strongest emotions. "Portia will send on my clothes, once I settle somewhere. Well, most of them. I doubt I'll have much call for ball gowns over the next little while."

He made himself smile, although he hated to think of her being an outcast. She'd adorned society, and society would be all the poorer for her lack. Granville was right about that.

Juliet accepted his hand and stepped into the coach. They were both wearing gloves. The contact shouldn't have had the power to steal his breath, but it did.

She settled on the seat facing forward, while he took his place opposite. He'd rather sit beside her, but he wanted her to know that he meant to make no demands. He offered her assistance to help her settle in to her new life. Anything else was up to her.

"There's room for your maid inside," he said, wondering where the girl was.

Juliet's stare was unreadable. "She's not coming."

Evesham paused in leaning across to close the door and regarded her in surprise. A lady never went anywhere without an escort. And Juliet would need a maid wherever she decided to set up home. He shut the door with a click, as his brain winnowed the implications of her announcement.

"Did your father forbid her to go with you?" That seemed unnecessarily spiteful.

"No. It's not the sort of thing he'd think about. I decided to leave alone."

Puzzled, Evesham studied her through the gloom, while light rain pattered on the roof. "I'm not complaining. Conversation is easier if we're on our own."

Conversation and other things. But Juliet had rejected him over and over. He couldn't imagine that she joined him with a view to consummating their chaotic relationship.

To his great regret.

You're here to give her your support and aid, man. Nothing else. Don't start building castles in the air. Or bedrooms at the next inn. Helpful, gallant, and respectful. Those are your watchwords for today.

As she untied her gray bonnet, she sent him another assessing look that he couldn't interpret. She brushed the raindrops off the high crown and set it on the seat beside her. "Thank you for picking me up on the drive. That obnoxious Celia Edgecombe is still hanging around like a bad smell. I didn't want her to see me go off with you. She's got the nastiest tongue in Mayfair."

After Evesham's knock on the roof, the carriage rolled forward. "What did Portia say about your father throwing you out?"

He supposed that this was none of his business. He and Juliet weren't friends. To be honest, he wasn't sure what they were. Not lovers, to his sorrow. In his opinion, they suffered the unpleasant aftermath of sin without any of the preceding delights. The best description that he could muster for his relationship with Juliet Frain was companions in adversity.

Evesham waited for Juliet to put him in his place, but she sighed and answered readily enough. "I didn't see Portia. Papa has forbidden her any contact with me. He ordered her to her room and placed a footman at the door to keep her there."

"That's rotten," he bit out.

He still had difficulty equating the tyrannical father with the exuberant fellow he'd come to know during rehearsals. Although he supposed the man had always had a taste for histrionics.

He'd come to like Lord Portdown – until the man turned on his eldest daughter. Evesham was no expert on love, but he had an inkling that unless it was unconditional, it wasn't worth a farthing.

"He's making a point."

"Portia won't stand for that." Over the last week, Evesham had developed a great respect for Lady Portia's determination to be her own woman.

"She won't, but just now, discretion is the better part of valor. I've left a letter for her, telling her that I'm traveling with you. Once I've found lodgings, I'll set up some way for us to communicate."

Despite his stern lecture to himself, he couldn't help being far too aware that he merely needed to lean across the well between the seats to touch Juliet. By Jericho, if he sat beside her, it would be a snip to take her into his arms.

He forced himself to concentrate on practicalities as a distraction from what he really wanted to do. "I've asked Mulray to make for London, but we can go somewhere else if you'd rather."

"London might be best. I can get lost in the crowd there, and it will be easier to sort out the details of how I mean to go on."

"I've been thinking about where I can take you. If I put you up at Hebden House, we'll just stir up more talk. Although you'd be safe and comfortable there, and I'd enjoy your company."

Another of those bleak smiles lengthened her lips. He'd always admired her spirit, but never as much as now, when her life lay in utter ruin. She had such courage. Most women would bewail their fate, but Juliet faced adversity with her head up. "You speak as if I have a chance of coming back from this."

"One lives in hope. You obviously have hopes, too, or you wouldn't give a rat's arse about Celia Edgecombe."

"I'm also thinking about Portia. Papa was right about one thing – two scandalous sisters have spoiled her prospects."

"Two scandalous sisters, and a menagerie of animals."

It wasn't the greatest joke in the world, but he felt like a king when she responded with a brief laugh. "The irony is that I always thought Porsh was the sister most likely to get into trouble. Now she's the only daughter Papa's in charity with."

Evesham rolled his eyes with theatrical exaggeration. "Give her time."

Another huff of amusement. "You're trying to make me feel better."

"Is it so obvious?"

"Yes. And appreciated."

He leaned back against the leather upholstery and stretched his long legs out between the benches. Did he say that he felt like a king? No, by gum, he felt like an emperor.

The carriage turned out of the gates. He doubted that he'd be back, despite these few days at Afton Park changing his life. To think, his fate had hinged on losing a hand of piquet.

"I thought you'd hate my guts," Evesham said, as the carriage gathered speed on the road north.

Juliet had been staring out the window with a pensive expression. She must wonder if she'd ever travel these familiar roads again. Now she turned to him with her characteristic solemnity. "I went along with everything you did."

That prodded his rusty conscience. She wasn't the guilty one. He was. But as usual, the woman bore the brunt of the punishment. His hands closed into fists on his lap, as he yet again wished that he'd given her father a good shake.

"Yes, but everything I did drew you further along the path to destruction."

"You didn't tie me up and force me." She bit her

lip and avoided his gaze for the first time since they'd set out. "In fact, you could have taken me when you came to my bedroom. It didn't even occur to me to stop you. At least one of us kept a grip on reality. And that wasn't the proper lady, but the unrepentant rake."

"You'd never forgive me if I'd gone ahead."

She was back to looking like a sphinx. A tired and rather downhearted sphinx, but nevertheless beautiful. A beautiful enigma. "Perhaps."

Not perhaps. Certainly. "I don't want you to despise me."

"I don't. I never have, although I tried."

Evesham didn't deserve to bask in her answer. But he did. "I know you tried. Every night at dinner, I checked my soup."

As he'd hoped, that produced another glimmer of a smile. Since they'd left Afton, she'd lapsed back into looking doomed. Now she appeared a little more lively. "I'm glad I didn't poison you. This journey would be much lonelier without you."

"I live to serve you." That was no lie, although he spoke as if he was in jest. She wouldn't believe him, however he said it.

"It's thanks to you that I'm still a virgin."

He closed his eyes and stifled a groan. "Please don't say that."

"Thank you?"

"No, the other bit." He shifted on the seat to ease his discomfort. If he had to listen to her wittering on about her untouched state all the way to Town, he wouldn't survive the trip.

"The bit about being a virgin?"

"Yes." He opened his eyes, expecting her to look offended. Instead, he could see that she was curious. "It reminds me how much I want you, and how I have no right to have you, and how when I had my chance, I damn well let my scruples prevail."

Juliet's glance was warmer than usual. And she'd paid him a compliment or two without choking on the words. He had no idea why. After all, because of him, she'd been banished from her home and family. "Those scruples become you."

Another compliment? What on earth was going on? "They're an infernal nuisance. I swear today all I intend to do is to get you safely to London, and you keep talking about beds and kisses and being a deuced virgin. You make it tough on a fellow who hasn't had a lot of practice in doing the right thing."

"I think you're a better man than you want to be. At least sometimes," she said thoughtfully. "You're not who I thought you were when we met. I expected a leering Lothario, but you're more complicated than that."

Was complicated a compliment? To his shame, he wasn't brave enough to find out.

He made himself smile, although right now he felt like there wasn't enough air in the carriage. "And I expected to meet a woman as cozy as an ice cave."

Another exhalation that might have been a laugh. "All disapproval and moral messages, and no sense of humor at all?"

"Exactly. A walking biblical sampler, scolding me about the dangers of following the primrose path."

"Instead, you've shown her the primrose path, and she's realized how much she's missed out on."

Not what he needed to hear. He struggled to keep things light. "You can thank me later," he said with an airy wave worthy of her father.

"I loved kissing you." Sincerity deepened her voice.

Heaven help him. It seemed his trials weren't over. What in blazes was he meant to say to that?

This time his groan was audible. "Juliet, you

might feel like I'm your new best friend, but for the love of God, can we talk about something else? I'm not made of steel."

Despite part of him being hard enough to fit that description.

When he'd offered her transport to London, his intentions had been pure. But he hadn't counted on how he'd feel, trapped in this confined space with her. How her alluring scent would perfume the air. How he'd react to having her unchaperoned and close enough to touch. How the twilight intimacy of the carriage would inspire him to picture other, forbidden intimacies.

He wished that she'd stop staring at him. "But this is what I'm thinking about."

It was what he was thinking about, too. Not to mention, remembering how he'd squeezed her breasts and stimulated her to a climax. And how she'd stepped into his arms last night, before everything went to hell.

Evesham gritted his teeth until his jaw ached. He went on, determined to prove that she hadn't made a mistake of epic proportions when she joined him in this carriage. Practical arrangements. Practical arrangements. That's what he needed to concentrate on. Not how pretty she was, and how her skin felt like silk under his hand.

"If you agree, I thought I might take you to my old tutor and his wife." His voice scraped out over his tight throat. "They live in Bloomsbury, so you're unlikely to meet anyone from the beau monde. It's not an opulent house, but it's comfortable, and you'll like Mr. Trinder and his family."

She frowned. "But what will they think when you turn up with an unaccompanied woman? Won't they fear that you're parking an inconvenient mistress with them?"

At least she'd stopped talking about kisses. Thank the Lord. "They're broad-minded people. And frankly, Juliet, you're the most unlikely trollop in the history of the world. One glimpse of you in that dashed nun's rig, and they'll know that you're a lady of the most virtuous type."

She glanced down at the ensemble covering her from chin to booted feet. "It's the height of fashion."

"It's gray and it's frumpy, and my grandmother could have worn it." If only the dreary rag quelled his interest in what lay beneath it.

"I wanted something warm and hard-wearing. I'm sorry it doesn't fit your tastes in traveling companions."

She sounded miffed. Excellent. If she was annoyed with him, it would distract her from reminiscing about what they'd done in her bedroom.

"I'm just saying that you don't look like a scarlet woman. The Trinders are sensible folk. They'll understand you're not a doxy, the minute they set eyes on you. Anyway, they know that I'd never do that to them. If I ask for their help, they'll give it. No questions asked."

She continued to observe him with a steady gaze that he really shouldn't find arousing. "You're fond of them."

"I am."

"Then thank you, that sounds like a solution. I didn't want to have to find a room in a hotel. It seems ridiculous that at twenty-six and financially solvent, I can't just march up to London and arrange a roof over my head. But that's the contradictory world we live in."

He managed a smile, although he understood her frustration. Juliet was a million times more capable and responsible than he was. Yet as a man, he enjoyed a freedom of movement denied to the female half of the population. "If you'll permit me, I'll get my man of business to look into finding you a more permanent home. Unless you have someone who takes care of your business affairs already?"

"Papa's solicitor has always been in charge of my inheritance."

"We need to separate you from him as soon as possible, then. There's a conflict of interest. I'll introduce you to my chap, and he'll handle everything. If there's any problem laying your hands on your funds, I'll cover your expenses in the meantime."

When she talked about kisses, she'd turned soft and melting. Now the onslaught of pragmatic information left her looking bewildered. "You're...you're very thorough. Thank you."

Evesham tilted an eyebrow in her direction. "You aren't going to kick up a fuss about accepting my help?"

This time, she offered him a real smile, if a little ragged around the edges. Given the way her life as she knew it had disintegrated within the last twenty-four hours, that was understandable. He was pleased to see her looking less desolate with every second.

"I'm truly grateful. As long as you allow me to pay you back every penny, once I gain access to my inheritance."

Repayment was an argument for another day. As far as he was concerned, she was welcome to everything he had. And not just because he was to blame for her current predicament.

Him, and a certain William Shakespeare. How could he – anyone – resist taking her into his arms after that balcony scene? Every word that they'd spoken had been incitement to a kiss.

"I'll see my solicitor keeps records."

She accepted that at face value, thank heaven. He

didn't want to fight about money. He didn't want to fight at all.

"Thank you."

By now, rain pounded on the roof. Mulray, his coachman, would be cursing him. To keep the conversation away from dangerous areas, Evesham reverted to a good old British staple. The weather. "We'll be very late into London with this downpour."

"Perhaps we should stop at an inn on the way and wait for it to clear."

Although he was sure that the remark held no salacious intent, his asinine heart started leaping about like an overexcited hare. He said a silent prayer for restraint. "I don't think that's a good idea."

"Your driver will be soaked."

Better Mulray copped a drenching than a delay exposed Evesham to impossible temptation. It was difficult enough keeping his paws off Juliet as it was. "He's a hardy soul."

"Nobody is expecting me. There's no special urgency for me to arrive."

There was, if she wanted to stay chaste. His hands gripped the edge of the leather seat. "Juliet, for pity's sake..."

She lowered her eyelashes and started to pleat the wool of her pelisse. It was the first sign of nerves that she'd shown. Perhaps she was worried that he might overstep the boundaries. She wasn't the only one. "I'm not expressing myself very well," she mumbled.

He sucked in a shuddering sigh. This was torture. "We can't stop on the way," he said in a strangled voice.

She glanced up with a meaningful look. But for the life of him, he couldn't work out that meaning. "Because somebody we know might see us?"

He couldn't help sounding grumpy. "No. Because

I want you, and a nice cozy inn with nice cozy bedrooms gives me too much opportunity to do something about that."

Evesham waited for Juliet to tell him to go to Hades, but to his utter astonishment, she lifted her chin and spoke in a steady voice. "In that case, let's find that inn."

CHAPTER NINETEEN

*I*f Juliet hadn't been quite so on edge, she'd have burst out laughing at the complete astonishment on Evesham's face. For once, she had the advantage over the worldly duke.

Oh, she was wicked to enjoy this so much. Although not as wicked as she intended to be.

The man who sat across from her had dressed with more care than usual for his meeting in her father's library. Not to mention, a deep purple bruise marred his sculpted chin where Granville had hit him last night. But he was still the man she wanted above all others, even if she was damned for it.

She linked her hands in her lap and spoke calmly, as if she wasn't breaking every rule that she'd lived by for twenty-six years. "I seem to have taken you by surprise, Your Grace."

"You... We... I..."

At his continued speechlessness, she did laugh. Amusement helped to counter the nerves that fluttered like sparrows trapped inside her.

He sucked in an audible breath and managed to get a sentence out, even if in a raspy croak. "By Jove, Juliet, do you know what you're saying?"

"I believe I'm in full possession of my wits, sir."

He raked a trembling hand through his hair and stared at her as if she was likely to disappear in a puff of smoke. "I'm not sure you are."

A cowardly part of her had hoped that he wouldn't ask for explanations. The man she'd once judged him to be would just jump on her and have his way. She probably wouldn't even need to wait for a convenient inn.

But he'd never been that man. If she was honest with herself, she wouldn't be having this conversation with that ruthless seducer.

He stripped off his gloves and leaned forward. When he took her hand, her heart gave a great thump that made it difficult to speak.

"Last night, I spent a lot of time thinking about my life," she said in a low voice. "I was still thinking, while I packed to leave my home after Papa threw me out."

One of those wry smiles that she loved. "I'm sure."

"I thought about always being a model of propriety."

"Until you met me."

"Until I discovered what temptation was."

The smile turned tender. "Thank you for that."

"For what?"

"For admitting that I don't yearn alone."

"Of course you don't. That can't be a secret to you."

"It's still nice to hear you say it." He drew off her gray leather glove and brought her hand to his lips. "It's nice that you aren't fighting the attraction anymore."

A grunt of bleak amusement escaped, as her fingers tangled around his. The brush of his lips made her shiver with anticipation. "I wasn't very successful."

"What conclusions did you reach during all this soul-searching?"

He lowered her hand, but kept hold of it. That warm, steady clasp gave her the courage to continue. "After twenty-six years of exemplary behavior, I was cast out just as finally as I'd have been cast out if I'd run off with the gardener's boy at sixteen. In the end, a lifetime of prudence did me no good. If I have to pay the price anyway, I may as well enjoy the crime."

"Are you offering to become my mistress, Juliet?"

"No." Heat crept into her cheeks. "It may be unlikely, but one day, I hope to restore my reputation, at least to a point where I can do charitable work and see my sisters and lead a useful life. If I enter a liaison with you, all of that will be denied to me."

He looked disappointed, but didn't argue with her conclusions. "Then what are you offering?"

"One night where we meet as equals, and you show me everything I've been missing."

Faint mockery arched his eyebrows. "That might require more than one night."

She swallowed to moisten a scratchy throat. "One night is all I can give you. Will you accept the bargain? I...I hunger for you, and this is my only chance." She swallowed again. "I'm not made for intrigue. The events of the last few days only prove how useless I am at subterfuge."

"I may disappoint you." Still holding her hand, he crossed to sit beside her. "A virgin's first time isn't always pleasant."

Embarrassment made her mutter, "When you...when you came to my room, you did something to me that..."

She wasn't used to talking about such intimate things. Good heavens, soon she wouldn't just be talking about them. If Evesham accepted her terms, he'd become her lover. The thought flooded her with a churning mixture of excitement and apprehension.

A smile eased the stern line of his lips. "I gave you a climax."

"You can do that again. If it hurts afterward, I won't mind."

His brows drew together. "Juliet, darling. I'm not worthy of you."

Mortified, she stared at him. "Are you saying no?"

He released a huff of sardonic laughter. "If I were a gallant knight like that idiot Granville, I'd refuse. You deserve better than a quick swive in an obscure inn."

"I don't want Granville. I want you." She pulled her hand free. "Please don't say I've made even more of a fool of myself."

"I've wanted you from the first. I never thought you'd consent to be mine. As if I'd say no."

A great sigh of relief expelled all the air from her lungs. It had taken every scrap of her bravery to reach this point. If it had turned out that Evesham was no longer interested, it would hurt even more than hearing her father pronounce her dead to him.

"Then..." she started in a shaky voice as she removed her other glove. "Then do you think perhaps you might kiss me? I'm never afraid when you kiss me."

Emotion filled his eyes. Desire, as always. And something else that made her nitwit heart ache with poignant longing. Something that looked like affection and care and need. "My dearest girl..."

He pulled down the blinds, deepening the darkness. Then he slid closer along the bench and looped his arms around her, as if she was made of the most delicate glass. When his lips touched hers, the moment held all the tremulous enchantment of their first kiss, except that, this time, she knew what was to come.

As he continued to toy with her, she made a complaint against his mouth and scraped her teeth across his lower lip. He deepened the pressure, sweeping his tongue over her lips before venturing inside. With a growl of satisfaction, she tangled her hands in his hair to bring him nearer.

His gentleness threatened to break her heart, and today had already held too much heartbreak. Now she wanted heat and excitement. Wild and demanding passion to incinerate the last of her qualms. Vigorous masculine energy to extinguish the memory of her humiliation and banishment.

Panting, he raised his head and stared down at her, eyes glittering in the shadows.

Juliet stroked his face with a boldness that she'd never shown before. Beneath her palm, his cheek was warm and she felt the slight roughness of his whiskers. She was careful not to press on his bruise.

It felt good not to guard every action. Losing her reputation delivered a freedom that she'd never experienced. Perhaps this new life wasn't going to be all bad, after all.

"I'll tell Mulray to find us an inn." Raw need grated in his voice.

"Off the main route. Anyone on the highway to London knows me." It was an effort to think of practicalities, when she ached for more kisses, for Evesham's hands on her. "I've brought a veil, but it would be better to go somewhere I won't cause a local scandal. Or at least another local scandal."

A more thorough kiss. By the time he drew back, her toes curled with pleasure in her half boots.

"I'll have you to myself until tomorrow," he said. "It's more than I ever thought you'd grant me."

A slow smile curved her lips. "I can kiss you as often as I like."

"And I can touch you and hold you." His hand drifted over her head with a light touch before he kissed her again. "You'll have to move away while I talk to Mulray. He's easily shocked."

In a daze of pleasure, she disentangled herself. Evesham reached up and rapped on the roof.

Mulray opened the sliding panel to look down into the carriage. Water dripped from the wide brim of his hat, and he looked cold and miserable. "Yes, Your Grace?"

"Sorry the day's so vile, old man."

"Lovely weather for ducks, sir."

"It is that. Do you know an inn on the Salisbury road where we won't make much of an impression?"

"Salisbury, Your Grace? I was heading for London."

"A small change of plan. Also I'd like you to take the shields off the doors."

"Very good, sir." Soon after the panel shut, the carriage jolted to a stop.

Juliet heard a few bumps and scrapes, as Mulray removed the wooden panels displaying the ducal arms and stored them in the luggage compartment at the back.

"He'll know what we're planning," she said, once the carriage started moving again.

"He won't betray us." Evesham's arms curled around her shoulders. Ridiculous as it might be, the embrace made her feel protected. "He's been with the family since boyhood, and he's unshakably loyal. But if you're having second thoughts, we can continue on to London."

A smile twisted her lips, although it warmed her heart to know that Evesham was letting her decide what happened between them. "Then poor Mulray might drown."

"Or we could stop at an inn and have a meal and

wait for the weather to pass. Two travelers seeking temporary shelter."

She tried to read his expression through the darkness. "That's not what you want."

His grunt expressed fervent agreement with that remark. "Hell, no. However the choice remains yours."

She raised her chin. "If I don't take this chance, I'll regret it for the rest of my life."

He caught her up for another kiss, over too soon. "Your courage humbles me. Never think I take this gift for granted."

How she wished that he didn't sound as if she was the answer to his every wish. She fought so hard to keep a grip on stark reality. That stark reality was that while she'd remember what they did for the rest of her life, he'd move on to other lovers. He'd soon forget Juliet Frain.

Fate delivered her to Evesham for a single night. No more. If she persuaded herself that this extended beyond satisfying their attraction, she was asking for trouble. And she already had enough trouble to keep her busy into the next century.

She stared up at him through the gloom. "I wish we were already safe in a room somewhere, with just you and me and nobody to judge us."

"Still a few misgivings?"

"One or two, but I won't be a reluctant lover."

"The first time I saw you, I thought of a captive flame. You contain such passion, Juliet. Tonight will be a glorious adventure."

Heaven help her. Trouble had well and truly found her. What was the use of pretending otherwise? How could she resist him? How could she shut her emotions out? The blunt answer was that she couldn't.

"What things you say," she said on a melting sigh,

sliding one hand up his chest. "I find myself quite overcome."

When he stroked her cheek, the heat of his touch eddied in her blood. "Are you overcome enough to call me Lucas?"

He'd asked her once before, after that shocking encounter in her bedroom. Shocking and magical. And frustrating. As she now admitted.

That night, she'd attempted to maintain some distance. Today, she had no choice but to surrender with her whole heart, come what may.

She smiled back at him and for once didn't try to hide her enchantment. "Lucas, I want to be your lover. I want it more than words can say. Let's hope that inn isn't too far away."

CHAPTER TWENTY

Upstairs at the George and Crown Inn, Evesham knocked softly on the door connecting his room with Juliet's. It was early afternoon, but the downpour outside made it seem much later. He wore only shirt and breeches.

Mulray had outdone himself, finding this place within half an hour of receiving his orders. It was a quality establishment, but unused to aristocratic patronage, as Evesham soon realized. At the arrival of such an expensive carriage, the landlord and his wife went into a complete spin. Even without the identifying escutcheons on the coach, there could be no doubt that the occupants came from society's highest echelons.

Juliet had emerged from the carriage, veiled and silent. They'd settled into a private parlor while their rooms were readied, and enjoyed an excellent luncheon. After eating, he escorted her upstairs, then left her to go to his room to wash and shave.

The old inn was mercifully empty. The foul weather must have discouraged the regular patrons from leaving their hearths. He was glad about that. If he and Juliet aroused too much curiosity, she might lose her nerve.

Right now, he reached such a pitch of excitement, he'd shatter like an overheated cannon if she sent him away. This anticipation was delicious and fed his arousal. It made him aware that for far too long, genuine hunger had been lacking from his amours. Everything had become a matter of routine.

He knew the steps of the dance, and so did his partners. There wasn't an ounce of suspense in any of it, unless he counted the suspense of how long he'd take to move on to a new conquest.

Evesham didn't feel like that now. This encounter offered such high stakes that his jaded heart skipped and cavorted in his chest like a circus pony. He felt ready to jump out of his skin. No woman had made him feel like this since...

The truth was that he'd never been as het up about a woman. In the coach, Juliet was lucky that he hadn't moved from kisses straight to seduction. It was a blessing that Mulray had found the inn so fast.

At her soft command to enter, he was shocked to see his hand shake when he lifted the latch and pushed the door open. His heart crashed to a stop when he crossed the threshold and saw her standing waiting for him.

He had fond memories of the pink peignoir from the night that he'd invaded her bedroom. With her golden hair flowing loose around her shoulders, she looked pure and lovely.

Mixed with his surging lust was wonder that such an exquisite being should offer herself to a miscreant like him.

Juliet eyed him uncertainly and drew the peignoir closer to her body, revealing that beneath the frail silk, she was naked. The clinging material provided a breathtaking impression of a voluptuous form with full, firm breasts and curved hips.

He'd been right that first day. She did have

spectacular legs.

Another jolt of arousal struck. Not for the first time, he told himself that he couldn't fall on her like a starving lion. He owed it to her – hell, he owed it to himself – to introduce her to pleasure with all the finesse that he could muster.

"Juliet, you're beautiful," he said in a husky voice. Awe tightened his throat and threatened to steal his ability to speak.

"Th-thank you," she said on a whisper.

The polite response was so true to Juliet that he couldn't help laughing. Not to mention that he was happy in a way he couldn't recall feeling in years. He strode forward and swept her up in his arms.

This time, her kisses tasted of unconditional surrender. She wrapped her arms around him and joined in the passionate interplay of lips and tongues and teeth. Her untrammeled ardor threatened to blow his head off.

Still kissing her, he shuffled her backward, until she tumbled down onto the carved oak bed that dominated the room. She gasped as she hit the mattress and dragged him down to follow her.

He straddled her thighs and rose to his knees above her. "You drive me mad. You've always driven me mad," he growled, as he hauled his shirt over his head and flung it to the floor. Only his breeches remained.

"The insanity is mutual." She stroked his bare chest, combing her fingers through the scattered black curls. Everywhere that she touched, she set off explosions of heat. "By heaven, you're a gorgeous man, Lucas."

He loved to hear her say his name. But not as much as he loved her fascinated discovery of his body. When she traced the line of his pectorals, the brush of her fingers over his nipples made him shiver.

A frown knotted her forehead, as one caressing hand glanced over the red welt of scar tissue high on his left arm. "What's this?"

He glanced down, although he knew what she was looking at. "A souvenir from my duel with Granville."

Wide blue eyes, dark with consternation, met his. Overmastering emotion made her voice shake, too. "You could have died. I'd never have known you."

"He was certainly angry enough to kill me. But I came through all right. The devil looks after his own."

The glance of her fingers across the raised flesh flashed through him like lightning. Because she was right. His life could have ended in that field in Camden. Just now, the thought that he might have missed holding Juliet Frain in his arms was unbearable.

"I'm so glad he didn't kill you."

Evesham prepared to make some careless response, because he was the rakish duke and he greeted trouble with a grin and a quip. But the meaningless riposte died unspoken, when Juliet leaned in and kissed his ugly scar.

The action carved a rift through his pretense that this was just another sensual escapade. More intense than usual, certainly, but at heart the same as all his other affairs.

This encounter wasn't like anything else. Juliet was unique. Even if he lived to a hundred, she'd remain unique.

"Right now, so am I," he said fervently and caught her face to hold her for a desperate kiss.

He'd loved kissing Juliet from their first embrace on the empty stage at Afton Park. But these kisses were different. Not just because she'd learned how to stir him up.

Every kiss was a prelude to a more profound joining. Evesham raked his hands through her lovely hair, bunching it as his mouth plundered hers. He slid the silky robe away from her shoulders to bare her breasts.

She gave a murmur of discomfort. So far, his kisses had lulled her into following where he led, but now he caught the flare of shyness in her eyes. She lifted trembling hands to cover herself.

"Will you let me see?" he asked, his voice gruff.

She bit her lip but after a moment, she lowered her hands. "As you wish."

"Juliet..." Once again, words escaped him.

She was all woman. Creamy flesh. Jutting raspberry nipples. Her hair rippled across her shoulders, providing a fragile modesty. But under his admiring gaze, she raked her hair back, until she was revealed in all her glory.

Reverently, he shaped his hands to her lush shape and discovered the warmth of her skin. She sighed and tilted up with such eagerness that his overexercised heart took off on another gallop. He squeezed and stroked her, and when he could bear no more delay, he bent to take one sweet, beaded point between his lips.

Juliet cried out and angled closer. Her hand burrowed into his hair, urging him nearer. He needed no further encouragement.

Evesham used teeth and tongue to torment her into trembling arousal. While he teased, he caressed her, running his hands down her flanks and hips. She moaned as his mouth suckled her other nipple.

When he lifted his head from her breast, she lay across the sheets in magnificent disarray. Her eyes were closed and a flush colored her cheeks.

He took her lips in a brief, fierce kiss. When he

pulled away, her eyes fluttered open and he found himself drowning in sultry blue.

"Time to drop the last barriers, my darling," he murmured, sitting up to undo the knot at her waist that kept her in her peignoir.

He hadn't fumbled undressing a woman since he was a beginner. But for the life of him, he couldn't manage the pestilential sash.

"Damn it," he muttered between his teeth.

Her expression mirrored his desperation. "Tear it."

He didn't hesitate. The sash shredded, and she wriggled out of her robe.

The breath jammed in his throat at the first sight of her nakedness. She was all gold and white, from her lustrous fall of hair to her flawless skin to the darker gold curls covering her mound.

As his ravenous gaze drank in the sumptuous details of Juliet's body, he recognized that it was time to let physical needs rule. Her languorous gaze and swollen red lips showed that she was ready. The preliminaries had been delectable, but now his blood drummed with an insistent rhythm and he was harder than an iron pole.

"You're perfect," Evesham whispered, placing a kiss on each breast.

Desire had always been present, but with every moment, desire merged with a more unfamiliar feeling. Worship perhaps. Certainly gratitude.

What a fool he was. He'd assumed that the pupil in this encounter would be Juliet. But as she drew him deeper under her thrall, he discovered a new world. Where pleasure resided as much in heart and soul as in his body.

Her hand fluttered to cover the hair at the junction of her thighs. "The way you look at me..."

"You feel self-conscious?"

Her lips quirked. "At the very least." She paused. "And excited."

His smile broadened. "I approve of excited."

She rolled her eyes. "Good. Because I feel like my skin is about to burst into flame."

By Jupiter, she was brave. When she gave herself, she did it without stinting.

He caught her hand and lifted it to his lips. "Such pretty skin, too."

Her shaky amusement didn't match the softness in her eyes. "Now you know better than anyone."

"I feel blessed that you're with me like this."

Another twitch of her lips. "Whereas I feel—"

"Awkward?"

"A little. But mostly I feel...desired."

"You're most definitely desired, my darling. Shall we continue?"

"Yes, please."

He kissed her hand again and rolled out of the bed. Thank the Lord, his breeches caused him less trouble than her robe. Juliet pushed up against the pillows, her attention fixed on him. Her wide-eyed astonishment had him blushing. Another first.

"I'm a big sod." Her gaze felt like a caress, and he hardened, when he'd assumed that he was already as erect as he could get. "Say something, Juliet. I'm afraid I've terrified you into a swoon."

Still, she stared. Did she have any inkling how that concentrated attention made him burn?

Her throat moved as she swallowed. "Lord above, Lucas, I had no idea."

His laugh was fond. "You're not swooning?"

She brushed a wing of hair back from her shoulders. Her curiosity had stopped her worrying about her nakedness. Which suited him very well. "I'm far too interested to swoon."

What could he do, hearing that, except dive into

the bed and kiss her until she was panting and trembling?

His caresses became more purposeful. Soon, he lay between her legs. She moaned as he stroked her cleft, reveling in the slick heat.

She wanted him. And God knew he wanted her.

"Oh! That's…strange," she said when he slid his finger inside.

"Does it hurt?"

"No." She didn't sound sure, and her hands pressed hard into his shoulders.

Evesham moved his finger in and out in a tantalizing rhythm and watched her eyes darken as pleasure rose. Her response dissolved into a long, shuddering sigh, and she angled her hips up.

He kissed her, as he used two fingers to penetrate her. She was so tight, so very tight.

Juliet wrapped her arms around him. When he came up for air from the kiss, she bestowed a shy smile on him. "Don't make me wait any longer, Lucas. Make me yours."

CHAPTER TWENTY-ONE

uliet watched Lucas's expression change from eager excitement to overwhelming emotion. Desire remained. He'd looked at her with desire from the first. On stage, he'd made such a powerful Romeo because he'd done nothing to hide his craving for her. On stage, she hadn't had to hide how much she wanted him either.

On stage. And now.

She stretched up to kiss him. To her surprise, the kiss was as sweet as it was passionate. Just as the glow in his eyes spoke of feelings that extended beyond physical hunger.

Juliet warned herself against tumbling into a fool's paradise, where the man she gave herself to genuinely cared for her. But what else could she think, when Lucas gazed at her as if she made every dream come true?

He rose on his elbows and stared down into her face. "Hold onto my shoulders."

Her fingers clutched the top of his arms. His skin was hot under her touch, and he breathed hard. Even in her innocence, she recognized his fight for control.

Juliet bent her knees, cradling him between her

thighs. "I'm ready," she whispered.

He dipped his head for another kiss of such unabashed appreciation that it made her arch upward. When she felt heated pressure between her legs, she released a whimper against his lips.

More pressure. A tinge of discomfort.

At the sight of his nakedness, she'd wondered how her body would cope with his size. Now she knew, and it wasn't as easy as she'd hoped.

Her fingers dug into his straining arms, as he pushed further. The stretching sensation sharpened, and she bit her lip until she drew blood.

His entire body had gone rigid, not just the part that penetrated her. His words emerged in jerky gasps. "Is it too bad?"

"No," she forced out.

He kissed her quickly, his tongue soothing the sting of her torn lip. "Such a pretty liar, my love."

His love? No, she wasn't that. But his humor leavened the painful intensity. Her body lost some of its stiffness. When he pushed deeper, it wasn't so painful.

"Don't...don't stop," she said, desperate to know his possession, in spite of the awkwardness. She'd ventured too far along this path to lose her nerve now.

"You're marvelous."

She didn't feel marvelous. She felt needy and restless and inept.

He bent and kissed her with a fervent passion that went some way toward banishing her fear that she made a mess of this.

When he plunged forward, she opened to welcome him. The pain was brief and close to forgotten by the time that he raised his head. His kisses always swept her away into another more radiant world.

He stared down at her, as if he'd never seen anything as perfect in his life. "Juliet, are you all right?"

While he joined his body to hers, she'd held her breath. Now she released the air pent up in her lungs and hefted a great breath. The musk of their arousal tinged the warm air.

When she shifted, he growled with approval. Her frantic clutch at his shoulders loosened, and she stroked down his arms and over his back.

Her theoretical understanding of what happened between a man and a woman crumbled under the impact of the act itself. The closeness was indescribable, beyond even her wildest imaginings. Breathtaking in its completeness, as though she and Lucas became one in the flesh, but also in heart and spirit.

"I feel...made anew," she murmured, adjusting to this glorious invasion.

Juliet watched his eyes change. Concern vanished, replaced by a masculine satisfaction that assured her he found no complaint with her inexperience.

She'd always imagined this act taking place under cover of night, but she loved being able to track the nuances of his expression. Especially when, as now, she could revel in his pleasure in her.

"There's more."

She trailed her hands down that firmly muscled back and dared to trace the firm globes of his buttocks. Carnal curiosity had tormented her from their first meeting. It dawned on her that he'd given her the right to explore his gorgeous, vigorous body.

"Show me."

His gaze was questioning. She loved how closely he watched her, gauged her reactions. The focused attention had made her uneasy when they'd first met. Now it felt like...caring.

"I don't want to hurt you."

She bumped her hips higher, surprised at her boldness. "I was a little uncomfortable at first, but now it's..." Words failed her.

Lucas must have understood what she tried to say, because he kissed her. Then he started to move.

As he slowly withdrew, Juliet sighed with pleasure. Every nerve came alive. "Lucas, that's wonderful."

She gasped again as he slid back inside. Smoother this time, although her inner muscles clung just as snugly. Passionate heat enveloped her, turning the sting at the start into a mere memory. What had felt so foreign started to become familiar.

"Oh, yes," she hissed and tilted her hips.

He set up a compelling rhythm. Soon her enjoyment changed to something more insistent, disturbing, overwhelming. It was like when he'd put his hand between her legs and made her see stars. But because this time, he shared his body with her, the result was immeasurably more powerful.

"Don't fight it, Juliet. Let it happen," he crooned, dipping his head to nibble his way down a sensitive nerve along the side of her neck. She shivered and cried out as the spiral of response tightened to ravishing agony.

For a tremulous instant, she poised on the edge. Before, on a great burst of flaring release, she flew across the barrier and into a cascade of blinding light.

"Lucas!" she cried. Her nails scored his back, as overpowering sensation stretched her on a rack of ecstasy.

Through her quaking, she was aware of him pulling back and leaving the bed. "Lucas?" she asked tentatively.

"It's fine," he said.

Which would have been more convincing, if he didn't sound like he was in pain. Juliet fought her way through the mists of pleasure and pushed herself up against the pillows to watch him disappear behind the screen in the corner.

Seriously worried, she wrenched the sheet off the bed and wrapped it around her. She scrambled out of bed and went after him. Her legs were shaky, and her knees felt like water. Ripples of response still combed through her like waves up a beach.

At the sound of a muffled groan, all impulse to grant Lucas privacy vanished.

"Are you sick?" She rushed around the screen, then slammed to a halt as she caught him spilling his seed into a towel. His fist closed hard around his swollen rod, and his features were taut as if he was in torment.

"No." As he lifted his hand away from himself, his dark gaze turned rueful. "I couldn't hold back any longer."

While he wiped himself off, she observed with fascinated eyes. "You didn't have to hide."

His lips turned down. "I thought you'd be disgusted if I spilled on your stomach."

She hitched up the sheet, which showed a tendency to sag. "You protected me from a baby."

He shrugged, as if it was nothing. "Of course."

She studied him with puzzled eyes. "For a heartless rake, you're a very considerate lover."

A blush heated his cheeks, which pleased her no end. When she'd met him, she'd judged him as too jaded and sophisticated to be embarrassed at anything, no matter how outrageous. "I'm not a bloody heartless rake."

"No, you're not," she said softly. Now her nerves had settled, she let her gaze wander over his body.

This was her first chance to take in his full physical splendor. And splendid he certainly was. "You're a very handsome rake, though."

"What a lot of nonsense."

She laughed at his obvious discomfort with compliments. "I can't be the first woman to tell you that."

He tossed the crumpled towel to the floor. "It means more, coming from you."

It was her turn to blush, and what she said next made her blush hotter. "May I look at you? I've never seen a naked man before today."

"If you must."

"I think I must."

Her thorough survey covered every hard line of his torso. The firm pectorals. Ridges of muscle across his flat stomach. Bronze-colored nipples nestled among dark curls of hair.

The curls arrowed down the center of his body to a thicker nest of hair at the base of his belly. Even now, his rod looked too large to fit inside her.

But of course, it had. With superb results. The afterglow of those extraordinary moments made her blood swirl like a lazy river. Subjecting him to this slow, sensual inspection stirred more of those feelings.

In the confined space behind the screen, she breathed in the spicy scent of virile male. A rush of damp heat between her legs had her pressing her thighs together.

He groaned, and his hands opened and closed at his sides, as if he fought the urge to grab her. A wanton thrill ripped through her at the thought.

"Maybe you should go back to bed," he said through his teeth.

"Will you join me?" Her fall from grace meant she could be as brazen as she liked.

The glance that he sent her seared her skin. "In a moment."

His interest was stirring, too. The flesh between his legs showed signs of coming to life.

"May I touch you then?"

He clenched his jaw so hard that a muscle danced in his cheek. "Juliet, it's your first time. You might need to recover, before I start bouncing about on top of you again."

She realized with a spurt of warmth that had nothing to do with heightened excitement that he was being considerate again. "I don't want to waste our time together."

"And I don't want to cause you any physical harm." He sighed and ran his hand through his hair in the characteristic gesture. Her eyes fastened with utter fascination on the way the muscles of his chest moved. He groaned again. "Stop it, or I'll forget my good intentions."

She gave him the sort of assured, sensual smile that she'd never imagined herself capable of. But she wasn't the restrained, careful lady she'd been all her life. Or at least until she met this enticing example of masculinity. Lucas's hunger for her lent her a confidence in herself as a woman that she'd never known.

It might be wicked, but she'd never been so happy. Until now, she'd lived her life behind a pane of glass. Now she lived in the moment.

"I speak from experience when I say good intentions are overrated."

His grunt expressed wry amusement. "Let me have a wash, then we can talk about it."

That sounded promising. She hitched the sheet up and returned to the bed. Her body felt different, too. Panic had swamped her immediate awareness of the way that her muscles protested at any sudden movement. Muscles that she hadn't even known she possessed.

"Why are you laughing?" he asked from behind the screen. She heard the splash of water as he washed.

She propped herself up against the pillows. "I was remembering how the night before her wedding, I told Viola what her husband would do to her in bed. It turns out that I had no idea. What you did to me went way beyond anything that I ever imagined."

He emerged from behind the screen, carrying a large bowl and with a couple of towels draped over his arm. To her regret, he'd wrapped another towel around his waist.

"In a good way?"

Her lips quirked. "Are you chasing compliments?"

Lucas set the bowl on the nightstand and shot her a smiling glance that made her stomach knot with helpless longing. "Given some of the things you've said to me, can you blame me?"

She touched his arm. "I'm sorry. You made me afraid that—"

"That we'd end up doing what we just did?"

"Perhaps not in so many words, but I'd never been attracted to a man before. I didn't know how to handle it. I didn't know how to handle...you."

"You have my permission to handle me as much as you wish." His lips twitched. "Once I've made you comfortable. You'll feel more the thing after a wash. May I remove that frightfully becoming sheet?"

Given what he'd just done to her, it seemed silly to balk at revealing her nakedness. "Yes."

"You don't sound very sure." The tenderness in his gaze turned her blood to molten honey.

Juliet had imagined the sexual act would dominate the day's events. It turned out that it was only one of the snares awaiting a yearning heart. She hadn't expected this poignant sweetness after Lucas bedded her. A sweetness that ripped away the last of her ragged defenses.

"You've already seen me." She made an apologetic gesture. "It shouldn't matter."

"I'd like to see more. Will you allow me that privilege?"

Her hand shook, as she loosened the sheet. Her cheeks felt like fire. Clearly, despite abandoning her chastity, she hadn't lost the ability to blush.

"Juliet, you beggar my dreams," he said when at last she lay bare. The raw emotion in his voice went a long way toward vanquishing timidity. That, and the glow in his dark eyes.

"I'm…I'm glad," she whispered.

He dipped the cloth in the warm water and skimmed it over her breasts and stomach. When her nipples tightened in swift response, she exhaled in soft surprise. She waited in tantalizing suspense for him to devote his attention to her breasts, but he moved on to her arms and legs.

Then with a gentleness that threatened to break her already tattered heart, he parted her legs and began to wash her there, where his body had joined with hers.

His face was set with concentration. No hint of prurience. Whereas with every touch, her blood rushed hotter, and her skin burned for the touch of his hands.

Having him washing her in such a private place – good heavens, looking at her there – she should be in an agony of self-consciousness. She had been at first, but soon arousal drowned embarrassment.

On an incoherent complaint, she shifted against the sheet.

Lucas looked up with a frown, and his hand went

still. "Am I hurting you?"

She bit her lip before confessing the shameful truth. "No, you're making me...want you again."

The delight in his smile left her feeling as if the sun came out from behind a cloud and shone just for her. "Juliet, you make me so happy."

He dropped the flannel in the bowl and came down over her for a fierce kiss. Even as she gave in to the demands of his mouth, she reached down and tugged the concealing towel away from his waist.

He was hard and ready. She waited for him to unite their bodies again.

But when his lips shifted from hers, it was to trail more kisses down her body. Discovering places that in her innocence, she'd never imagined might send her up in flames.

His lips traced a meandering path down to her navel. Her protest this time was louder, and she dug her fingers in his silky hair, as he dipped his tongue into the small indentation.

Lucas dropped a line of kisses above her pubis, then shifted lower to bury his head between her legs.

Consternation slammed through her. She was aware of heat and suction, and the flicker of a tongue in a place where she'd never thought a man's mouth would venture.

Helpless to resist, her thighs splayed out on either side of his head. Each touch, each kiss set off a fresh burst of pleasure.

"Lucas!" She went rigid, and her knees rose around him.

When he looked up, she wasn't so sure anymore that she appreciated the daylight. His eyes were heavy with desire, and his lips glistened after that intimate kiss.

"Let me do this, Juliet."

"But...it's perverse."

He turned his head to place a kiss on her thigh. "I promise you'll like it."

"But why would you..." Her capacity for speech evaporated, when he dipped his head to lick her cleft with a voluptuous appreciation that she couldn't mistake.

"Want to taste you there, where you're most a woman? How can I resist?"

His words punched their way through her, demolishing inhibitions and leaving only curiosity behind. She sucked in a deep breath, and the tension leached out of her muscles. "Very well."

"Thank you," he said with a fervor that she couldn't doubt he meant, however bizarre this activity seemed.

He caught her knees and held her legs apart. He began to kiss her. When his tongue teased that mysterious place that turned her blood to fire, she bit back a moan. She dug her hands into the rumpled sheet, as another bolt of searing response sizzled through her.

The scrape of teeth had her moving under his mouth. Not away, but closer. He responded with a murmur of encouragement.

Soon the onslaught of cascading reaction was continuous, like being suspended in the middle of a storm. A return of that surging wave that lifted her up to bliss. She raised her hips, and one hand raked through his hair in an unsteady caress that was a silent plea to continue.

He concentrated on that sensitive place, until she panted for air. Surely she must detonate into flaming embers. Then on a husky cry, Juliet abandoned herself once more to the heights of rapture.

Every muscle in her body convulsed, as he shifted up to kiss her on the mouth. The salty flavor of his lips hinted at the taste of her body. The thought was thrilling. Even more thrilling, the irresistible spasms had barely subsided when she felt a hard, seeking pressure between her legs.

"Yes, oh, yes," she sighed. She kissed Lucas with all the excruciating longing in her heart as he pushed forward.

CHAPTER TWENTY-TWO

This time, Evesham slid into Juliet's body as smoothly as if she'd been created to take him. The eager grip of her muscles threatened to blow his head off.

After he filled her to the hilt, he paused to bask in the ineffable connection. There was physical pleasure. More than he could remember finding with a woman. Yet somehow with Juliet, an act that he'd always enjoyed before became...more.

She tightened her arms around him, as if she never wanted to let him go. With a long, luxuriant sigh, she bowed up toward him.

"That's lovely," she murmured, kissing him with a quick passion that sent another jolt of heat flaring through him.

For a long moment, he rested in the radiant closeness. Taking her virginity had been an unforgettable moment. He'd imagined that might be the greatest experience this world could offer. But lying here inside Juliet and knowing that nothing could separate them was even better.

This felt like coming home after a long and dangerous journey. For nine years, he hadn't had a home. If he was truthful, he hadn't had much of a home before that. Now Juliet became his home. His meaningless wanderings ended at this instant, when she accepted him as her lover.

Evesham closed his eyes and buried his head in the curve of her shoulder. The very air that he breathed turned into Juliet. Warm, aroused woman. A trace of lemon soap from her wash. He and this woman were bonded in a way that reached beyond the carnal into something that felt like transcendence.

But the carnal exerted its demands, too. And the carnal was miraculous.

With an incoherent sound that expressed pleasure and encouragement, she wriggled down in the bed. Her hands fondled his back before sliding lower to caress his buttocks. On a muffled groan, he pulled back, then pushed forward again to discover that same shattering welcome.

Her body still clenched and released from the mighty climax that she'd enjoyed when he'd used his mouth on her. He knew that letting him kiss her between the legs had been a gesture of trust. Hell, everything she did with him today was a huge gesture of trust.

She yielded so sweetly. No hint of reluctance. No hint of fear.

His heart brimming with thankfulness, he started to move with more purpose. Even while he regretted breaking that wordless communion as he poised deep inside her. When her body had made vows in silence that he doubted she'd ever speak aloud.

But yielding to his male impulses provided its own joy, especially when she gave a luscious little murmur and angled to meet his every thrust.

"Do that again," he grated out, as he withdrew.

She'd kept her eyes shut, as if allowing her other

senses to feast on this unfolding pleasure. When she lifted heavy eyelids, he stared down into smoky blue irises with dilated pupils. She looked as if she drifted in a world beyond the everyday. "Do what?"

"You squeezed me. I like it."

More than liked it. The sensation of her muscles contracting in an intimate embrace had set off fireworks.

She suited her actions to her words. "Like this?"

"Hell, yes."

He bent to kiss her with a rough enthusiasm that somehow still retained traces of tenderness. Her body clasped him so tight that he felt ready to burst into flame.

Evesham rose on his elbows and increased the pace. His balls throbbed for release, but he wanted Juliet to find her peak first.

She kept her gaze fixed on his, so he watched her eyes widen and turn glassy as she approached her climax. Her lips parted with a struggle for breath, each exhalation emerging on a sigh of yearning.

Then, as easily as a petal tumbled from a rose, she slipped over into her climax. The soft moan that escaped her at that moment of surrender was the most beautiful music that he'd ever heard. For as long as he could, he held himself still as she spasmed around him.

But soon, too soon, the demands of his body claimed him. Evesham began to shift faster, more deliberately, until he reached the limits of restraint. He wrenched free of her body and prepared to leave the bed.

"Don't go," she said in a husky voice. "Stay with me."

"Juliet, are you sure?"

He forced his reeling mind to function beyond sheer animal hunger. Almost impossible so close to his crisis.

She didn't mean for him to spend himself inside her. But he'd felt like a lost dog when he'd gone behind the screen. Staying with her was better. Not as good as flooding her womb with his seed, but he couldn't risk giving her a child, not until they had some plans in place.

With greedy hands, she hauled him down and kissed him again, threatening to send him over the edge. "I'm sure."

He thrust once more, then pulled free to pump onto the pale curve of her stomach. Her hands flattened on his chest, over the place where his heart thundered with the sound of her name.

He collapsed at her side, laboring to fill his lungs. Sex had always seemed an easy pleasure. With Juliet, importance weighted every action. But the pleasure, too, was richer, more substantial.

She took his hand. More trust. Another wrench at a heart unaccustomed to playing a part in his affairs.

"That was...remarkable," she said in a hushed voice.

"Yes, it was." More remarkable still that the man of the world had to fight back a huge wave of emotion.

He'd thought copulation had no more secrets to reveal to him, the notorious rake. It turned out that he'd been an arrogant fool. Because every moment with Juliet deepened the mystery. And his fascination.

He rose on one elbow to kiss her with a leisurely enjoyment that expressed thanks and pleasure, and the promise of more pleasure to come.

When he drew away, Juliet regarded him as if she'd never seen anything so marvelous. The tender way that she cradled his jaw sliced yet another chasm through his soul. No woman had ever had this power over him. After that magnificent swiving, he'd returned to himself enough to understand that she had the ability to destroy him.

"I had no idea it could be like this," she said, her voice laced with wonder.

"Neither did I," he said. While he knew that she wouldn't believe him, it was the unadulterated truth.

Another quick kiss, then he was out of the bed. "Let me clean you up."

She hoisted herself against the pillows and pushed back the heavy fall of golden hair. His teeth and beard had marked her fine white skin. She looked tired but glowing, and so lovely that she stole his breath.

He bent to collect the towel to cover himself, but she made a pleading gesture with one hand. "Don't. I like to see you."

He let the towel drop. "I like to see you, too."

"I liked feeling you...on my skin."

He sucked in a relieved breath. Despite her cooperation, he'd feared that his masculine release might repulse her. "You're a goddess, Juliet."

Her lips quirked with the self-deprecating humor that he'd liked from the first. He'd arrived at Afton Park expecting to meet a woman with no laughter in her, a woman who took herself too seriously for smiling. "You flatter me."

"On my oath, I don't."

This time, her smile held a touch of sorrow. "A goddess could make time stop."

"When I'm inside you, I feel like time stops."

Her eyes darkened, and he glimpsed some profound emotion that he couldn't identify. He knew what he wanted to see, but wanting it so much meant that he couldn't trust himself to interpret her feelings.

"So do I."

He set the bowl on the nightstand with such haste, water splashed over its edges. But he had to kiss her now or perish.

There had been so many spectacular kisses since she'd promised to be his, but this one trumped them all. It spoke of longing and admiration and gratitude. And of something else that as yet Evesham didn't have the courage to put into words.

He stared down into her unforgettable face in wonder. "A goddess, Juliet."

She studied his features, as though she strove to imprint every line on her mind. But to his regret, the joy drained from her eyes, replaced by something that looked like apprehension.

It seemed that the strength of the emotion between them troubled her, too.

Evesham stirred in the tumbled bedclothes and opened eyes dry with tiredness. Bright sunlight poured through the open window, and birds sang outside. It wasn't late, but he could tell that dawn had passed several hours ago.

In his arms, Juliet slept. She was pale and drawn, and her lips were full and bruised after hours of kissing.

After the eventful night, his limbs ached with weariness. Sublime weariness.

He was in no hurry to get up, so he closed his eyes and nestled her closer. Her back was pressed into his chest, and she was loose with exhaustion. With a tender gesture, he cupped her breast. She was a woman of sumptuous curves.

Evesham was nearly asleep again, when she shifted with a muffled protest. His hold on her tightened. He didn't want her moving. He wanted her staying just where she was.

But she was awake. She turned in his arms to kiss him softly on the lips. He found himself staring into eyes cloudy with drowsiness.

"Good morning, Lucas."

"Good morning, Juliet," he murmured in return and brushed the heavy tangle of hair back from her face with sleepy appreciation.

After the night's excesses, her features were subtly changed. Her expression conveyed a new sensual awareness. She looked like a woman who understood passion. It made her even more exciting. She'd always been beautiful. Now that beauty blazed like a beacon.

"I didn't mean to go to sleep." Her voice was husky with tiredness. It reminded him of how she'd sounded when he was deep inside her. After everything that they'd done to each other into the early hours, he shouldn't have the energy for sexual interest.

He shouldn't, but he did.

Nonetheless, he wasn't a barbarian. He'd tried to be as considerate as possible, but by the end, he'd noticed Juliet's discomfort. So when his dick surged into life, he told it to behave.

"Nor did I," he said ruefully. "Are you hungry?"

He was desperate to keep to the most prosaic topics. Because he was deathly afraid that despite everything that had happened, she might still mean to leave him.

He'd learned to respect her will. Hadn't she defied two dukes and a furious father to face her disgrace alone?

"Yes," she said.

He'd arranged for an extravagant supper to be served in the dressing room last night. An empty bottle of champagne that they'd drunk in the early hours sat on the chest near the door with a half-eaten tray of pastries beside it.

"I'll dress and go down to arrange breakfast. Shall we eat up here?"

Wanton mischief lit her eyes. "I don't mean I'm hungry for food."

"Juliet..." The rest of the sentence disappeared in a frantic gulp, as she shaped her fingers around his stiffening cock.

Last night, at first she'd been shy, but she'd soon picked up on his endless appetite for her and she'd become bolder. He'd loved watching her lay claim to herself as a woman with physical needs. He'd loved satisfying those physical needs even more.

Somewhere before midnight, he'd given her a breathtaking lesson in how to touch his prick. The lesson hadn't lasted very long, but now she demonstrated that she'd understood the essentials. She ran her hand along his length, squeezing and releasing him in a way that drove everything but need from his mind.

Her grip tightened, and she leaned in to kiss him again, with more purpose. So far, while she'd been gratifyingly cooperative, he'd taken the lead. It seemed that the tables had turned.

"You're out to seduce me?" he grated out.

"Is it working?"

"Yes, it is."

"Good." She pushed him flat on his back with a brazen enthusiasm that turned his blood to steam.

Only a madman would resist. She shoved the sheets out of the way to reveal his body. As that also exposed her magnificent Norse goddess form, he had no complaints.

With flaring interest, he watched her straddle his hips. She bent and kissed him again, with a rising passion that matched his. He caught her full breasts in his hands, squeezing the warm, firm flesh.

Evesham watched her eyes change. She had exquisitely sensitive breasts, he'd been pleased to discover. When his thumbnails scraped pearled nipples, her breath caught.

Too soon, Juliet wriggled out of his hold and began to kiss his chest, using lips and tongue and teeth. Her hands played a concerto of caresses over his arms and shoulders.

When she kissed his stomach, for a dazzled moment, he wondered if she might take him in her mouth. He might have kissed her quim, but this was a variation that he hadn't broached. Less than twenty-four hours ago, she'd been a virgin. Despite her blatant enjoyment of everything that they'd done in this bed, sucking his prick was a step too far.

He'd just started to get excited at the prospect – he'd enjoyed a thousand fantasies of his cock inside Juliet's mouth – she sat up again.

Before he could feel disappointed, she rose and in one smooth glide, took him inside her. Lightning flashed in his head, his blood surged like a tidal wave, his heart threatened to crash free of his chest.

"Dear God, you're killing me," he growled, setting his hands on her hips. The hot, pulsating slickness of her body surrounded his.

The confident, wanton smile on her lips would have been foreign to the Juliet he'd met. This was a woman who owned her power. By heaven, he'd never seen a more beautiful sight than her sitting astride him, naked, while their bodies joined in sultry promise.

"Poor Lucas," she said with insincere pity.

When she circled her hips, all he saw was exploding suns. "By Jericho, do that again," he managed to say through a throat as tight as a drumhead.

She did, then began rocking forward and back on top of him in a way that sent fire rushing along his veins. The urge to lose himself inside her was nigh invincible, but he fought it back. He didn't want this extravagant pleasure to end so fast.

Juliet rested her hands on his chest and moved up and down with a deliberate slowness that threatened to make him insane. Every shift of that magnificent body promised to send him up in smoke.

Evesham caught her luscious rump in his hands and pressed his fingers deep into the luxuriant flesh. He'd always liked women who were all soft roundness, and Juliet's lush body struck him as just perfect.

Her movements became less controlled as she strove for relief. He loved the way her features tightened and her eyes went opaque as her peak approached. Knowing her crisis loomed so close built his arousal into an unstoppable fever.

"Shall I help?" he asked, as she teetered on the brink without finding relief.

Bending forward until her hair fell about his face in a gilt curtain, she kissed him hard. When she pulled back, she smiled. "Yes."

With a shaking hand, he touched her sex, rubbing hard as she descended with clumsy eagerness. She clenched around him, then jerked into climax.

Evesham gritted his teeth and tensed every muscle to stillness. If he moved now, he'd lose control.

He managed to last until she collapsed on his chest in boneless exhaustion.

With a groan, he rolled over, taking her with him. He was too close to tarry. He wrenched free and lost himself in the sheets.

For a long while, he lay with closed eyes, as his

body recovered from that massive orgasm. In time, his breath came more easily and his heartbeat steadied. He wiped himself off and hauled Juliet into his arms for a long, intense kiss.

He didn't want to acknowledge it, and she didn't say the words. But the shattering fuck and even more, this kiss, felt like goodbye.

CHAPTER TWENTY-THREE

The moment Evesham opened his eyes, he realized that Juliet had left the bed. A quick glance around the room proved that he was alone. With his heart racing, he surged up in alarm.

Surely she wouldn't go without a word. Not after that resplendent night.

But her gown no longer draped over the back of the chair, and her half boots had disappeared from beside the hearth.

"Damn it all to hell," he muttered, staggering out of bed and tugging on his breeches.

If she'd hired a carriage from the inn, someone must know where she'd gone. Or perhaps she'd taken the mail coach.

He had no idea how much money she'd had when she left Afton Park. If she was short of funds, the stagecoach was the more likely choice. He loathed to think of her alone and unprotected on the road and subject to insult, as was wont to happen to unaccompanied women in public conveyances.

He'd grabbed up his shirt, ready to go roaring downstairs to interrogate the staff, when the door to the dressing room opened. Juliet stepped through, catching him mid-panic.

"Lucas? What is it?"

He drew an uneven breath to ease his galloping terror. Although what he saw didn't cheer him up much.

She was dressed in that damned nun's habit of a traveling ensemble. She'd tied her hair back in a simple but severe knot, and she held her bonnet in one hand.

"You weren't here when I woke up."

The pathetic response stung his pride. But he had a sick premonition that his pride was about to receive a drubbing, whatever he did.

"I wanted to dress. If we're going to make London today, we're already late leaving." She glanced out the window. He couldn't help thinking that she tried to avoid his gaze. "The weather's better, but after yesterday, the roads will be a quagmire."

She sounded bright and practical and not at all like last night's husky-voiced siren. He'd had the occasional lover who, in the light of day, had found the excesses of the previous evening an embarrassment. While Juliet's inexperience might make that likely, that wasn't what he believed happened here.

He hauled his shirt over his head, obscurely feeling like he needed the extra armor. "We don't have to travel today. The morning's well advanced, and the roads will be a mess. Neither of us has had much sleep. We could stay."

When she glanced at him as if he was a stranger, it cut him to the quick. "Lucas, we...we said this would be one night."

His hand sliced through the air. "No, *you* said that."

Her flinch confirmed that her composure was purely superficial. He wondered how many times

Juliet had bluffed at control to hide her turmoil. Just so must she have taken charge of her sisters and the estate after her mother's death. Just so must she have responded to the news of Bolton's accident. Just so had she listened to her father cast her out into the world.

She pretended that she could handle anything, but the calmer she appeared, the harder she struggled to conceal the inner storm.

That gave Evesham hope that he might have a few weapons of his own in this fight. Because he had no doubt that this was a fight. A fight to the death.

"Yes, I said that, when I asked you to stop on the way to London." She sounded resolute, despite the unhappy line of her lips.

He raked his hand through his hair in frustration. "It's not enough for me. Tell me it's not enough for you either."

"It has to be enough. Just because the world derides me as a fallen woman doesn't mean I'm taking up a career as a courtesan." She swallowed, her slender throat working above the pelisse's high collar. She was as white as milk now, and strain tightened her features. "I have all the more reason to guard my reputation. Or what's left of it."

He told himself to settle down. Losing his temper wouldn't help. But when he replied, his tone carried an edge. "For pity's sake, Juliet, if your reputation means so much to you, bloody well marry me."

She faltered back as if he'd attacked her physically, although he hadn't moved. "I can't marry you."

"Yes, you can. Easiest thing in the world. If you do, all your troubles will disappear. Society will embrace you, your father will take you back, Portia will have a duchess for a sister, and her marriage prospects will be bright. Devil take it, you'll even have a home of your own. Several.”

She looked under siege. “I can't say yes.”

He made a bewildered gesture. “Don't tell me that you don't like me. Don't say that you don't trust me. Unless you trusted me not to hurt you, you'd never have come to my bed.”

“I knew you wouldn't hurt me,” she muttered, staring at the floor. “I knew you'd be a marvelous lover. And you were.”

That should make him feel better. It didn't. “So you spare me a single night. How generous.”

She paled under his sarcasm and raised a devastated gaze to his. All the brittle poise that she'd adopted to keep him at a distance was gone. “It didn't seem too much to ask. One chance to find out what it's like to desire something and reach out to grab it.”

“You make me feel cheap.”

He wasn't exaggerating. In all his wild days, he'd never felt so crushed as he did right now. That her rebuff came after the most spectacular night of his life just added to his misery.

She recoiled. “I'm sorry. I thought you'd leap at the chance to get me into your bed.”

He straightened and sent her a searing glance. “I did. Because I wanted you from the start.”

She glared back. “Well, now you've had me.”

He sighed. “It's more complicated than that, Juliet.” He summoned every last scrap of his courage and confessed the truth that lay behind every action. “I'm in love with you.”

Juliet whimpered as if he'd punched her. Her proud defiance crumpled. “You can't.”

Her vulnerability made him hunger to wrap his arms around her and tell her that everything would be all right. But her posture made it clear that she didn't want him to touch her.

"Of course I can." His voice rang with the force of his emotions. "And do you want to hear something even more shocking? I think you might love me back."

He waited for a denial, even though he'd wager half his fortune – hell, all of it – that she loved him almost as much as he loved her.

A lightless blue gaze settled upon him. She looked as though she'd never be happy again.

She curled her hands over her bonnet and held it in front of her like a shield, but she replied in a steady voice. "Yes, I love you, Lucas. I don't want to, but I do."

Despite everything, he sucked in a relieved breath. He'd been sure, but he'd thirsted to hear the words. Even if his beloved sounded like she announced the end of the world.

He surveyed her in baffled frustration. "Then why in the name of all that's holy won't you marry me? Are you afraid I'll be unfaithful?"

She squared her shoulders, and the look she sent him stripped away every threadbare defense. "I can't rely on your honor."

He frowned. "Yet you gave yourself to me? That makes no sense."

She swallowed again, and her grip tightened on the broad brim of her bonnet. "I couldn't resist coming to your bed. Not when it was my only chance. Not when I was paying the price for a scandal, without having any memories of...love to compensate for the punishment."

"Now you'll have memories and nothing else," he said with a hint of savagery. "Will they keep you warm at night?"

He hated himself the minute he spoke. She looked ready to shatter. "They'll have to."

"Yet you could have me in your bed every night.

You could bear my children. You could be my beloved duchess. You could step into a future where we live and love together for the rest of our lives. Doesn't that tempt you even a little?"

"Don't be cruel. You must know it tempts me." Anger flared in her eyes. He supposed it was an improvement on the desolation that it replaced. "But I can't trust you."

"If I make promises to you, I'll keep them. I've never broken an oath. I never will."

"Did you say those same words to Vanessa Gould?"

The name crashed down between them like a landslide. He straightened and squared his jaw. "Juliet, I can't talk about that. It means breaking another promise. But for the love of God, believe me, it's not what you think."

"So you say." Her shoulders slumped, and she made a weary gesture. "But you ruined that girl's name and did nothing to make it right. How can I marry a man I don't respect?"

By Jupiter, that smarted. That smarted like being flayed alive. "You respected me enough to give me your virginity."

She stiffened. "That's a low blow," she said coldly.

Evesham bowed his head in acknowledgment. "You're right. It was."

When he didn't apologize – be buggered if he would – she made a helpless gesture. "You must see that we have to part."

No, he didn't see that. He wasn't giving up. Not when she loved him. Not when he loved her. Not when she represented his only hope of happiness.

"Juliet, I beg you, I beg you with every drop of blood in my body, to trust me." Urgency roughened his voice. "I promise on my life that I'm the man you want me to be. I won't betray you. I won't break your heart. Believe me. For God's sake, believe me. Take me as your husband, my darling."

Her eyes were great pools of grief. "But what about Vanessa?"

It was too much. Evesham couldn't bear not touching her. He strode forward and tugged the bonnet from her, tossing it to the floor. His shaking hands clutched hers. "Forget Vanessa."

He waited for her to pull away, but she returned his frantic grip and stared up into his face. "That's not possible."

"But you love me."

"Yes, I love you," she said, as though she confessed to a crime. "I can't help it. I could never help it. Even against my better judgment, I love you."

He bit back a snarl of protest. "It's not against your better judgment. I can make you happy. You can rely on me. I'll never let you down."

Anguish crimped her lips, and she turned ashen with distress. Damn his eyes, he should be kinder to her. He would, if he wasn't fighting for his very life.

She made a sound of distress. "But don't you see? That's just what a liar would say."

"I'm not a liar."

"Then why did you ruin Vanessa Gould?"

Dear God, she tortured him. "I can't tell you. It isn't my story to share. Not to mention there's danger to the people involved."

The irony didn't escape him that his only real claim to honor led the woman he adored to deride him as a man without any honor at all. Somewhere a spiteful fate was having a good laugh at his expense.

"Danger?"

His gut clenched in frustration. "I've said too much. Don't ask me."

Juliet made a half-hearted attempt to pull away. "Then we have nothing more to say to each other."

His grasp tightened. "No, I won't accept that."

"You must." She sounded weary and sad. But adamant. He came up against the invincible force of her will, just as her father had yesterday.

Evesham released a shuddering exhalation. "I haven't always been a good man. I haven't always done the right thing. But I've never let down a friend, and I've never broken my word. I never have, and I never will. If I did, I wouldn't be worthy of you. Again, I plead with you to trust me. Trust me, my love. Trust me."

That uncompromising blue gaze continued to search his face. He prayed with all his might that what she saw convinced her to relent. But when she disengaged her hands from his with a care that broke his heart, he understood that he'd lost. "I can't."

He knew he'd lost, and that made him want to rampage and shout and curse. But what good would that do? He tried again, even as he recognized that there was nowhere he could go from here. "You're consigning us both to endless wretchedness."

She bit her lip and tangled her hands in her gray skirts. "I know."

"You won't give me a chance?"

"I can't," she said again. She sounded older than her twenty-six years. "If you've committed this terrible sin, you're not the man I want to spend the rest of my life with."

"I've told you not to believe everything you've heard."

Even her lips were white now. She suffered. He couldn't doubt that. But her suffering wouldn't shift her stubbornness. "And I've told you that's just what a liar would say."

Unable to bear that probing stare any longer, Evesham swung away to the window. He grabbed the sill and bent his head as he fought for control.

"You're wrong about me, Juliet. You're wrong about this decision."

"So you say." Her response emerged dull with misery.

He sucked in a deep breath and struggled to make sense of what was happening. After all the joy and all the passion, it was over. He had to accept that.

No, no, no, his soul cried out in agony.

But he needed to learn to silence his soul. And his heart. And all his hopes.

Juliet wouldn't have him, so he must go on without her. If, right now, that sounded worse than a death sentence, so be it.

Blindly he stared out the window, as he struggled to find the will to say the next word, take the next step. Without his beloved, everything seemed so futile. Why bother?

He couldn't help thinking once more about unconditional love. It seemed neither Juliet nor her father understood the concept. Was it childish to believe that if she truly loved him, she'd take him? If she truly loved him, she'd know that he'd never wrong her.

But the sad fact was that he'd take her on any terms he could get her, with unconditional love or not. The even sadder fact was that she meant to leave him.

When he swung back to face her, she was eyeing him with dazed anguish. She'd picked up her bonnet and had gone back to clutching it in front of her as if it would save her from all the world's monsters. Among whom she clearly counted the man she claimed to love. "Must we part as enemies?"

Evesham told himself that he wasn't the first man rejected by the woman he loved. For pity's sake, it wasn't even the first time that Juliet had rejected him. She'd refused him four times now.

People didn't die of thwarted love. Give him a few years – maybe fifty – and he'd look back with a nostalgic smile on his pursuit of the unattainable Juliet Frain.

The problem was that right now, he felt like she knifed him and left him to die in a puddle of blood.

He braced his shoulders, as if he faced a dangerous foe. Because despite how much he loved her, Juliet was his foe.

"I'll ask one more time, Juliet. Then I'll never ask again." His voice was a harsh rasp. He didn't sound like a lover, even if he loved her beyond reason. "Before you answer, think of what you're giving up and also think what you'll gain. Not least a place as a duchess, which you were born to hold. Will you marry me?"

Juliet surveyed him out of blind eyes. Her features set in a way that sat oddly with the corroding despair that she couldn't hide.

Her answer emerged as precise as a cut diamond. "Thank you, Your Grace. My answer is no."

CHAPTER TWENTY-FOUR

Hampstead outside London, three months later

The hammering at the front door woke Juliet and had her scrambling out of bed and flinging on her wrap before her mind started to work.

A quick glance at the mantel clock told her it wasn't late. Only ten o'clock.

These days, she went to bed earlier and earlier to escape the dreary loneliness of her days. Perhaps the happy occasion might arise where she just slept the clock around and never had to wake up to survey the horrid mess that she'd made of her life.

By heaven, she hoped that day arrived soon.

As Juliet stumbled along the landing, the din stopped and she heard voices in the hall. Her maid Lizzie must have answered the door. She heard a door shut and assumed Lizzie had put the visitor in the parlor.

Juliet had rented this house shortly after her arrival in London, following a tense and largely silent journey up from Salisbury with Lucas. She still shuddered to remember back to the torture of those hours in his carriage. Having him close enough to touch and yet knowing that she could never touch him again. He sat mere feet away from her on the opposite seat, but it felt as if he was as far out of reach as the moon.

After that heartbreaking quarrel at the inn, she'd have much preferred to go her own way. But he'd insisted on honoring his offer to take her to the Trinders. She'd hated having to accept, but her broken heart didn't banish the practical problems of leaving her father's roof.

Nonetheless, she'd been determined to strike out on her own as soon as she could. She'd only stayed with the Trinders for a few days, and she'd used her interview with Lucas's man of business to get the name of another solicitor to oversee her interests. Mr. Baxter quickly arranged to take management of her inheritance from Papa's lawyer and had helped her to find this comfortable house in the pretty village of Hampstead.

Mr. Baxter had protested that the house was too modest for the wealthy daughter of an earl, however disgraced. But it seemed silly to pay for reception rooms that she never used. Silly, and an inescapable reminder of everything that she'd lost.

Portia hadn't been allowed to leave Wiltshire to see her, but they exchanged frequent letters via an animal-loving friend in Afton village. Viola had offered Juliet a place at Brazey Castle with her and Renfrew, but while she appreciated the gesture, Juliet had put her sister off.

Against all expectation, Viola and Renfrew appeared to be making a success of their marriage. The last thing Juliet wanted was to see two lovers find happiness, when she remained so far from that fortunate state herself.

She hadn't trusted Lucas to stay away, although

he must have known that she'd said her final word on their future. But to his credit, he hadn't come near her since introducing her to the Trinders all those long weeks ago. According to Portia, who heard more gossip than she did these days, he'd retreated to his estate in Devon and hadn't been active in society.

That made two of them.

Every day, Juliet prayed that she'd wake up without hungering for his presence. So far, those heartfelt prayers hadn't been answered.

And here she was thinking about the rogue again, when she should be wondering about her mysterious caller.

"Who is it, Lizzie?" she asked, when the maid appeared at the bottom of the steps.

Only now did it occur to her that it could be news from Afton Park, some trouble with Papa's health. Although hadn't she heard a woman's voice? If a messenger came from home, it would be a footman.

"It's a Mrs. Brandon, madam. She was most insistent that she see you."

"Brandon?" The name sparked no memory. And this was a very strange time to call.

Lizzie picked up her doubt. Worry darkened her pretty, freckled face. "Should I have refused her entry, my lady? She was sure you'd want to see her. She's…a lady. Or at least she sounds like one. I thought she might be a friend."

If she was, she was the only friend to call at this house. Juliet had no idea if Lizzie was aware of her mistress's disgrace, but she was a clever girl. She'd notice the lack of callers.

"Is she alone?"

"Yes, madam. But there's a smart rig outside with a coachman."

A smart rig indicated someone from the wealthier

classes. No wonder Lizzie had decided to let the woman in.

Juliet tightened the belt on her pink peignoir and came down the steps. "I'll see what this is about, Lizzie. But perhaps you should wait in the hall, in case there's any trouble."

Lizzie bobbed into a curtsy. "Yes, my lady."

Juliet went through to the parlor, where a tall woman wearing a stylish, but subtly exotic dark green traveling ensemble stood in the center of the room.

"Mrs. Brandon?" Juliet asked.

Even with her face veiled, the woman was obviously a stranger. But Lizzie was right. This was no penniless beggar.

Juliet could feel eyes studying her through the concealing veil. "It's Brandtner, actually."

The German name had clearly confused Lizzie. It confused Juliet, too. She didn't know anyone in Germany, and the woman spoke with the same crisp upper-class English accent as she did. "I don't..."

Mrs. Brandtner raised gloved hands to her veil and lifted it. "Although I suspect you might be more familiar with me as Vanessa Gould."

Juliet found herself staring into wide hazel eyes in a face of startling beauty. Nobody had told her that Lucas's first love was so lovely.

Unworthy jealousy stirred in her heart, even as she recognized its futility. After all, Lucas was lost to her. What did it matter if the woman he'd run off with as a young man turned out to be this vision?

Yet somehow it did matter.

So much about this encounter left Juliet floundering, yet the question that emerged was hardly the most important. "You're in England?"

Lady Vanessa's lips twitched. "I arrived back this week. I'm sorry to call on you at such an uncivilized hour, but Lucas's letter only arrived this morning. He sent it to the last address he had for me, and it's chased me all the way back to London. That's why it's taken me so long to respond."

Juliet struggled to make sense of what was happening. "Lucas's letter?"

Juliet's confusion made her caller frown in concern. "Perhaps I should come back tomorrow."

Good heavens, she'd once run Afton Park. Heartbreak hadn't just turned her into an emotional wreck. It seemed to have stolen all her social polish as well. She straightened her shoulders and strove to sound like a hostess instead of a moonstruck ninny.

"No, please stay." Her curiosity reached a point where it outweighed her astonishment – and her astonishment was immense. Having to wait another day for the explanation behind Lady Vanessa's visit would drive her insane. "I'm sorry. You caught me by surprise. Please, sit down. I'll order some tea."

As Lady Vanessa took a chair by the unlit fire and removed her gloves, Juliet went outside to where Lizzie waited with wide eyes and a barely hidden curiosity of her own.

"Mrs. Brandtner is a schoolfriend," she said, which was a lie but a better explanation than saying that at different times, they'd shared the Duke of Evesham's bed.

Impossible to imagine what the notorious Vanessa Gould could have to tell her, but she meant to find out. If the woman planned to warn her about Lucas's irresistible charm, she was far too late. "I didn't recognize her married name."

Lizzie, bless her, accepted the story without question. "Shall I make up the other bedroom, my lady?"

Goodness, was the woman expecting to sleep over? That seemed a step too far. Then Juliet recalled the smart rig outside. "I don't think so. But can you please bring in a tea tray? Then you can go to bed. If Mrs. Brandtner means to stay, I can prepare her room."

"Should I do the fire?"

"No, thank you. It's not a cold night."

Lizzie curtsied and headed down to the kitchens. Juliet, eaten alive by questions, rushed back into the parlor.

She couldn't help taking a quick peek at her visitor's hands. There was a wedding ring on her left hand. Either there really was a Mr. Brandtner, or Lady Vanessa took the trouble to make it seem that way.

"Did you have a good crossing?" Juliet asked, subsiding into a seat on the other side of the hearth.

How absurd to make small talk when she was agog to find out what had sparked this meeting. But she wanted Lizzie safely out of the way before they got down to business. Not for the first time, she was glad that the intrusive old biddy she'd engaged as a chaperone had left three weeks ago to live with a sick relative.

Lady Vanessa's lips twitched again. She looked like a woman who enjoyed life, not at all the shamed, downtrodden creature of Juliet's imaginings.

She clearly also thought that social niceties right now were absurd, although she did answer. "No, it was terrible. Luckily, I'm a good sailor. I'm in lodgings in Russell Square for the moment, while I look around for something suitable."

Juliet noticed that she spoke of her plans in the singular. "Will Mr. Brandtner be joining you?"

Sadness doused the humor. "Johann died a year ago."

"I'm sorry," Juliet said, even as the unworthy thought struck her that perhaps Lady Vanessa had returned to her homeland to rekindle her affair with her first protector.

It's none of your business, Juliet Frain. You set Lucas free when you refused his last proposal.

But her hands fisted in the loose peignoir, as she fought back a furious command for this woman to keep away from him. The last few months had been packed with unpleasant discoveries about herself. Now it seemed she needed to add dog in the manger to a list that included judgmental, self-righteous, and unchaste.

"Yes, it's been a difficult time."

Juliet, however unsympathetic she might be, recognized genuine grief in the response. She felt a pang of guilt. Difficult, she was sure, must be an understatement.

Lady Vanessa went on before Juliet could express a more sincere regret. "I'm here to see what it's like to live in England again. Germany has too many sad associations for me."

That traveling ensemble was the height of fashion, and Lizzie had commented on the expensive conveyance outside. Clearly Lady Vanessa was rich. But riches weren't enough to restore one's good name.

Did this woman hope to rejoin society? If she did, she was living in dreamland. The beau monde never forgot or forgave a scandal, as Juliet was discovering for herself. She'd imagined that one or two of her friends might try to make contact, but it seemed she'd been banished forever from decent company.

Lizzie came in with she tea and, after fiddling around setting it up, headed off to bed. Juliet picked up her cup, then put it down untasted. "Why have you come to see me, Mrs. Brandtner?"

Her visitor took a sip of her tea, before setting the cup and saucer on the table between the two chairs.

"For Lucas's sake, of course."

As Juliet considered the implications of this visit, she felt sick. The only way that this lady could know of her existence, let alone where she lived, was if the letter she'd received had mentioned her.

Had Lucas written to his former paramour to boast of bedding the virtuous Juliet Frain? Disappointment as sharp as a saber pierced her. Disappointment and humiliation.

Raising her chin, she spoke with a trace of hauteur. "The duke and I are only the most distant acquaintances."

She prayed that Lady Vanessa wasn't au courant with the latest gossip. If she was, she'd know that Juliet was a liar.

Lady Vanessa made an apologetic gesture. "I can't blame you for feeling that I've invaded your privacy. You must have heard that Lucas and I caused a great fuss nine years ago. But once I finally got his letter, I had to come and see you straightaway. I would have come earlier, but it took me an age to discover that Baxter is your man of business. Then it took me even longer to persuade Baxter to give me your direction."

"As I said, I can't imagine why you persisted. There's no special friendship between His Grace and me."

Her visitor studied her with perceptive eyes. She wasn't just beautiful, she was clever. Altogether an impressive woman. But then, she'd have to be, if Granville had been so keen to make her his duchess. Granville had the highest standards, after all.

"But that's not true, is it? I know I'm speaking out of turn and you must be wishing me to the devil. Lucas told me in his letter that he loves you and wants to marry you, but you won't have him because of what he did for me."

Juliet stumbled to her feet, heartbroken anew

that Lucas had betrayed her like this. "I'd like you to leave. You have no right…"

Mrs. Brandtner rose more slowly. "Won't you hear me out?"

"What? So that we can both commiserate about our experiences as mistress to the Duke of Evesham?" Juliet turned away and squeezed her eyes shut to keep the tears from falling.

"I was never Lucas's lover, Lady Juliet."

The quiet words sliced through her rising hysteria like a knife through butter.

Shaking, bewildered, she turned to face the woman. "I don't understand."

"I'm sure you don't. Nobody other than Lucas does. He's a man of unshakable honor, so much honor that he risked losing the only woman he's ever loved for the sake of a solemn vow he made to a friend nine years ago."

"A v…vow?" Juliet's hands twined at her waist, as she wondered what was to come.

"Yes, he swore he'd never speak a word of what passed between us when I ran away from Granville. But back in June, he wrote to ask for permission to tell you the truth about what happened between us all those years ago. That's the letter that arrived at my rooms tonight."

Juliet remembered him back at the inn in Salisbury, saying that she was wrong about his dealings with Lady Vanessa. Could she be about to discover the truth at last? And if she did, where did that leave her after three months without a word from him? "So will you give him permission?"

"I thought you'd get a truer picture of what happened if I spoke to you in person. He's inclined to play down his heroism."

Heroism? His Dis-Grace, Lucas Hebden?

Juliet was more baffled than ever. She gestured

toward Lady Vanessa's chair as she sat down. "Tell me everything."

CHAPTER TWENTY-FIVE

Dover, Kent Coast, 10 days later

The storm outside lashed the port, but the Duke of Evesham was safe and snug in Dover's best inn. Not that he was in a frame of mind to enjoy the luxury. This evening, as on so many other evenings, he stood at the window in his shirtsleeves, watching the world outside with a heavy heart.

On the table, most of an excellent dinner awaited clearing away. An open bottle of brandy, almost certainly smuggled in from France across the Channel, sat on the sideboard. So far, it remained untouched. Evesham had an inkling that it would stay that way, although none of his wild friends would believe it.

During the last barren months, he'd sought refuge in alcohol from time to time, but it never helped. He'd finish the sleepless night drunk and miserable and face the next day still miserable but with a headache.

Over the crashing of thunder, he almost missed the soft knock on the door. The servants come to take away his uneaten meal, he supposed.

But when he gave permission to enter, it was the innkeeper himself who appeared. "Your Grace, a lady is below, asking to see you."

By George, the bawds of Dover were getting pushy, if they fronted up at a man's lodgings to tout for business. And desperate, if they were out in this weather. But then, he was a duke with a reputation for both lechery and generosity. They wouldn't get many chances to procure such a client.

The libertine he'd once been would have greeted this news with pleasure. What better way to while away the hours before his ship sailed for France than with a good fuck? He was bored as well as unhappy, given that he'd been stuck in this godforsaken town for nearly a week while rough seas halted shipping.

But the man he was now had no interest in Dover's frail sisterhood. Since his days at Afton Park, he had no interest in women at all. Apart from the one woman who wouldn't have him under any circumstances.

These days, he was almost as bloody monkish as His Grace, the Duke of Granville.

"Send her away, man."

The man looked put upon. "She was most insistent, sir."

Evesham sighed and stared out the mullioned window at the lightning that split the sky. "She can insist all she likes. I'm not in the mood for a strumpet."

Jenkins hesitated as if he wanted to protest. He must get a cut of the bawd's fee. "I wouldn't have troubled you, except that her manner indicates she's a lady."

So not a street girl, then. A courtesan seeking custom, perhaps offering to become his mistress. His bad reputation was the gift that kept on giving. "Not even a high-class strumpet, Jenkins. Pour her a brandy on my account and tell her to ply her trade elsewhere."

Evesham swung away from the window to give the man a sharper order if need be, but Jenkins bowed. "Very good, Your Grace."

He didn't watch as the man collected up the remains of the meal and left. The innkeeper didn't query whether the food met Evesham's standards. After a week of having the duke in residence, the staff here was used to carrying away plates that had been barely touched.

Evesham sighed again with a weight of despair that he hated but couldn't shift. He was in a lather to leave England and all its gloomy memories. This delay in his plans grated. Perhaps with the English Channel between them, he could start to forget Juliet.

And fairies might fly him to Calais tonight, singing the "Hallelujah Chorus." He had a grim feeling that a broken heart knew no geography and he'd be as dismal in Paris as he was in London.

"Lucas?"

He frowned at his reflection in the glass. Damn it, he'd finally gone mad.

He could swear that he'd just heard Juliet say his name. Unless he got out of this slump soon, his wits might never recover.

Evesham closed his eyes and told himself to smarten up. He'd heard that voice in a hundred dreams, but never before during waking hours.

"Lucas, look at me."

His frown deepened. That sounded like Juliet when she was cross with him. In his fantasies, she was all blissful surrender, as she'd been during their one unforgettable night together.

Slowly he turned to face the doorway, afraid that

there would be nobody there.

Shock slammed through him, stole every ounce of breath. A tall, blond woman surveyed him from the threshold with a cool expression that he remembered all too well. The modest gray traveling ensemble was familiar, too.

The sight of the dreary garment convinced him that Juliet was indeed here in the flesh. She never wore that monstrosity when he fantasized about her.

"Juliet..." On rocky legs, he took a step forward, then stopped as if he ran into a pane of glass. His hands clenched into fists at his sides, as he reminded himself that he couldn't seize her up in his arms and kiss her into next Wednesday. Not given how they'd parted. Not when he had no idea why she was here.

"You were the lady downstairs."

He'd wanted like blazes to see her again, but he couldn't help fearing that this last glimpse before he left England forever would prove the fatal blow to any chance of peace.

"Yes." She untied her rain-bedraggled bonnet and set it on the chest near the door.

His fevered gaze devoured her. Water darkened the gray wool of her pelisse, and she looked cold and wet and out of temper. And beautiful. Oh, so beautiful.

That pure, delicate face had haunted every moment since she'd left him.

Were the features finer drawn? The traveling ensemble hung looser than it had three months ago. He hadn't suffered alone, it seemed.

"I told Jenkins to send you away."

To his surprise, wry humor twisted her lips. She suddenly looked human. All too human. Up to now, she could have been carved from marble. "He couldn't resist two hundred pounds."

Two hundred pounds? By Jupiter, that was a

fortune. More than most people saw at once in a lifetime. "No wonder he let you upstairs."

"I'd have paid more, but that's all the cash I'm traveling with. If he said no, I'd have bartered my jewelry."

She was so keen to see him? After all this time? None of this made sense.

"How did you find me?"

She released a soft exhalation and moved further into the room, shutting the door behind her. "You're not going to throw me out?"

"And have you waste all that money? Perish the thought." He knew that prolonging this meeting only worsened his agony. But he'd craved the sight of her. He felt like he breathed for the first time in months, even if he didn't understand what she was doing here.

"I'm glad. I've been on a merry chase over half of England in search of you. The gossip is that you were hunkered down at Lancers."

Amazement had him gaping at her. "You went all the way to Devon?"

"I did. And I had a devil of a time getting anyone to tell me where you'd gone. Your staff are all loyal, despite how you've neglected them."

He was guiltily aware that she was right. About both the loyalty and the neglect. His servants had welcomed his return after all this time, and he'd felt the burden of their disappointment when he left as soon as he'd sorted out the mess that his previous bailiff had left behind.

"Clearly not all of them were loyal, or you wouldn't be here."

"Your old nurse ended up taking pity on me."

"Gertie? I'd have thought she'd be the last person to break. How much did you pay her?"

"Nothing. Which is a good thing, or else I

wouldn't have so much left to bribe the landlord."

"You must have been very convincing."

"Believe me, I was."

Her arrival had sent his mind into utter disarray. How could he think when his heart ached with such longing?

But now, his brain started to work again. To his regret.

For one dazzling moment, Evesham had wondered against all expectations whether she was here because she'd decided that she couldn't live without him. That she'd found the last months as lonely and cold and generally unbearable as he had.

But she didn't act like a woman itching to fling herself into a lover's arms, heedless of the consequences. She was the same self-contained, composed lady he'd first met. Even the signs of suffering that he read in her face could result from living as a social pariah since she'd left Afton.

The surge of euphoria that he'd felt at seeing her had lasted a mere instant. This wasn't the passionate woman who had filled one night with rapture, before plunging him into the depths of hell where he'd howled ever since.

So why the deuce was she here? Evesham could only think of one reason. And he was pathetic enough to hope that he was right. Although if he was, she must be seething with anger. Not to mention consigning him to perdition.

To his shame, his voice cracked as he asked the obvious question. "Are you with child, Juliet?"

She went white and took an unsteady step back. Her trembling hands linked at her waist and twisted.

It seemed he was right. He'd been careful that one unforgettable night in Salisbury, but no prevention method was foolproof.

He should hate that carrying his baby was the

only thing that brought her to him. But he'd sunk to such depths, he'd take Juliet on any terms. Even if she only stayed to avoid the ultimate shame of bearing a child out of wedlock.

It was a humiliating admission for the dashing Duke of Evesham. But then, he was no longer the dashing Duke of Evesham. He was a broken relic of a man, who would sell his soul for a kind word from the woman he loved.

"No, I'm not pregnant." Her voice was so low, he wasn't sure that he heard her correctly.

"You're not?"

"No." She was back to looking like a pure, bloodless statue.

"Then why are you here?"

She wasn't carrying his child. Yet she'd gone all the way to Devon, then tracked him across the many miles to Kent. For the love of heaven, she'd paid a fortune to Jenkins for the privilege of seeing him. Hope, which he could have sworn was forever dead, sparked once more, made his heart pound with wild anticipation.

He strode across the floor and at last touched her. When his shaking hand curled around her arm, his heart constricted and warmth seeped into his blood. Since the day that he left her, he'd felt cold. The glorious summer just past had felt like an arctic winter.

"Juliet, why did you come?" he asked. "Tell me."

She was so pale that her blue eyes were huge orbs of darkness in her face. Her voice emerged as a hoarse whisper. "I...I came to ask you to take me back. If you'll have me."

Evesham sucked in a great breath, but still his mind reeled, as he struggled to come to terms with how she'd just changed his life. He was too distraught to be happy yet. Even if at last happiness hovered as a possibility.

"If I'll have you? What bloody drivel is this?" His hand tightened on her arm as he confessed the truth. "For pity's sake, you broke my heart, woman. Every day you're gone just breaks it anew. Living without you will torment me until I'm dead and buried. Even then, I fear my spirit will linger this side of the afterlife, just in the hope of hearing you say you think of me now and then."

Astonishment widened her eyes and wiped away the uncertainty that made him want to punch something. "Then, Lucas, for the love of heaven, why don't you kiss me?"

What the devil? It was too much for flesh and blood to stand. With a muttered curse, Evesham wrenched her into his arms and his mouth crashed down on hers.

The sensation of holding her again hurtled through him like one of the thunderbolts outside. The taste of her. Her scent. Her sumptuous shape. All so familiar, all so desired. All so forbidden.

He devoured her like a starving man. Because without her, he had starved. It had been so blasted long since he'd kissed her. He felt like he'd been alone for a century. She clung to him and kissed him back with a desperation to match his own.

"My God, I've been dying by inches without you." Then his pride in ruins, he spoke the words that he'd never said to another woman. "Don't leave me, Juliet. Don't go away again. I can't live without you."

Juliet went still and to his excruciating regret, struggled out of his arms. She no longer looked like the pallid, woebegone specter that she'd been before he kissed her. Color flushed her cheeks, and her lips were full and red.

He waited for her to make some declaration of her feelings, but instead she glared at him as if she was livid. "You gallant, ridiculous idiot, why on earth didn't you tell me the truth?"

CHAPTER TWENTY-SIX

*J*uliet watched incomprehension flood Lucas's features. "The truth? I just did. I love you, Juliet. I can never change that."

She believed him. That wild, clumsy, ravenous kiss had reassured her that he'd missed her as much as she'd missed him. After all the empty days, hearing his vehement avowal felt like a miracle.

"I don't want that to change." Her voice was choked. "Because I love you, too."

She watched a fragile faith seep into his expression, replacing strain and confusion. This time, when he drew her into his arms, there was more tenderness than fury, but the effect on her vulnerable heart remained as powerful.

Instead of a tidal wave of desire, this kiss was as sweet as honey. When she emerged from bliss, she was cuddled up next to him on the chaise longue in front of the blazing fire.

"Are you really here to stay?" Lucas stared down into her eyes. "I couldn't survive if you left me again."

She examined his beloved features and recognized the harm she'd done. Guilty regret knotted her stomach. "I'll never leave you while I have breath in my body."

She'd suffered during their awful separation. She saw that he had, too. Perhaps even more than she had. The deep lines between nose and mouth and the hollows in his face told a story of loss and longing.

Her promise to stay eased the tension in his features, but shadows lingered. Mere words weren't enough to heal the wounds that they'd suffered.

"You should have told me that day in Salisbury," she said again, exasperated with him, even as she loved him. Although part of her couldn't help admiring the stubborn valor that had so nearly divided them forever.

He studied her face, as if he cherished every feature. "That I love you? I did. Over and over. It didn't seem to make much difference."

Juliet winced to recall her behavior at the inn. On that abysmal day, she'd been so sure that she occupied the moral high ground. Yet all she'd done was consign them both to three months of soul-shredding wretchedness. She shuddered to think how close she'd come to losing him.

"It should have. I'm sorry. But that's not what I'm talking about." She paused. "Vanessa came to see me."

A dawning realization sharpened his features. "You know what happened all those years ago?"

"I do. She told me everything."

"I wrote to her for permission to tell you. By God, I must have written to her fifty times. I assumed the letters didn't reach her."

"They almost didn't. She's moved back to London. Your letters followed her from the Rhineland. Ever since she called, I've been trying to find you to beg your forgiveness – and tell you I could box your ears."

She saw that the threat didn't worry him. Not now

that he knew she loved him. "You nearly missed me here. I should have sailed last Tuesday."

Despite the moment's solemnity, she couldn't contain a dismissive snort. "As if the English Channel could stop me. I'd track you down to the ends of the earth if I had to." Her voice lowered to seriousness. "But you should have trusted me with the truth."

His expression hardened to reveal the strength of character that she ought to have recognized long ago. It had been a humiliating blow to discover that the man she'd always disdained as a hedonistic wastrel was much more principled than she, the supposed paragon of virtue.

Lucas's tone was as austere as hers. "I gave my word to Vanessa that I'd never reveal what happened when I helped her to run away from Granville. Never under any circumstances."

"Up to and including facing Granville in a duel." Her hands clenched hard in his crumpled shirt. Adore him as she might, the thought of him risking his life made her want to clout him. "He could have killed you, you stiff-necked idiot."

To her surprise, humor curved his lips. "You really shouldn't dote on me with such sweet endearments, my darling."

"You're lucky I don't wring your neck." Juliet glared at him, although she didn't pull out of his embrace.

How could she forget seeing his scar for the first time? For pity's sake, she could have lost him before she found him. The thought turned her blood to ice.

"The man's too honorable to murder me," Lucas said with an unconvincing attempt at lightness.

"And you're too honorable for your own good."

His expression turned grave. "Vanessa and I were never lovers."

"I know that. Now."

Juliet couldn't help recalling that night in London, when thanks to Vanessa, she finally realized just what a special man she'd rejected.

"She and I had always been best friends. We grew up together. In so many ways, we were both misfits. I couldn't stand by and watch her parents bully her into marrying Granville without doing something about it."

"Not when she was in love with her music master." Juliet felt such compassion for the innocent young girl, trapped in the web of family ambition.

"Johann Brandtner was a fine man, but he couldn't win against the Goulds, who were a grasping, ruthless bunch. They were ready to do anything, including commit murder, to get a duchess in the family. If they'd had the slightest idea that Vanessa was respectably wed and living near Cologne, they'd have hunted her down and done away with Johann. It was more difficult to threaten the powerful Duke of Evesham. Not to mention, if the world thought that Vanessa had given her maidenhead to a roué who wouldn't marry her, she lost her value on the marriage market."

"But you must have known I'd never betray her secret."

"I'd given her my word." His jaw set. "You trusted me enough to come to my bed, Juliet. You should have trusted me the rest of the way. You said you loved me, but it was love that had too many limits."

Another stab of guilt. Because, curse him, he was right. "I wasn't brave enough," she said in a low voice.

"No, you weren't."

She should have been more generous. She should have been more perceptive. She'd spent all her life listening to her head and ignoring her heart. In

Lucas's case, her heart had always known best.

Tears sprang to her eyes. "I've been so wrong about everything, and I've caused you such unhappiness. Can you forgive me?"

Lucas leaned in and kissed her with a thoroughness that soothed her self-hatred. His kiss spoke forgiveness even before he uttered the words. "I love you, Juliet. Of course I forgive you. And you're right. I should have told you."

Still hardly able to believe that they were together at last, she surveyed his beloved face. "I'm not sure I could have gone on without you, even if Vanessa hadn't visited. These last months have been intolerable."

His smile promised eternal love. "Let's make up for that with joy."

"Joy sounds good." Emotion thickened her voice, and a tear escaped to trickle down her cheek.

"You don't look very joyful." Wry amusement lightened his expression, as he caught the tear on one finger. "You look like you're about to cry your eyes out."

A soggy laugh emerged, and one hand sneaked up to tug at a curl at his nape. His hair was a complete mess. That was her Lucas. "I used to pride myself on my self-control, but since a certain ramshackle duke barged into my life, I'm at the mercy of my feelings."

"Not the proper and restrained Lady Juliet Frain?"

She gave another waterlogged giggle, torn between poignant emotion and the laughter that had always been Lucas's gift to her. "I don't think anyone calls me proper and restrained these days. I'm free to decide what I want and where I go."

He arched his eyebrows in mock dismay. "I'm hoping you've decided that you're coming with me."

She dredged up a misty smile. "Never doubt it."

For a long moment, they held each other in silence. A healing peace descended. Juliet hadn't known peace since she'd met Lucas, but now she was with him and set to stay that way.

"To think, if Papa hadn't cheated at cards, we'd have missed out on this."

She felt surprise ripple through him. "What the devil?"

Juliet started to laugh, in a way that she hadn't laughed in months. "Lucas, don't tell me you never guessed."

"The old rogue sharped me?"

"Of course he did. He's very good at it."

"And he looks as innocent as a lamb, which helps. That's an infernally dangerous trick to play. Men have been shot for less."

"He only does it for the sake of art."

Lucas shook his head in disgust. "I can't believe I was such a downy bird that he put one over on me. He beat me ridiculously fast, and I'm known as a dab hand with the cards."

"He wanted you to play Romeo, by hook or by crook. Shakespeare demanded it."

Self-mockery tugged at Lucas's mouth. "Then by all means, I must forgive him. After all, the deception brought me the love of a lifetime."

Juliet sighed and tilted her face up. "I adore it when you say those things."

"That's good. Because you've got about fifty years of similar avowals ahead, my love."

This time, the kiss held more passion than sweetness, although sweetness lingered below the heat, the way love flowed like a river beneath their desire. Juliet made an incoherent sound of delight when Lucas lifted her to straddle his lap. As the kiss deepened, she felt him swelling between her thighs.

With a boldness born of love given and returned,

she shaped her hand to that hardness. "I can't tell you how many nights I stayed awake, remembering what shameless things you did to me in Salisbury."

He closed his eyes, and she read the ghost of agony in his face. "It was hell, knowing I'd only ever see you in my imagination. I'd wake from dreams that felt so real, only to find my arms empty and heart aching."

His confession threatened to rip her own heart to pieces. She rested a hand on his lean cheek in a gesture of apology. "Lucas, you should hate me."

He kissed her quickly. "I could never hate you, although there were times when I wanted to give you a good shake and tell you to think what you were throwing away."

She stroked his chiseled jaw. "True love."

"Yes."

"I pledge myself to you." The depth of her feelings turned her voice hoarse.

"Do you?"

"With all my heart."

He studied her with a frown. "I've asked you to marry me four times. You've always said no."

Juliet understood now how those rejections had wounded him. She swallowed to shift a lump of painful emotion from her throat. Then swallowed again before she managed to answer. "If you ask me again, I'll say yes."

He caught her head between his hands, so she couldn't evade his somber dark eyes. Despite having already given Lucas her answer, despite knowing what he was going to ask, her heart began to race with giddy excitement.

"My one love, my forever love, I want to spend the rest of my life with you. I want us to make a family and grow old together. I want your face to be the first thing I see every morning. I want your voice to be the last thing I hear every night. I want us to link hands and step forward into a future that we create together. I never want us to part. I swear that from this moment on, you will be my cause and my beloved and my care." His throat moved as he swallowed. He wasn't immune to the moment's profundity. "My darling, make me the happiest man in England. Say you'll be my cherished wife, my duchess, my dearest. Say yes, Juliet. It's time."

Drat it. More tears. Despite blinking to clear the mist from her vision, it was hopeless. Her voice emerged as a shaky rasp. "Everything you say, it's like poetry."

"All that Shakespeare must have rubbed off." His voice lowered into earnestness. "Please answer me, my darling."

"I'd be honored to be your wife, Lucas. How could you think otherwise? The answer is yes."

"No hesitations?"

"None."

"No regrets?"

"Only that it took me far too long to trust what my heart knew to be true from the beginning."

Elation lit his face. "Juliet..."

Lucas kissed her with a hunger that echoed her rising need. She wrapped her arms around him, hardly able to believe that they'd found their way to each other at last.

Juliet closed her eyes in an ecstasy of surrender. Velvety darkness enveloped her, crammed with heat and love and Lucas. His rich, spicy scent fed her famished senses. His hard, glorious body beneath her caressing hands made her crave the ultimate union.

"Take me," she whispered, running her teeth down his neck and combing her fingers through the silky hair at his nape. "I need to feel you inside me."

Lucas grasped her waist and lowered her to lie on the chaise longue. As he kneeled over her, the skin clung tight to his features. "I love you, Juliet."

"And I love you. Let me show you how much."

His hands shook with urgency, as he tugged her drawers down. Then his hand slipped between her legs.

She grabbed his wrist to stop him. "Don't wait."

He went still. "I want to give you pleasure."

A cracked laugh escaped. "I'm already on fire, my darling. And I've been so cold and empty without you."

"Oh, my love." He ripped at his breeches until his rod sprang free.

Juliet's eyes widened. She'd spent three months remembering his body and what it had done to her, but even so, the sight of his virility made every drop of moisture evaporate from her mouth. The heavy pulse between her legs sharpened to the edge of pain.

With an unsteady gesture, her hand encircled him. She felt like she held all the power in the world within her grasp.

He gave a grunt of protest. "Too much of that, my girl, and we'll have to start all over again. Lift your knees."

She released him with a yielding sigh and tilted to accept a long, relentless thrust as he plunged forward. He filled her so completely that he left no room for anything but love.

"You're mine now." His voice was a throaty rumble.

She angled higher, feeling the thrilling change inside her. Her hands circled the arms that he braced against the chaise. "And you're mine. Mutual possession."

"The best kind." His smiles appeared more

naturally now.

When she tightened in intimate welcome, he groaned and bumped his hips forward. "Do that again."

When willful, independent Juliet Frain obeyed with alacrity, his growl of pleasure vibrated in her bones. He began to move with a powerful purpose that banished the last of her loneliness. He soon reached a place inside her that had her moaning with ascending pleasure.

With dizzying speed, the expanding rapture gathered her up and flung her out to the stars. She cried out, as she found her dazzling peak on a blast of sensual heat.

Lucas bent his head and kissed her, then shifted inside her. On a guttural moan of release, he filled her with his seed. She clung to his shoulders and joyfully accepted this gift.

After what felt like an eternity flying across the fiery edge of the cosmos, Juliet wafted back to earth. An earth forever changed. In those moments of glory, she and Lucas had formed an unbreakable union.

Perhaps they'd even made a child. A baby born of a love that triumphed against the odds.

She wrapped her arms around Lucas. Their bodies were as close as physical reality allowed. But after that extraordinary joining, their souls merged even closer.

He shifted. "Am I too heavy? Should I move?"

"Not yet," she said, her voice rough with a gratitude so fierce that it felt like a knife in her heart. She closed her eyes and said a silent prayer of thankfulness that this wonderful man was hers.

Lucas's kiss told her that he, too, had measured the dimensions of heaven in her arms. For a long time, they lay entangled, as the heights of emotion receded. The storm continued outside, but in this room all was contentment.

When he shifted, Juliet didn't protest. He sat up and dragged her into his arms. Snuggling into his side, she rested her head on his shoulder. She laid her hand over his heart, knowing that she could trust it at last.

"I'm looking forward to seeing France," she said idly.

Lucas kissed the top of her head with a quick tenderness that thrilled her. "Marrying you will be easier in England."

She shifted until she could see his face. "We can find an Anglican chaplain in Paris."

"We can find a thousand here."

She frowned, although she was too happy for real displeasure. "You're not going to elope with me, are you?"

"No. I'm going to whisk you back to London as soon as this pestilential storm dies away." Determination filled his voice. "I'm going to find you a chaperone, then I'm going to marry you in the full glare of society's approval."

"You mean to restore my reputation," she said with a hint of flatness.

"I do. I hope you'll forgive me."

He kissed her again. She kissed him back, although he wasn't saying what she wanted to hear. She'd liked the idea of the two of them becoming fugitives from the beau monde and its cruel judgments.

"I'll have to go back to watching my step, and I'm not sure I want to." She sighed. "My respectable self couldn't have chased you across England."

"Once you're my duchess, you can act as you like."

"Hmm, perhaps."

Another kiss chased away most of her discontent.

But not quite all of it.

He watched her with a hint of a smile. "Juliet, you've spent your life preparing to shine in society."

"But then I met you."

"I intend you to glitter as you were born to."

"You probably want to invite Papa to the wedding," she said in a long-suffering tone. That really was a sore point. She was a long way from forgiving her father for throwing her to the wolves.

"Yes. Because then Portia can be your bridesmaid. You'd like that, wouldn't you?"

Curse him for knowing her so well. "She'll bring her beagle."

He laughed. "We'll tie the ring to his collar."

"You'll call the banns rather than get a special license."

His voice became all silky persuasion. "Juliet, it will kill me, waiting three weeks to have you in my arms again, but it will be worth it in the long run. I want the world to watch you become my bride. I want everyone to see how proud I am of you."

That went a little way toward appeasing her. "You know, none of my so-called friends got in touch after Papa tossed me out."

"They probably didn't know where you were."

"They could have written and asked Portia. She always knew."

"Then to Hades with them. We'll find you some new friends. You can do so much good in the world. Isn't it worth swallowing a little pride in return?"

This time, her sigh indicated surrender. How could it not? He spoke good sense, even if she regretted losing the chance to tell society to be damned. "Three weeks?"

"Yes. And I'll take you to Paris for our honeymoon."

"We could go to Paris tomorrow and forget all this

fuss. We could share a cabin on the boat, then set up in an apartment near the Champs-Elysées."

"Don't tempt me." He closed his eyes and heaved a profound sigh. "I hope you appreciate my sacrifice. It's in a good cause, but it will be torture to play propriety until our wedding night."

She studied his face. "I'd never realized that you were such a political animal."

He opened eyes bright with self-mockery. "I've always known how our world works, my darling. Up until now, I've had no real reason to follow the rules. Now I have your good name to protect. I don't want anyone saying nasty things about the woman I love."

"They will, you know."

"Once we show the world that we're the happiest couple in England, the gossip will die away. By the time our first baby arrives, nobody will remember you kissing me in the bushes."

A nostalgic smile curved her lips. That evening had ended up in chaos and recrimination and tears. But his kisses had been enthralling. "I'll remember."

"And so will I." His expression remained serious. "Come on, Juliet, admit it. You don't want to be an outcast. The Duchess of Evesham will rise above criticism, once she takes a few simple steps to claim her place in the beau monde."

She cupped the side of his face and pouted in a way that sensible Juliet Frain would never have done a couple of months ago. "I was looking forward to being wild and scandalous with you."

His answering grin conveyed an intriguing hint of the rogue that she'd once judged him to be. He hauled her onto his lap. "I most sincerely hope that you'll fulfill that ambition. Behind closed doors. But in public, I want the world to say that the love of a good woman reformed the incorrigible Duke of Evesham and turned him into a pillar of society."

"So I still get to be wicked?"

His audible inhalation betrayed excitement. To her surprise, he started to harden under her rump. A pillar, indeed. "Often. Always."

"Then I believe, Your Grace, we have a plan."

His visible relief told her how much her rehabilitation meant to him. "Thank you."

A little wriggle made his interest grow. "But we can be reckless tonight?"

His laugh rang with love, as unmistakable intent gleamed in his eyes. "No need for either of us to turn over a new leaf until at least midday tomorrow, my love."

She kissed him with every drop of her overflowing happiness. "Then there's no time to be lost, my dearest duke."

EPILOGUE

Venice, Italy, a year later

The moon shining down on the rippling Grand Canal created an unforgettable scene. Juliet Hebden, Duchess of Evesham, leaned back against the tall, powerful man standing behind her and drew in a deep breath of the salty air.

"I loved Paris," she murmured as Lucas's arms lashed her closer. His hands settled over her midriff, warm through the slippery silk of her cream nightdress.

He bent to kiss the shoulder bared under the ribbon strap that held up her nightgown. "I know you did. Which is odd, because you didn't see much beyond our hotel suite."

It was true. After all their time apart, then the weeks that it took to plan a wedding that shouted defiance to everyone who had snubbed her, she'd been in a fever to give herself over to uninterrupted revels with her virile husband.

"That's one of the reasons I liked it."

A wry grunt of agreement. "No argument from

me."

They stood between French doors opening onto a small gothic balcony projecting over the silvery water. The breeze that whispered around them was blissfully warm. October in Italy was balmy. In England, cold autumn weather had set in by now.

She continued to muse on their travels. "And I liked Vienna."

"We saw a little more of Vienna."

Spring in the Austrian countryside had been glorious, an explosion of color that echoed the joy in her heart. She cherished the memory of making love in a secret dell beside a rushing stream, where the fresh scent of crushed flowers had mingled with their cries of pleasure.

"And I'll never forget seeing the Forum by moonlight when we were in Rome."

"Yes, Rome had its charms." His embrace tightened, making his deep voice reverberate against her back.

They'd recently enjoyed a passionate interlude. If she turned around, she'd see an elaborate bed carved in the form of a gilt seashell and a chaos of lace-edged linen sheets.

But right now, she couldn't look away from the enchanted scene before her. The line of ornate palazzi across the water formed dark shapes against the sky, with here and there the glow of a candle to prove that she and Lucas weren't the only people awake after midnight.

She set one hand upon where both of his rested over her stomach. "This is the best by far."

"I thought you'd like it."

"I do. So much."

A companionable silence fell, as Juliet took in the view – and basked in her husband's nearness. She loved these quiet moments, when she and Lucas communicated without words. His touch spoke of love and protection and pleasure in her company.

To think, she'd once dismissed this marvelous man as shallow and careless. How wrong she'd been. He was everything that she'd ever wanted. He was everything that she'd never even thought to want.

As if Lucas read her thoughts – it was uncanny how often he tracked the workings of her mind without her saying anything – he stroked the plain of her stomach. "Don't you have something you'd like to tell me?"

She smiled out over the dreaming city. "I wanted to be sure."

"Are you?"

Her smile broadened. "Yes."

His grip firmed, and he turned her to face him. The candelabra on either side of the doors shed enough light for her to read the elation in his expression. "You're carrying our child?"

"Yes. I'm so happy."

"Oh, Juliet..." He hauled her into his arms and kissed her with a clumsy ardor that betrayed his joy. By the time that he came up for air, she was breathless and trembling.

"My darling, I hoped. But then you didn't say anything. I wondered if perhaps you didn't recognize the signs."

She gave a short, shaky laugh. " Of course I recognized the signs. Was I not the source of all marital information for my maiden sisters?"

Lucas responded with his own laugh. He caught her waist and stared down at her, as if she was a miracle that he could hardly believe he witnessed. "You could tell them a lot more now."

She gave a dismissive huff. "I suspect these days, I don't have to tell them a thing."

"No, perhaps not." Her dry response made him

smile, but she could see that he had no attention to spare for Portia or Viola. "When?"

Juliet had no trouble interpreting his question. "Around Easter, I think."

He still looked like a man who had bent to pick up a penny and found himself in possession of a guinea. "A baby in the spring."

She studied him. "You're genuinely pleased?"

"A child born of our love is the crowning blessing."

"A baby will curtail our freedom."

"A baby makes us a family."

She blinked away tears, as the last of her lingering worries disappeared. Worries that she now realized had been unnecessary.

As ever, Lucas was too perceptive to miss her reaction. "Did you think I might resent becoming a father, you silly girl?"

He sounded fondly exasperated rather than upset, thank goodness. "I married a rake, after all," she said in a thick voice.

"No, you married a reformed rake. There's a difference."

"You won't mind settling down?"

He leaned in and kissed her with a reverent adoration that made her heart clench. "I look forward to a lifetime of love with you, my darling – and to the arrival of as many children as the good Lord grants us."

"Lucas, I don't deserve you," she said. To her dismay, she began to cry in earnest.

He surveyed her with wry affection. "Of course you do, you beautiful goose. You're my reason for living. You're everything to me. You must know that."

Hearing that only made her cry harder.

With a groan, Lucas bundled her up in his arms

until his warm, spicy scent surrounded her. That scent would always be the smell of home to her.

By the time she'd regained control, they shared a tapestry-covered armchair and she was sitting on his lap.

"Better?" he asked with a loving smile that threatened to make her cry all over again.

"Yes," she managed to say through the emotion clogging her throat.

He dug around in the pocket of his dressing gown and produced a clean handkerchief. "Here."

"Thank you." She wiped her eyes and blew her nose.

"You weren't really worried about my reaction to your news, were you?" he asked gravely.

She crushed the handkerchief in her hand and nestled close enough to hear his gallant heart beating through the silk dressing gown. "We've been so happy since we married, wandering from country to country, pleasing ourselves, living with no purpose but love. I wasn't sure how you'd feel about taking on responsibility for a new person. We'd never talked about having children."

One dark eyebrow quirked upward. "We did plenty to ensure that offspring were more likely to arrive than not."

Stupidly her cheeks heated, when after the excesses of this last year, she should have moved beyond blushing at anything. "I can't get enough of you."

He shifted to settle her more comfortably. "I feel the same. It's no surprise that two such passionate people made a baby. I'm proud that you'll be the mother of my children." He regarded her with masculine perplexity. "By Jericho, that can't make you cry."

She gave a watery giggle. "I'm a little

overwrought."

He released a forbearing sigh. "I'll have to start carrying extra handkerchiefs."

Lucas sounded so comfortable with everything. More confirmation that her qualms had been needless. "That's a good idea."

Juliet rested her head on his shoulder and closed her eyes, picturing her husband devoting that practical good sense to raising their child. The thought was unaccountably moving.

She'd long ago forgiven herself for misjudging him when they first met. Now she realized yet again that she'd underestimated the outstanding man she'd married. He'd make a wonderful father.

She was half-asleep before he spoke again. "Perhaps it's time we went back. I'd like the baby to be born at Lancers."

Juliet stirred and forced her mind to work. "I was glad to leave London when I married you. I couldn't bear how all the people who had spurned me toadied up, once we decided to wed."

"I know. The world is a wicked place full of wicked people. But on the other hand, I'd love to show you Lancers. You've never been there. You'll love it. And you'll love putting your touches on the house. It desperately needs updating. Not to mention that you miss Portia and Viola. You can show the sycophants that they have no power over you. A happy life is always the greatest revenge."

She sat up to examine his features in the last of the flickering candlelight. "You want to go home?"

His smile was rueful. "It seems I do, much as I've enjoyed crisscrossing the Continent."

She put aside her misgivings. "Then we must go home."

He subjected her to a probing look. "It's time you made your peace with your father. After all, if he hadn't cheated at cards to secure the perfect Romeo, you and I would never have met. At the very least, he deserves our gratitude for that."

Her stomach knotted with the mixture of hurt and anger that the thought of her father always aroused. Once her engagement was announced, Papa had welcomed her back into the family. Then he'd paid without complaint for an extravagant wedding at St. George's in Hanover Square.

But Juliet could never forget the way that he'd treated her at Afton Park. She'd stayed with Viola before the ceremony, and while both she and Papa had done their best to appear reconciled, under the surface, the bitter estrangement lingered. At least on her side. With his usual optimism, he'd assumed that everything was forgiven.

"Juliet?"

Her lips turned down. "You're right."

Lucas laughed with more of that devastating fondness. "You don't say that very often."

His teasing didn't make her smile. The pain of her father's rejection would never leave her. But as Lucas said, more was at stake here than her injured feelings. "I'd like our children to know him. He's their only living grandparent."

"I understand how he hurt you. I'm not playing that down. He doesn't have to move in with us, but it's time we mended fences. You know the rift in the family preys on your mind."

It was her turn to sigh. "Pity the woman who marries a wise man."

Lucas bent his head and kissed her. He knew that she'd relented. The kiss spoke of love and support – and sympathy for her contradictory feelings about her wayward parent. "So?"

The kiss went a long way toward easing the tumult inside her. "So perhaps we might leave visiting Naples for our next trip?"

"We can bring the children," he said.

Her laugh was genuine, if a touch cracked. "You keep talking about children in the plural. Let's worry about this one first."

"Thank you for agreeing to go back to England. Let's show the world what a magnificent duchess you are."

She sent him a sardonic look. "The duke's not too bad either."

He made a theatrical gesture of protest. "Not too bad? I'm superb, don't you know?"

Juliet's laugh resonated with love. "You *are* superb. I congratulate myself on having the extreme good sense to marry you."

Lucas still looked at her as if she delivered the stars to his door. "I love you, my precious duchess."

"And I love you, my glorious duke."

This time, the kiss lasted much longer and soon deepened into a passion that turned the whole world to fire.

ABOUT THE AUTHOR

Australian Anna Campbell has written 11 multi award-winning historical romances for Avon HarperCollins and Grand Central Publishing. As an independently published author, she's released more than 35 bestselling stories. Right now, she is working on a new series called Scoundrels of Mayfair, set amidst the glamour and sensuality of Regency London. Anna has won numerous awards for her stories, including *RT Book Reviews* Reviewers Choice, the Booksellers Best, the Golden Quill (three times), the Heart of Excellence (twice), the Write Touch, the Aspen Gold (twice), and the Australian Romance Readers' favorite historical romance (five times).

Anna loves to hear from her readers. You can find her at:

Website: www.annacampbell.com

facebook.com/AnnaCampbellFans

x.com/AnnaCampbellOz

bookbub.com/authors/anna-campbell

The Worst Lord in London:
Scoundrels of Mayfair Book 1

Headlong into the unknown...

Independent, willful Kate Starr has cherished a penchant for handsome Lord Shelburn since she was sixteen years old, but as a mill-owning industrialist, she moves in a different world from the libertine earl. Then one fateful day, Shelburn invites her to accompany him in a scandalous race, and immediate physical attraction swiftly turns into blazing passion.

The hunter caught...

Leighton Anstey, Earl of Shelburn, glories in his reputation as the worst lord in London. His fame as an irresistible seducer is unrivaled, although his amours are notable for their explosive heat, not their longevity. The dashing lord has never met a

woman who can hold his wandering attention, until
he tumbles into a liaison with a mysterious woman
who enthrals him, body and soul.

A brief encounter or a forever love?

Neither Kate nor Shelburn views their torrid affair
as more than a shooting star, flaring red-hot for a
brilliant instant, then destined to fade to nothing.
But does the fiery desire raging between them blind
them to the chance of finding lifelong happiness
together?

The Trouble with Earls:
Scoundrels of Mayfair Book 2

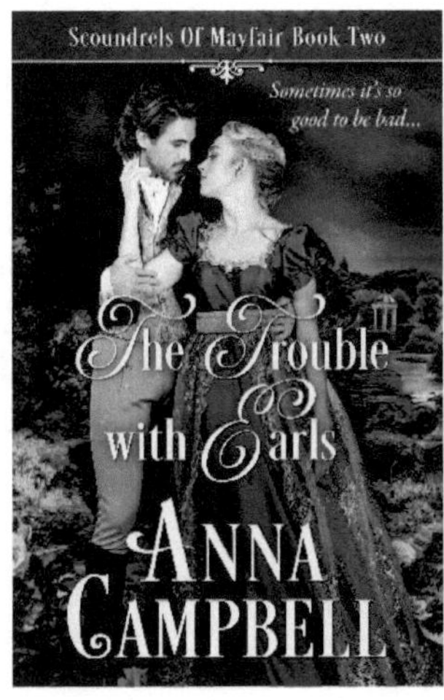

The wild rogue and the wallflower!

Toby Sutton, Earl of Renfrew, is a notorious libertine with no interest in marrying a wellbred young miss and making her his countess. But when he meets lovely Lady Viola Frain, irresistible desire creates an explosive mix with his native recklessness. Within a matter of days, he and Viola are joined in a hurried marriage of convenience, patched together to scotch an almighty scandal.

Marry in haste, repent at leisure?

With two spectacular older sisters, shy Viola Frain is used to being the overlooked member of the family. When handsome Lord Renfrew literally falls at her feet, Viola finally meets a man who thinks she's special. But before the fragile bloom of attraction can flower, she finds herself wed to Renfrew and whisked away to brooding Brazey Castle, where shadows of old tragedy threaten her frail hope of happiness.

The trouble with earls...

Society watches avidly, forecasting disaster for an alliance between two people so mismatched. Can passion unite the rake and the recluse? Or is the truth just as Viola fears? That the trouble with earls is that they're bound to break your heart.

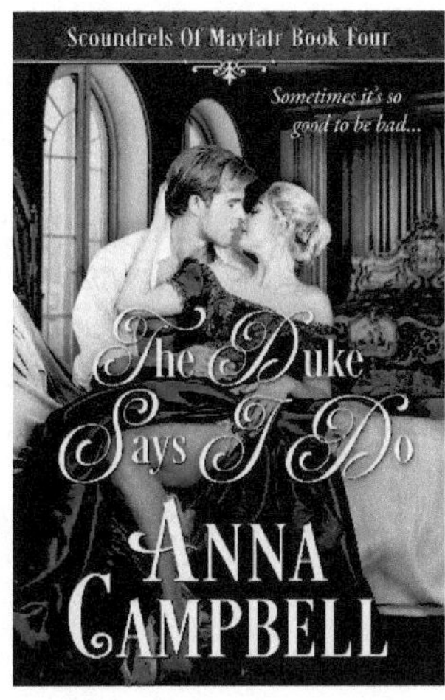

The rescuer rescued...

In a world that doesn't care, Lady Portia Frain devotes herself to rescuing mistreated animals. Her dedicated crusade means forsaking any plans to marry, not to mention the risks of standing up to bullies in London's mean streets. It's inevitable that one day, she bites off more than she can chew. When she encounters trouble saving a mongrel dog from a dogfighting ring, the Duke of Granville is her only hope – to her regret. Not only is he the suitor her sister jilted under scandalous circumstances, he's also, in her words, "the most boring man in Britain."

She's his worst nightmare and his only desire!

Alaric Dempster, Duke of Granville, would be delighted never to see another Frain again as long as he lives. They're nothing but trouble, including his former fiancée Juliet and her nincompoop younger sister. But when London's perfect gentleman stumbles upon Portia in a dangerous confrontation, honor requires him to step in, whatever his low opinion of the lady in question. After his reluctant gallantry, he and this featherbrained do-gooder are forced into close quarters and much to his irritation, he's forgetting how much Portia annoys him and remembering just how beautiful she is. It's a devil of a dilemma for a duke determined to keep his distance – and his sanity.

A love that breaks all the rules.

But passion has plans for these unlikely lovers. Reckless Lady Portia and the straitlaced duke discover opposites attract in the most delicious way and festering dislike provides the surest path to irresistible desire. Is this a case of first impressions being right? Or will difference prove the spice that sparks a lifetime of happiness?